Gina was completel  the bed in front of her i But he was a dead ringe Korolev.

How many hours had she spent as a teenager, gazing in rapt adoration at his poster on her bedroom wall? It showed him dancing in his most famous role, Spartacus, wearing nothing but a gladiator's leather shorts, his bronzed chest crisscrossed by leather bands, his powerful muscles gleaming with oil. His face hadn't changed: the square jaw, the straight nose, the wheat-colored hair flopping over his high forehead. The mesmerizing lagoon-blue eyes.

Suddenly, she understood why she'd found Nick so irresistible. He had Alex Korolev's eyes.

"You were in my studio?" the man asked, in a deep voice like Nick's, but with only a ghost of his accent.

She'd been standing there with her mouth open like a goldfish. She gulped, trying to find her voice—then the switches clicked in her head.

His studio. Built for a professional dancer.

Omigod omigod omigod.

He didn't look like Alex Korolev. He was Alex Korolev.

Praise for Marisa Wright

"An engaging romp from start to finish"

~ Jacqueline Falcomer,
author of 'Forget Me Not'

A Dance with Danger

by

Marisa Wright

A Dance with Danger

Cover Art by *Tina Lynn Stout*

The Wild Rose Press, Inc.
PO Box 708
Adams Basin, NY 14410-0708
Visit us at www.thewildrosepress.com

Publishing History
First Edition, 2022
Trade Paperback ISBN 978-1-5092-4265-8
Digital ISBN 978-1-5092-4266-5

Published in the United States of America

Dedication

With thanks to Gary van der Walt, on whose legs my hero walks.

Chapter One

September 2002

Gina Williams ran naked from the bathroom, struggling into a cream terrycloth bathrobe three sizes too big for her frame. By the time she got down the stairs to the door of the villa, Nick Rostov had already crossed the beach and stepped onto the wooden jetty. She caught up with him as he was unhitching the cruiser's mooring rope.

"Nick, wait!" She put her hand on his arm to make him look at her. "What's going on?"

"I told you. I have business today. Urgent."

"But—how long have you known about this?"

"Dimitri tell me last night."

She thought back to their arrival at the marina, late last night. Nick had spoken—in Greek, or maybe Russian—with a stooped, gray-haired man, before they took the short boat trip to the island. She hadn't understood a word, of course.

So he'd known all this time but hadn't bothered to mention it. And he'd let her laze in bed, and take her time in the shower, without saying a word. "Why didn't you tell me?"

He shrugged. "Is my business. You here to enjoy beach, swim, lie in sun."

Did he understand her so little? Lying on the beach

1

all day was the last thing she'd want to do. Besides, he had no right to make assumptions on her behalf. Still, having an argument might not be the best way for her to get on that boat. "I'd really rather come with you," she said. "If you give me five minutes, I'll grab my stuff. I can get dressed on the boat."

"No!"

She stepped back, shocked by his scowling eyebrows and hard-set mouth. His face relaxed, a little. "You must stay. I go now."

"Five minutes, honestly, that's all I need! And I won't get in your way. Just give me a lift to the mainland, I'll go sightseeing by myself."

"Not possible. You stay." He pulled her to him and bent to kiss her forehead. His beard tickled her nose. "Maybe tomorrow." With that, he vaulted onto the gleaming white cruiser

"Nick!" she wailed, her frustration bringing out her Australian accent. "I came here to be with you, not sit on a bloody beach all by myself!"

"I back tonight," he called to her as the boat pulled away from the pier.

With a huff of annoyance, she sank down onto the jetty and hugged her knees, confused by Nick's dismissive attitude. He'd been so different in Thessaloniki, eager to fulfill her every whim. Perhaps she should have accepted that theirs was just a holiday romance. He was Russian and lived here, in Greece. She lived in England, but her real home was ten thousand miles away in Australia, how could that ever work? When faced with the choice of being single and unemployed in damp, gray-skied London, or spending a few more sun-kissed weeks with a handsome Russian, she had weakened. Wouldn't anyone?

She leaned back on her hands, gazing up at the clear, jewel-blue sky, and felt the tension in her neck ease. Even in mid-September, the sun was bright, the air was mild, and the fresh aroma of pine mingled with the salt tang of the breeze. If only the island had been as she'd imagined, she'd have waved Nick off without a word of complaint.

When Nick had said, "I have a luxury villa on a Greek island," she had imagined somewhere like Mykonos, with neighbors and restaurants and ferries and telephones. The reality had turned out to be a great lump of barren rock in the middle of a bay, with no transport and no phone signal.

She swiveled to glare at the building behind her. When she'd first arrived, she had been mightily impressed by the Hampton-style mansion, gleaming white in the moonlight with a small crescent of beach in front, and the great cliff looming darkly behind. But then she'd discovered it was divided into three two-bedroom villas, and Nick owned only the one on the far right. And apart from the fake mansion, there was absolutely nothing else on the island, unless you counted the generator shed and the water tank. There wasn't even a garden, just a wide wraparound deck. Nothing to do but swim and sunbathe, and—now that Nick had taken the cruiser—no way to leave.

A movement caught her eye. A woman emerging from the center villa, which belonged to Nick's brother. Nick had warned her that Sasha and his girlfriend were weird recluses who hated visitors.

The girlfriend was coming towards the jetty, no doubt coming to board the stylish Venetian-style runabout moored there, all burnished wood and shining chrome fittings. A way for Gina to escape the island too, perhaps.

She stood as the woman approached. Wow, she was tall, and her tailored shorts made her legs look even longer. Her flaming red hair was perfectly groomed. Gina groaned inwardly, thinking how her own uncombed mop of boring-brown curls must look to such a Glamazon.

Holding out her hand, she noticed her bathrobe had fallen half-open and had to use both hands to pull it close around her. "Hi, I'm Gina! You must be Monika?"

The woman nodded but her face remained impassive. "You're Nick's guest, I suppose."

"Yes. He had to leave on business unexpectedly so I'm kind of stuck here. I wondered…"

Monika was already climbing into the runabout, as if Gina hadn't spoken. But she wasn't ready to give up yet. "It would only take me a few minutes to grab my things, if you could possibly give me a lift to the mainland?"

"I'm sorry," Monika said, not sounding sorry in the slightest. "I'm meeting someone at the airport. I can't wait."

Gina watched her steer the runabout out to sea with a twinge of jealousy. Monika had hair that hung in a pin-straight bob, legs up to her armpits, a rich boyfriend and a beautiful boat. Some people had all the luck.

Sighing, she crossed the white sandy beach and slumped into one of the wicker chairs on the deck, considering what to do with her day. There was one silver lining of Nick's absence: she'd have plenty of time to do her daily ballet practice. The only difficulty was *where*. The four-poster bed took up too much room in the master bedroom, and even if she moved all the furniture in the lounge and rolled up the Persian rug, it would hardly be enough space.

But the third villa would have space. Nick had told her it was empty, abandoned when the owner went bankrupt. Empty meant no furniture. If one of the rooms had a finished floor…

She walked over to the villa entrance. A chain was threaded through the handles of the double doors, but the padlock was missing. She removed the chain, pushed the doors open and found herself in a small hallway—with a finished floor, she noticed. *Promising.*

Facing her was another door. She opened it, and stopped on the threshold, awestruck. The room was enormous. Beams of sunlight slanted in through skylights in the double-height ceiling, onto a vast expanse of honey-colored floorboards. The only furniture was some built-in cupboards at the far end— and fixed to the wall opposite her, a ballet barre. The other two walls were unfinished, their battens still visible.

Unmistakably, a dance studio. She stepped into the room and tested the floor by jumping up and down. It was properly sprung, not laid on concrete, to protect dancers from injury. Built by someone for whom dancing was a business, to be worth going to all that expense.

Her feet left footprints in the dust and sand. The place hadn't been used for ages. She must ask Nick if he knew anything about the previous owner…but wait. Why hadn't Nick told her about the studio? He knew she was a dancer and how useful it would be to her.

Another bone to pick with him when he got back from his trip. But in the meantime, she had more important things to think about. She would need to find a broom, a bucket and a mop for a start. That floor would take a lot of cleaning—but it would be worth it. With a gleeful skip, she left the studio, looking forward to a glorious morning of dancing.

****

Alex Korolev sat up in bed. Music filtered clearly through the wall between his bedroom and the villa next door. Someone was in his studio.

He reached for the buzzer by his pillow. Nick must be doing this, as revenge for refusing to increase his allowance. Alex put the buzzer down slowly. He wouldn't give his brother the satisfaction of knowing how much it upset him.

No point trying to sleep now. He pressed the remote control to open the blind, letting in the morning light, such as it was. The window, at the back of the house, looked out onto the cliff face only a few feet away.

He closed his eyes. If only he could sit quietly and listen to the melody like a normal person, but he'd been dancing since he was three. His instinctive response to music was movement. Without wanting to, he could see the dance in his mind's eye. Unbidden, his shoulders swayed. He moved his leg—and gasped at the pain.

The music was from *Nutcracker*, which made him think of the last Christmas before the accident. The festive season was always a busy time, crisscrossing the globe as a guest artist. He had traveled nearly fifty thousand miles in two months.

How his life had changed. In the last six months, he'd traveled no more than a few meters, from his bed to the bathroom and back.

His world now was limited, but not without its comforts. A king-sized bed, goose-down pillows, a large-screen television—although satellite reception was unpredictable at best, and he didn't know enough Greek to understand the local broadcasts. He'd had the Persian rug removed from the floor. He would never need to walk on it, and it caught on the wheelchair's wheels.

The music died away. His muscles relaxed.

The swans' music from *Swan Lake* began. An inspiring Tchaikovsky score. He knew it too well. The ballet he and Louise had been rehearsing before the crash.

The first notes of the *pas de deux* sounded through the wall, and the memory of the accident flooded his brain—the squeal of tires, the screeching, grinding collision of metal, glass showering over him. Then silence, and the smell. Rain, gasoline, rubber, and a strange smell of copper. Blood. Louise's blood. Her broken body next to him, her head—.

"For fuck's sake!" He grabbed the lunch tray from the nightstand and hurled it in the direction of the sound. It ricocheted the wall, sending crockery shards flying. The violent movement sent a jagged pain through his legs as the bolts of the metal fixators grated against bone. He swore at them.

Minutes later, the bedroom door creaked open. "What the fuck do you think you're —" Alex stopped. He was not shouting at Nick, but a petite woman dressed in a typical dancer's ragbag of clothing, with a tangle of dark brown curls and huge dark eyes.

****

Gina was completely thrown. The man sitting in the bed in front of her must be Nick's brother Sasha. But he was a dead ringer for the famous dancer, Alex Korolev.

How many hours had she spent as a teenager, gazing in rapt adoration at his poster on her bedroom wall? It showed him dancing in his most famous role, *Spartacus*, wearing nothing but a gladiator's leather shorts, his bronzed chest crisscrossed by leather bands, his powerful muscles gleaming with oil. His face hadn't changed: the square jaw, the straight nose, the wheat-colored hair flopping over his high forehead. The mesmerizing lagoon-blue eyes.

Suddenly, she understood why she'd found Nick so irresistible. He had Alex Korolev's eyes.

"You were in my studio?" the man asked, in a deep voice like Nick's, but with only a ghost of his accent.

She'd been standing there with her mouth open like a goldfish. She gulped, trying to find her voice—then the switches clicked in her head.

His studio. Built for a professional dancer.

Omigod omigod omigod.

He didn't *look* like Alex Korolev. He *was* Alex Korolev. Why had Nick called him Sasha?

"Well?" he said.

"I'm sorry." She took a few steps forward so she wasn't shouting from the doorway. "I didn't know it was yours. The door was open and I didn't think—"

"Did Nick offer you the studio?"

"No, no, he didn't mention it." She felt the need to defend him, for some reason. "He had to rush off on business today. I'm sure he would have explained if he'd been here…"

That seemed to amuse him. A half-smile twisted his mouth. "No matter. It is not your fault."

She smiled, relieved that he seemed to have forgiven her.

He held out his hand. "I'm Alex. And you are—?"

"Gina." She took his hand, losing her ability to breathe as their fingers met. She was holding Alex Korolev's hand!

Gina Williams, you're twenty-three, not twelve! Get a grip.

Reluctantly, she let go. "Actually, I know who you are. I'm a huge fan. I saw you in *Spartacus* four times. It was the most amazing performance I've ever seen. I hope we'll be seeing you on stage again soon."

She stopped, noticing his mouth had set in a thin line, the muscles in his jaw tensing in reaction to her words. An awful feeling of dread crept over her. What an idiot she was, so overwhelmed at seeing him that she'd missed the obvious signs. He looked pale. The blanket over his legs was strangely lumpy. She knew he'd been in a car crash, but that was months ago. Some French ballerina had run her sports car off the road. She'd died, but he'd survived with minor injuries. Or so the newspapers had said. Still, to be bed-ridden after all this time…

Her stomach lurched as her gaze reached the corner of the room. The pair of crutches could mean a lingering knee or ankle injury, with a long recovery time. But a wheelchair…*oh, no, please no.*

When he finally spoke, his words confirmed her fears. "I won't be returning."

Her heart broke for him. At thirty, he should be at the peak of his career. She remembered his effortless leaps across the stage. How would she feel if she woke up tomorrow and couldn't dance? To hear the music she loved and be unable to express it. To be forever earthbound when her body wanted to soar.

Dancing is what I am, not what I do.

It was a trite phrase, trotted out by dancers to explain their dedication, without really thinking. But true, all the same. No one else could understand how completely the dancer and the dance were intertwined, how fundamental movement was to a dancer's very existence. For someone who could dance so brilliantly to suddenly lose that ability…

Tears welled over, and she ran her hands over her body, looking in vain for a handkerchief. He picked up a box of tissues from the bedside table and held them out to her. She grabbed one and blew her nose, trying to regain her composure. His eyes, watching her quietly, didn't help.

She broke the silence. "I'm so sorry."

"I'd be grateful if you don't tell anyone else about this. I don't want media attention."

"No, no, certainly not," Gina said, as if the thought of telling all her friends had never crossed her mind, "and I'm sorry about the studio, I won't use it again."

"Use it," he said.

"No, really, I—"

"You are a dancer, yes? You need a studio. I have one. It makes no sense to leave it there, gathering dust. Use it and welcome." He smiled at her.

"Thank you so much, I really, really appreciate it."

She felt such a fool, standing there with a huge grin

on her face and nothing to say, but she couldn't bring herself to leave his presence. "Well, I—I should go." She tried to adopt a more adult, ladylike expression but the smile kept escaping. "Lovely to meet you."

Belatedly, it occurred to her that she must look a fright. Medusa hair, no make-up, a pink ballet wrap-over she'd had since she was fifteen, the ancient leotard and holey tights. Embarrassment gave her the impetus to turn and scurry out of the room.

Outside the door, she closed her eyes. Had she really just curtsied before she ran out? He must think she was a complete twit. But oh, he was still gorgeous, even with dark shadows under those amazing eyes. What a pity she couldn't tell a soul about him.

****

Listening to the plunking of the *Sylvia* waltz through the wall, Alex chastised himself for offering her the studio. Now he would have to listen to that damn music every day.

He would never have agreed if she hadn't cried. She had looked at him with those huge velvet-brown eyes, moisture trembling on her long lashes, and then that smile had broken through her tears like a rainbow.

He wondered what kind of dancer she was. She'd been playing ballet music, but she lacked the flat-chested, anorexic look of a professional ballet dancer. Not nearly tall enough to be a showgirl either, and too classy to be a stripper— though she had the curves for it, from what he could see under that woolly warm-up gear. Mentally he tried to peel it off her.

Not that a woman like her would look twice at him now. In any case, she was his brother's girlfriend, and therefore off-limits, however much he'd like to fantasize.

But where was Nick, and what was he thinking, to bring a gorgeous woman like that to the island and abandon her the very next morning? Alex made a mental note to ask his PA, Monika, if she knew more about it, although he was not hopeful. She disliked Nick and did her best to avoid him, and any of the girlfriends he brought to the island.

The love theme from *Spartacus* began and was cut off after only a few bars. Thank God. The *Waltz of the Flowers* began. The notes swirled and eddied, the melody an irresistible stream of joy that lifted his spirits, carrying him along in spite of himself.

He had been avoiding music because it reminded him so painfully of all he'd lost. But the *Waltz* reminded him there were good memories, too. He had forgotten the power that music had, the energy it could create. Music was the engine that had fueled his dancing, that had enabled him to fly. As Tchaikovsky's boisterous finale galloped to its climax, he felt more alive than he had in weeks.

He wondered where Gina was from, how she had met Nick, what she was doing now. For the first time in months, he wanted to get out of this room, so he could find out more about her. He wanted to know what that mouth would be like to kiss. What those breasts would be like, crushed against him. What that—

His mind said, *she's Nick's girlfriend. Get over it.* His body wasn't listening.

Chapter Two

The bedroom door creaked. Alex prayed it would be Clara, bringing lunch, so he could ask her to clean up the broken crockery and coffee-stained wall before Monika saw them.

It wasn't.

Monika stopped with her hand on the door handle. "What the—? Alex, what the hell happened?"

"There is nothing to worry about." He raised a calming hand. "It's fine."

Monika stared at him. He wondered how to phrase his next sentence. If he got it wrong, she would storm out before he had a chance to explain, and he did not want to do that to Gina. "Someone was playing music in the studio. I over-reacted—"

"It was that girl, I bet. And I bet Nick put her up to it. I'll go and sort her out."

"No!" Alex's shout made her stop in mid-turn. "I have spoken to her. In fact, I've said she can use the studio for the rest of her stay."

"Are you serious?"

"Yes. She heard the noise, she came to investigate and…and we had a chat." He paused. "Seeing her…listening to the music…it made me realize I have been stubborn. You are right. I will get up today, for a few hours."

Several expressions chased across Monika's face—

surprise, disbelief and finally a grin. "You know, I met her on the jetty earlier, looking like a crazy woman. I wish I'd paid more attention. I've been trying to winkle you out of that bed for months, and she achieves it in a day! What's she got that I haven't?" She raised an eyebrow. "Apart from boobs, of course."

"It has nothing to do with—"

"You don't fool me, darling, I know you too well," she said, laughter in her voice. "I bet she leaned forward and looked at you with those big Bambi eyes, and you practically fell into that cleavage."

"No! If you must know, she—she has a nice smile." He held up a hand as Monika opened her mouth to scoff. "Okay, okay, I admit it, a nice figure too, from what I could see. It was hard to tell, she was wearing some knitted thing."

"Well, she's improved your mood, at least. You know, that's the first time I've seen you smile for weeks. Anyway, let's get you up."

She walked to the bed and drew back the covers, careful not to catch them on the fixators on his legs.

Every time Alex looked at them, he recalled the moment he'd first seen them at the hospital. Until that moment, he had been sure he would prove the doctors wrong. Never dance again? *Hah!* He'd show them. Those specialists had no concept of how hard he could work, or how dedicated he was to his career. No matter how bad the injury, he would return to that stage.

And then he had seen the circular metal cages encasing his legs from knee to ankle, the three great bolts skewering them in place…

"You're sure the music won't upset you?" Monika asked, bringing the wheelchair close to the bed.

"I'm sure," he lied. The music had upset him, but it had brought joy, too. "She's a dancer, she has to practice."

He braced himself. The fixators were heavy and he needed momentum to swing them off the bed. Trying to move slowly only made it worse. He clenched his teeth and swung. He sat on the edge of the bed for a moment to recover.

"Did she say what kind of dancing she does?"

"I didn't ask," he admitted.

"I can guess, if she's anything like Nick's other tarts."

Alex shook his head. "She's not a stripper. She's...different."

Monika leaned forward so he could put his arms around her neck. "I didn't say she was a stripper. I know exotic dancers who are very classy people. They're not the ones Nick usually associates with, that's all. But if you've talked to her...it sounds as though his taste has improved. Maybe he's finally growing up."

"My thoughts exactly." He used her support to stand up and swivel into the wheelchair.

Monika walked around to take the handles of the chair. "Let's get those dressings changed, and you can sit in the lounge and admire the view. Who knows, you might get lucky and she'll go for a swim."

Alex contemplated the idea. A swim. He'd almost forgotten there was water out there. What would Gina look like in a swimsuit?

Monika interrupted his train of thought. "I still think Nick engineered it. He probably told her to use the studio, just to upset you."

"She told me she was bored and went exploring."

"You give that brother of yours too much credit."

They reached the shower. Monika helped Alex onto the stool, helped him strip off his pajamas, and stood well back when he turned on the faucets.

Like most Greek bathrooms, there was no shower screen or curtain. Alex felt no embarrassment. Monika had been a dancer too, once. Dancers took nakedness for granted.

"I'm sorry, I forgot to ask you about Juliette," he said, as he lathered his hair. "You are back much earlier than I expected. Her flight was on time?"

"Amazing, isn't it? And she's absolutely thrilled with her cottage."

"She would be welcome here, you know."

"Don't be silly. She's here to write her novel, not to see me. Besides, that sofa bed in the lounge is fine for one night, but I wouldn't make anyone suffer it for a whole month."

Alex wiped the water from his eyes and gave her a look. "I was not thinking of the sofa bed."

She reached out as if to slap him on the head. He ducked. "Behave!" she said, but she was laughing. Then her expression grew serious. "She won't be sharing my room, Alex, much though I'd love her to. I told you, Juliette's straight. Or thinks she is. I love her to bits, but unless she can get over her hang-ups, she's never going to be anything more than my best friend. I'm resigned to it."

"A stunning redhead like you, I don't know how she can resist you. Especially wearing those shorts."

She pretended to slap him again, and he almost fell off the stool.

While Monika helped him dress, Alex reflected on how selfish he had been for the last six months. He had felt that if he couldn't dance, there was no point in living. He had given up, not even trying to look after himself. But he had never given a thought to Monika.

After the accident, he had offered her a generous payout, but she had insisted on staying on, even though he no longer needed a personal assistant. "I've spent eight years looking after you, Alex, and I'm not going to stop now," she'd said. "You'll need help with different things, that's all. I've checked with the doctors, and it's nothing I can't handle. Anyway, I quite fancy a few months on a Greek island."

He had said yes, of course, and given her a raise— it was only fair. She could so easily have found a job with another celebrity, handling charity fundraisers and TV interviews instead of pus-filled dressings and bedpans. But the money didn't give him the right to take her for granted the way he had. He owed her a great deal. He didn't want to think what life would have been like without her patient, smiling presence. She had been stuck on the island for far too long.

"While Juliette is here, you must take some time off, as much as we can arrange," he said. "If I use the wheelchair, I can manage without you for longer. We can work out a timetable."

Monika grinned. "Deal. But only if you'll let me give you some rehab exercises, too."

"Deal."

****

In Nick's villa, Gina cleared away the remains of her lunch and put her plate in the dishwasher, which was already full of dishes. She frowned at the smooth, brushed-steel front of the machine, and wondered how on earth to switch it on. All the appliances in this shiny white kitchen looked challengingly futuristic.

A dour-faced little woman, twice Gina's width and about twice her age, waddled in, laden with shopping bags. She stopped when she saw Gina. "Mr. Nick told me he have a guest. I am Clara, housekeeper."

"I am Gina. Let me help you with those bags."

Clara's expression softened a little, and she let Gina take some of the bags and set them on the breakfast bar. By the time Gina had helped her empty them all, stacking the groceries in the fridge and the cupboards, she was positively beaming.

"You are very helpful. Thank you, miss. Will you be staying long?"

"I'm not sure, really." Gina sensed Clara was curious about her and Nick, and she didn't want to discuss it. "You speak very good English."

"I worked in the big houses on Corfu when I was a girl. Many famous English people lived there in those days." Clara pulled an apron from her bag and put it on. "I am sorry, I must go next door. I am late today and I must make Mister Alex his lunch."

With that, she bustled out of the kitchen.

Gina climbed the stairs to Nick's bedroom. The decor was the same elegant terracotta and white as the rest of the house. Against it, his choice of bed struck a jarring note: a king-size four-poster in black wood, with red satin sheets. Of course, she knew why he wanted the posts.

She hadn't unpacked yet, and part of her questioned whether it was worth doing. Nick had been so moody since they arrived at Venetiko, not at all like the charmer he'd been in Thessaloniki. Still, she shouldn't make snap judgments based on less than twenty-four hours.

The closet was less than half full. Nick didn't have a lot of clothes, but what he had was expensive: Italian suits and shirts from Saville Row tailors. She felt almost embarrassed to hang her chain-store clothes next to his. There was no room on the shelves, though. Luckily, one of the bedside cabinets was empty apart from a scatter of loose change. She fished out the coins and managed to squeeze her undies and dance wear into the three slim drawers.

What to do until three o'clock? She pulled a paperback from her tote. She'd purchased the fat historical romance at the airport in London and intended to read it on the plane. So far, she hadn't gotten past the first chapter.

She opened the French doors onto the balcony under the gable, and settled on one of the white wicker sofas, adjusting the peaches-and-cream cushions to support her head. From here, she could enjoy a fabulous view of the beach, the turquoise water, and not far beyond that, the mainland. The red-tiled houses of Venetiko town marched up the hill, dotted with vivid splashes of pink and purple where bougainvillea rioted over their verandas.

She pulled a cream-colored knit throw over her knees and opened the novel. Within half an hour, she was fast asleep.

****

Monika opened the door to their lounge and waited while Alex wheeled himself in. He scanned the room, taking in the dove-gray sofas, the peach Persian rug, the silvery damask curtains—none of it to his taste, but elegantly done. The work of the millionaire who had bankrupted himself building the villas, allowing Alex to buy the whole island for a song.

Monika placed her hands on the arm of one of the sofas and pushed.

"What are you doing?" Alex asked.

"I'm—oof, these are heavy—moving the furniture out of the way. It'll give you some space to practice controlling that wheelchair yourself. It's all very well to wheel it along in a straight line, but you've got to learn to turn corners, too."

"Yes, teacher."

"I know I'm a nag, but you know you'll thank me later," she said, starting on the second sofa.

Alex hated to sit by and watch as she rearranged the furniture against the walls. Finally, she picked up a small coffee table and placed it at the window. "There. Now you can sit at the window and enjoy the delicious lunch Clara made for you."

She left to fetch the food. Alex wheeled his chair into position and gazed out at the sea, and the town of Venetiko beyond. Though no more than a ten-minute boat trip away, it seemed to belong to another world, another life.

In that life, he'd been so confident about the future, he had cheerfully spent the entire fee from his second movie to buy the island. Or rather, to make a down payment.

After the accident, the sensible thing would have been to sell the place and live in his London terrace house. The mortgage on the island was too much of a drain on his finances. But moving here had been a far more effective way of keeping out of the news; most people weren't even aware he had bought it. He had managed only a few visits, to supervise the building of the studio and take delivery of his "party boat"—what a waste of money that had been. He would have got rid of it, except that Nick was so in love with it.

The cruiser was not at the jetty.

Monika entered, carrying a tray. "You're in luck. Clara was late herself, so she was all set to apologize to me. Don't worry, I explained."

"Nick is still not back," Alex said.

"No." Monika placed the tray on the table. "Maybe we should ask your girlfriend to join you for lunch. She'll be all alone."

Alex's impulse was to leap at the chance, but the word "girlfriend" triggered a warning in his brain. "I don't think so. Nick is much too jealous. You know what he can be like."

"Yes, unfortunately, I do."

"I am sorry you and he don't get on."

Monika leaned against the window frame. "I just hate the way he sponges off you. Don't deny it, I'm the one who has to go to the bank for you. I know exactly how much you've spent on clearing his debts and indulging his spending."

"Nick had a hard life—"

"What does that have to do with anything?" She stood and paced across the front of the window, anger making her animated. "Why is it your job to make it up to him? It's not your fault he had an unhappy childhood, you weren't even there."

Alex didn't respond. Monika would never understand. Nick was the only family he had left in the world. As the older brother, it was his responsibility to keep the two of them together. Nick had suffered too much in his life. Though he had only dim memories of his late parents, Alex felt he owed it to them to look after his only brother.

Chapter Three

Finally, at dusk, the motor cruiser appeared out of the gloom. Gina ran out to the jetty to meet Nick. She extended her arms so he could throw her the mooring rope as he coasted up to the jetty, but he ignored the offer. She felt a stab of irritation. In Thessaloniki, where they'd met, it had felt wonderful to be with a man who insisted on doing everything for her—but there was a fine line between "goddess-who-deserves-to-do-nothing," and "little-woman-who's-too-helpless-to-do-anything."

He disembarked, crushed her in his arms and kissed her, but she found it hard to relax and enjoy his embrace. She was too wound up, thinking of how she would tackle him about Alex. How could Nick keep his brother's identity a secret? He'd done it deliberately, too, referring to him as Sasha instead of Alex. This didn't bode well for their relationship if he couldn't be honest with her.

Nick drank a beer at the smoked-glass kitchen table while Gina tossed the salad Clara had left for them and took the cheesecake out of the fridge. She had already turned on the oven to reheat the moussaka.

It was the strangest feeling, looking at Nick's face, now that she knew he was Alex's brother. They looked alike in more than just eyes and hair color, but Nick's military haircut and thick beard had disguised the shape of his face. Their bodies could hardly be more different: Nick's bodybuilding had created a thick neck and bulging biceps that looked nothing like Alex's streamlined dancer's physique.

She waited until he had demolished the moussaka and had almost finished the cheesecake before she broached the subject of Alex. "Why did you tell me your brother's name was Sasha?" she said, picking up her own fork.

"Because it is."

"His name's Alex."

"You talk to Monika?" Nick shrugged. "Sasha, Alex, in Russian both Alexander."

So he hadn't told her a deliberate lie about the name. "I didn't talk to Monika. I talked to Alex."

His eyes widened; his mouth dropped open. She had expected surprise, but he couldn't have looked more shocked if she'd said she'd just spoken to Santa Claus. "I tell you not see him." He shook his fork at her, spattering her shirt with strawberry sauce. "Why you go?"

"Careful!" She jumped up to fetch the sponge from the sink and dabbed at her sleeve. "I didn't mean to. I was exploring, I found the dance studio, and while I was in there, I heard a crash. I thought someone might've been hurt so I went to investigate."

"You not go again. Bad for Alex." He speared a strawberry and ate it, as if that was the end of the matter.

"Oh, I won't bother Alex again, of course, but I have to work out. It's my job, I have to stay in condition. The studio is there, and Alex said I could use it, and that's what I plan to do."

Nick didn't even look up from his meal. "I forbid."

Forbid? For a moment, Gina wondered if she had misheard. "Surely it's Alex's decision, not yours. I know who he is now, the secret's out. There's no reason I shouldn't use it."

The table legs scraped across the floor as Nick sprang to his feet. He stepped round the table and grabbed her arms. "You obey me. Or I punish you."

The words might be menacing, but the suggestive smirk on his face meant she couldn't mistake his meaning. "Nick, I know you like this master-slave thing, but it belongs in the bedroom. It doesn't give you the right to order me around in real life. If you think it does, maybe I should just go home."

She twisted away from him, pulling her arms from his grasp, and walked away. In the entrance hall, she stopped, feeling foolish. Where could she go? She heard his footsteps and felt his hand on her shoulder. "Forgive me, Gina. I have difficult day." He kissed her neck. "I told you. My brother very sick. If you use studio, he hear your music, he hear you dance, upset for him, yes?"

She opened her mouth to say Alex had already heard the music and didn't mind, but he interrupted her. "Also, villa is building site, dangerous. I will lock."

Gina thought about the beautiful, raftered ceiling with its huge skylights, the impeccably smooth wooden floorboards and the elegant cabinetry. A couple of the walls were unfinished, but there was nothing dangerous about the studio. Before she could say so, Nick had taken her hand and pulled her into the corridor, where he opened the first door on the left and flicked on the light. The room was kitted out as a gym, with a rack of free weights, medicine balls, a bench and a yoga mat.

"Here, you exercise," he said. "See? You not need studio."

She could use the weights for extra conditioning, but there was no floor space to dance in, so it wasn't a solution. But it wasn't worth ruining the evening by starting the argument again. No doubt he would see it differently in the morning after he'd had time to think it over.

****

Alex bolted upright in bed, the vision of the broken windshield fading into the reality of his large screen TV. He sagged against the headboard. Early morning was the most common time for his flashbacks, though this was the first for several weeks. Gina had made him think about Louise yesterday—no doubt that was the reason for the nightmare.

His relationship with Louise had barely begun when the accident occurred; but to hold and lift a ballerina meant touching her almost as intimately as if they'd already been lovers. He knew every inch of her. He remembered how feather-light her body had been, how effortless to swing into a fish dive. How easily the steering wheel had…he ran his hands over his face, as if that might wipe away the visions.

He had sometimes speculated about a future with Louise, if she had lived, but Monika said that was no more than survivor guilt. Deep down, he knew that was true. Louise would have been just one more of the ballerinas with whom he had shared a stage and a bed.

Yesterday's optimism had deserted him. Monika would arrive soon, expecting him to be eager to get out of bed and seize the day, but he had no appetite for it.

There seemed no point in all the pain and effort, if the best he could hope for was to stagger around with a walking frame like some doddering old man. Once upon a time, he could fly.

His bedroom door slammed. He squinted; the broad-shouldered shape approaching his bed could be only one person. He pressed the remote control to open the window blind. "Nick, if this is about your allowance—"

"No. I know you will not increase it," his brother said in Russian. "But I need an advance. Only a couple of thousand."

"Your allowance goes into the bank in less than a week," Alex said. "Can't you survive till then? You know I won't finance your gambling anymore—"

"It's not gambling. It's a cash flow problem, that's all. Thessaloniki was expensive."

Thessaloniki was on the other side of Greece. "What were you doing there?"

"I felt like it. Venetiko is boring."

Alex couldn't argue with that. For him, the whole attraction of Venetiko was its quiet, undiscovered beauty, but tranquility had never been Nick's style. Perhaps, if he'd been thinking straight, he would have encouraged Nick to stay behind in London—but he hadn't been thinking straight about anything much after the accident. He shifted, trying to find a less painful position for his legs.

"Alex, the money?" Nick said. "It's Gina's fault. She says you met her. Girls like that don't open their legs unless you wine and dine them, treat them like a princess. That costs."

Alex clenched his teeth. "The answer is no."

"But—"

"That's final. How many times do I have to explain?" *My career is over.* He still couldn't say it aloud. "We can't live like millionaires any longer. Your allowance is far higher than the salary I pay Monika. It should be more than enough."

Nick didn't have to speak. His response was written all over him. The jutting lower lip, the clenched fists. He turned to leave, then swiveled back. "I have told Gina not to see you. You will keep your hands off her. She is mine."

He slammed the door as he left.

Alex bit his lip, regretting his decision. Things were bad enough between himself and Nick already, and he had made it worse, all because he'd got angry on behalf of a woman he didn't even know.

****

Gina stood outside the third villa, hands on hips, staring at the door. The chain had been threaded through the door handles and padlocked. Nick had meant it when he said, "I forbid."

Now she had to decide what to do about it.

So as not to make a noise on the deck as she passed Alex's villa, she ran along the beach back to Nick's place. There was still no sign of him. She sat at the breakfast bar in the kitchen, trying to look as though she'd been eating her breakfast all along.

She had tried to discuss the subject early that morning, thinking Nick would be more agreeable while they were in bed—but he'd uttered a curt "no" and headed for the bathroom. Then he'd announced he was going to see Alex. Her first reaction was relief, because Alex had already given his permission. But something about Nick's manner made her doubt. Finding the studio locked only reinforced that feeling—it suggested he'd already made up his mind, and that what Alex said would make no difference. Though it flummoxed her why Nick should be so against the idea.

It was true that her dedication to dance had sometimes irritated Nick in Thessaloniki. With their busy schedules, finding time to meet had been difficult, and he resented it when she wouldn't give up a dance class to see him. Perhaps he was fearful that if she had Alex's studio, she would neglect him.

But in that case, *he* shouldn't neglect *her*.

Today would be a test. He was off to the mainland again, but this time he would have no excuse to leave her behind. She was ready, her handbag next to her under the bench.

Nick returned. He didn't look in the best of moods.

She poured him a coffee. "What did Alex say?"

"What?"

"About the studio."

"I not ask. Not necessary." He took one swig of the coffee, set it down and stood up. "I go."

"Wait a minute!"

He was already on his way, striding out of the kitchen. Gina clenched her teeth, determined not to lose her temper. "Please, let me come with you this morning," she said, catching up with him. "You can drop me anywhere. Just let me know when you're coming back."

"I not know when I come back." He finished his coffee and set off for the jetty. She grabbed her bag and hurried after him.

"I tell you what," she said as they walked, "if I

could borrow the runabout, I can go to the mainland myself, and I won't have to bother you at all."

He grunted. "Boat belong to Sasha. Monika needs today."

She had expected as much. Fat chance she had of borrowing it from grumpy Monika. "What about that one?" She pointed to a tarpaulin-covered shape resting on the sand by the generator shed, at the far end of the beach.

He released the mooring rope. "Engine broke. Wait for part."

She sighed. She should have expected that, too. Why else would Nick use an ocean-going cruiser for the ten-minute trip between the island and the mainland? The distance was so short, she could almost swim it. But not quite, unfortunately. "If I come with you now, I could get a water taxi back. Do they have water taxis?"

"No."

"Look, I'm sure I can find my own way back, somehow."

He was already on board the cruiser. When she stepped onto the swim platform to follow him, he stopped her with a hand on her arm. "Better you stay."

"This is ridiculous!" She struggled against his grip, but he responded by grabbing her round the waist with his other arm, picking her up and depositing her back on the jetty.

"You. Stay."

She watched, fuming, as the cruiser roared away.

She didn't understand Nick. One minute he was a charming gentleman, next minute a caveman. She was beginning to think the caveman was the real Nick—but against that was the evidence of all those weeks in Thessaloniki, when he'd given no hint of that side of his personality.

It wasn't fair to draw conclusions based on just two days. Perhaps the stress of his business emergency, whatever it was, was getting to him. All the same, she couldn't forgive his behavior. And she was positive that he'd lied about the studio.

With that in mind, she considered herself released from all her promises.

Chapter Four

Alex sat in his wheelchair at the picture window of the lounge. He looked up as Monika collected the lunch tray from the table in front of him. "I should have done this long ago," he said.

"The only possible answer to that is, 'I told you so'," Monika said with a wry smile. "I'm off to Juliette's. I'll be back in time for a late dinner. *Ciao*."

Monika was right. Against all her nagging, he had been pig-headed about staying in his bedroom; part of his fuck-the-world reaction to his injuries. Stupid, in retrospect: just looking at the view cheered him. Especially when this afternoon, the view included Gina. No more knitted layers, just a red string bikini that offered him a glorious view as she strolled away from the villa, across the sand to the jetty. She carried a sarong and towel, which she dropped on the weathered wooden surface before slipping into the water.

It was a pity the terrain around the house was rough. Rock and soft sand were impossible in a wheelchair. A few months ago, he hadn't cared. The outside world had been something he wanted to forget. Now he wished he could be out there, swimming with her in the clear water. It was frustrating to be so far away, able to see only her head and shoulders, and sometimes not even that.

There was something alluring about the way her

hair fell back, dark and seal-like, when she lifted her head out of the water.

Monika left the house, jamming her canvas hat on her head, handbag slung over her arm. She stopped on the jetty and called out to Gina, who came swimming over to speak to her. Alex couldn't hear their conversation. When Monika gestured toward the window, he wondered if she was talking about him. Gina's head swiveled in his direction and her face lit up with the smile he'd found so irresistible. He wanted to think it was meant for him.

A few minutes after Monika had driven the runabout away, Gina ran out of the water and up the beach. The sight had been worth waiting for. She had the tiny waist and flat stomach of a dancer, but above them her breasts rose high, round and firm.

She had to turn back to collect her sarong and towel, giving him a three-hundred-sixty-degree view— and the bonus of her bending over to pick up her things. He groaned. This was some kind of torture. Delicious, maybe, but still torture.

She was out of sight now, entering the house. *Phew.*

A polite cough sounded behind him. He used his left hand on the wheel to swing his chair around. Gina stood in the open doorway. Droplets still beaded her skin. Her thin sarong was tied low around her hips and clung to her damp thighs.

"I hope you don't mind," she said. "Monika said you were here."

"Not at all. Please, come in."

She stepped into the room. "I wanted to say how much I appreciate you allowing me to use the studio.

It's such a wonderful place to practice."

He had to make an effort to concentrate. "I wouldn't know, I've never used it. It wasn't finished when I had the accident."

"Are you sure the music isn't disturbing you?"

"No, not at all," he said. Disturbing him? She had no idea how much she was disturbing him now. The shape of her nipples was clearly visible through the soft fabric of her bikini.

He tore his eyes away and cast around for something else to talk about. "You must let me know if I can help you with your dancing."

For a moment, he wondered what he had said to switch on that smile again—then she spoke. "Would you really teach me? That would be unbelievable! Even if you could spare half an hour, twenty minutes, it would be wonderful." She was almost jumping up and down with glee, her eyes growing wide with excitement. "When were you thinking?"

She had misunderstood. He'd meant to offer a referral to his agent, or an introduction to—actually he wasn't sure what he'd meant, it had been the first thing to pop into his mind. But why not? The best teacher he'd ever had, Anton Lehtonen, had hobbled on two sticks. "Whatever time suits you."

"Fantastic!" Her smile dimmed, a frown forming between her brows. "Can I let you know tomorrow? Nick and I haven't managed to have much time together yet, I don't want to agree a time and find he's got something planned for us."

Nick. Damn. How could he forget? His brain was addled. "Maybe it's not such a good idea. Nick won't approve."

"*Approve?* He's my boyfriend, not my father!"

Alex hesitated. How to explain Nick's jealousy without making him look bad? "You know what it's like with brothers. We're competitive. He is convinced I try to steal his girlfriends. In my defense, I've never given him reason to think so. But it means I would not do anything without asking him first."

Gina pursed her lips. "I wouldn't want to cause a family argument. I'll speak to him, but I'll have something to stay if he tries to stop me."

"Let me talk to him first, if you don't mind?"

She seemed about to argue, then shrugged. "If you think it's best. I really appreciate the offer."

Before he could say more, she had put her hand on his neck and planted a kiss on his cheek. Water droplets showered from her hair onto his face, but he scarcely noticed. Her fingers against his neck were feather soft, but the surge of desire it sent through his body was anything but gentle.

"Oh heck." She was trying ineffectually to dry his face with her soggy towel. He turned towards her, raising his hand to stop her, and found himself looking straight down the swelling cleft of her breasts.

"It's okay," he said in something between a squeak and a groan. "A little seawater won't hurt me."

He touched his cheek as she left. The kiss had been the light thank-you peck dancers exchanged all the time, but the sensation of her warm lips lingered. She had a talent for making him agree to things against his better judgment. First the studio, now the class. It would never happen—Nick would be too jealous. He would know soon enough—the moment Gina mentioned having seen Alex, Nick would be at his door bellowing for an explanation.

Alex wasn't afraid of Nick's temper tantrums, but he didn't like the idea of exposing Gina to them. He hoped she wouldn't try to raise the subject with him before he'd had a chance to calm the waters.

****

Around eight o'clock, Gina gave up waiting for Nick, and ate dinner alone. The evening had turned chilly, so she abandoned her plan to read on the deck, settling on the cream linen sofa in Nick's lounge room instead. Her book lay open on her knee, but she couldn't concentrate. Alex's offer to coach her was priceless, but she could feel it slipping through her fingers.

Alex had asked her to wait until he'd spoken to Nick, but he didn't know Nick had already forbidden her to see Alex or use the studio. Alex didn't know she'd had to pick the padlock this morning. She should've confessed, but it was too late now. She could foresee them having a row, and she felt guilty at causing trouble between the two brothers.

No, it was her problem, and her responsibility to deal with it, even if that meant facing a tough confrontation with Nick. But she would have to pick her moment carefully.

When she finally saw the cruiser approaching, she hurried out to the jetty. Nick's kiss had the strong, lighter-fuel taste of vodka, and her mood dipped. She had pictured him working hard somewhere, but he'd been in some bar instead.

In the kitchen, she made him the vodka he asked for—but only a thimbleful of alcohol, disguised with a mountain of ice. "That was a long day."

"Yes." Nick pulled his bulging wallet from his back pocket and dropped it on the coffee table.

"I still don't understand how you can run an import-export business in such a small town.

"You know where is Albania?" Nick sat on the sofa, waving his already-empty glass towards the north. "Border only an hour from here. Albania is transitioning to market-oriented economy. There are wonderful opportunities for forward-thinking entrepreneurs. More vodka."

He stumbled over the long words, and not just because of the vodka. The words were obviously quoted from a marketing brochure. But she had never seen a brochure from his work, or any other paperwork for that matter.

Come to think of it, Nick never carried a briefcase, or a laptop. Just his phone and that wallet, bursting with cash. Gina bit her lip. "Tell me the truth, Nick. Do you have a proper business, or is it *all* black market?"

His eyes narrowed. Eventually he spoke. "I tell you already, is Greece. It is only way to make money here."

Gina nodded, sighing. She understood the Greek economy was a mess. She'd guessed, from the way Nick flashed wads of banknotes in Thessaloniki, that some of his business was cash in hand, a nod and a wink. The black market seemed epidemic in Greece, even in businesses like the dance festival where she'd worked, and the theatre where they'd staged the final show. But she had assumed his under-the-counter deals were part of a larger, legitimate operation. She couldn't see how small-time smuggling could pay for his fancy suits. Or his fancy boat.

He reached up, caught her arm and pulled her onto

the couch beside him. "Better to not ask questions."

"But—"

He silenced her with his mouth, but she was too distracted to respond. He stood, still holding her arm, and hauled her up off the couch. "Come to bed."

At the bedroom door, she tried to pull away towards the bathroom, but he urged her forward to the bed. She wasn't in the mood for sex, but she wasn't in the mood for a row, either. They fell together onto the satin quilt.

Although her brain felt disengaged, her body betrayed her. She had never experienced bondage before Nick, but the idea had always aroused her. The power of his arms holding her down, and his insistent, demanding tongue, made her quiver with anticipation.

Nick flipped her over and fastened her wrists to the bedposts with soft silk ties.

Her breath hitched as his hand caressed her buttocks—but instead of a light spank, there was a sharp, vicious sting. She yelped.

She craned her head around. He had a belt in his hand. "Nick, what are you doing?"

"You need discipline, woman."

"No, Nick. You'll hurt me. No belts."

"You obey me." He raised the belt.

She twisted, pulling her arm out of the silk tie, yelling, "No!" The end of the belt struck her on the thigh.

"Bring that ass here!" Nick tried to grab her leg, but she had shed the other tie now and scrambled off the bed. He glared at her. "Woman, you obey me!"

She planted her feet, bracing herself in case he tried to force her back on the bed. "No, Nick. this is too much. Stop."

His eyes glowed under furrowed brows. She held her ground, returning his glare.

He whirled, threw the belt into the corner of the room, and stalked off to the bathroom.

Her knees buckled and she slumped on the edge of the bed, trembling, all too aware how close she had come to a beating. If he had decided to press on, she wouldn't have been able to stop him. Those arms were far too powerful.

Nick emerged from the bathroom, climbed into bed and pulled up the quilt, his back to her. What was she supposed to do? She went to the bathroom and brushed her teeth, listening for any sign of movement in the bedroom. Nothing. She poured a glass of water and wrapped herself in one of the white waffle bathrobes hung on the door. Still nothing. Her bare feet making no sound, she slipped out of the bathroom and through to the balcony.

The moon gave her enough light to find her way to the sofa. She curled up among the cushions, huddling into the woolen throw for warmth. She sipped her water, waiting for Nick to appear at the door and apologize. He didn't.

Staring out at the sea, she scolded herself for being so willfully dumb. She'd known, right from the start, that they had nothing in common; but the fire he could ignite with just a look had seemed too significant to ignore.

Until she'd met Alex and discovered the simple explanation—that Nick had Alex's eyes. Deep down, she had known she was lying to herself. All that bullshit about "not judging based on two days." In any other place and time, Nick's behavior yesterday would've been a clear signal for her to pack up and leave. Even more so today. All the warning signs had been there, but she hadn't wanted to admit it, because she couldn't bear the thought of leaving Alex so soon. She would have to give up on the master class now, because she couldn't possibly stay with Nick. Not after this.

She knew he liked BDSM, but up till now, their play had been mild—soft ties, light spanking. He had never forcibly restrained her or hit her hard. Now, her thigh still stung where the belt had struck. There would be a bruise. Had he picked up the belt out of anger, or was it a sign of his true tastes? Perhaps up till now he'd been softening her up, not wanting to scare her off until he'd got her isolated on the island.

A chill ran through her. All he had to do was wait until Monika was off on some errand, and he could do whatever he liked. Alex wouldn't be able to do a thing about it. He might not even know anything had happened—would he hear her screams at the other end of his villa? Perhaps that was why Nick had been so keen to keep her away from Alex and Monika. If they didn't know her, they wouldn't wonder if she disappeared…

She stood and walked to the window, shaking her head as if to clear away her thoughts. She was being ridiculous, reading far too much into the situation. He'd been angry and drunk and picked up his belt. No doubt once he was sober, he'd be full of apologies. That didn't excuse what he'd tried to do, but it was an explanation. There was no need to start turning him into some kind of monster.

All the same, she couldn't stay with him.

If this was anywhere else, she would wake Nick, tell him it was over, pack up and walk out—but here, she had no way to leave the island without Nick's cooperation. Recalling the fury in his eyes as they'd faced off in the bedroom, she very much doubted she would get it. She was stuck on the island until morning and she'd have to make the best of it.

Her mind revolted at the thought of sharing Nick's bed again. But if he woke and found her sleeping on the sofa, it might only make him angrier. She tiptoed back into the bedroom, shrugged off the dressing gown, and slipped under the quilt as quietly as she could. Thankfully, Nick didn't stir.

She lay awake for a long time.

Chapter Five

The next morning, Gina woke with a start after Nick tossed aside the covers and strode to the bathroom. He didn't even look at her. She considered following him but then thought better of it. As it was difficult to have a civilized conversation in the nude, she decided to wait and gauge his mood over breakfast.

Even then, it was bound to be awkward, and after last night's *contretemps*, she feared it could get nasty. Best to be ready in advance, rather than endure Nick's glowering while she packed up later.

She opened the top drawer of the bedside cabinet and scooped out an armful of underwear. Something clinked on the tiles at her feet, and she hesitated, but there was no time to investigate. She needed to pack as much as she could before Nick returned.

Her suitcase sat on the floor of the closet. She opened it and crammed the underwear into the mesh pocket inside the lid. A gush of water told her Nick had started the shower.

Hauling clothes off hangers into the case, she wondered what she'd dropped by the bed. If it was one of her favorite earrings, she'd hate to leave it behind. They weren't valuable in money terms, but her grandmother had given them to her. Now she thought of it, she *had* left them on top of the cabinet. Careless.

She returned to the bed. Sure enough, one of the

pair sat on the cabinet, but its twin was nowhere to be seen. Getting down on all fours, she checked the floor, peered under the bed…and found the earring, resting against something covered in plaited leather. She retrieved the earring, but something about the object looked familiar. She reached for it and pulled.

As she'd suspected, it was a handle—and the leather plaiting continued, snaking under the bed in a coil. She didn't have to pull it any farther to know what it was. Her father had used something similar in his circus act. A bullwhip.

The water stopped. She shoved the whip back under the bed, scrambled to her feet, slid the closet door across to hide her suitcase and dived back under the quilt. Seconds later, Nick appeared, rubbing his hair with a towel. She made a show of stretching and yawning.

"Hurry," he said, tossing the towel aside. "Five minutes, we go."

"What?"

"You want visit mainland, you come." He pulled a t-shirt over his head and reached for his trousers.

Shit. "Can't we have breakfast first?"

"No time, very late." He shoved his feet into a pair of loafers and headed for the door. "Five minutes."

She hopped around the room, swearing, trying to get into her shorts, pull on her blouse and find her shoes all at the same time. It seemed pointless, going to the mainland when she'd have to come all the way back to fetch her things, but what choice did she have? He was in a tearing hurry; she could only imagine the explosion she might trigger if she said, "Wait, we need to talk."

By the time she reached the jetty, Nick was already

starting the engine, leaving her scrambling to get on board before the boat leaped forward. "Nick—" Her voice was lost in the roar as he opened the throttle.

The sea spray splashed cold on Gina's arm where she gripped the rail at the stern of the cruiser. She could use the few minutes of the short journey to talk to Nick, but her nerve failed her. Last night she'd made him angry, and she had barely gotten away with it. She wasn't game to risk it again, especially not after finding the whip. If he could use such a vicious weapon for pleasure, what might he do in anger? She had no idea how and where she could safely broach the subject of leaving—but alone on a boat, in open water, was definitely not the best choice.

They were almost at the port. She tried to appreciate the gorgeous day, but her mood was as somber as the ruined Venetian castle brooding on its high cliff above the town.

Nick didn't offer his hand for her to disembark.

They walked along the paved waterfront promenade to his BMW.

A stocky police officer, his jacket straining around his middle, approached. She expected him to say, "You can't park here," then slap Nick with a fine, but the two men embraced in a back-slapping hug.

Then Nick turned to her. "Gina, meet Stelios, my good friend."

Stelios saluted her in what might have seemed a polite gesture, except for the way his eyes raked her up and down. She crossed an arm over her chest, wishing she had worn a blouse with less cleavage.

"I will be moment only," Nick said.

Gina went to stand under one of the squat, knobbly

palm trees on the edge of the promenade, well away from the greasy policeman. For a town, the place was remarkably quiet—no car engines thrumming, no tourists babbling, no muzak playing. Only the breeze rustling through the fronds of the palm trees, and the high bell-like clink of rigging from the yachts bobbing in the pale water.

To her right—northwards—she could see the island of Corfu, too far away to discern any houses. Directly ahead of her, and much closer, she recognized the island they had just left, a mountain jutting out of the sea with the pseudo-mansion at its foot, on its crescent of sandy beach.

She turned to see if Nick was ready to go, just in time to catch him pressing a wad of cash into Stelios's fat fingers. Stelios saw that she saw, but he didn't seem in the least embarrassed. Giving her a cheery wave, he sauntered off along the promenade.

"Stelios keeps eye on my car while I not here," Nick said as he crossed to the BMW.

"He's a policeman, isn't it his duty to protect property?" she asked, stung by Nick's casual attitude to crime. "I don't see why you have to bribe people to do their job."

He shrugged. "In Greece, thief pay little something, police look other way. My boat, my car, they are special. I pay Stelios little something, he *not* look other way."

They wound their way steeply up through the narrow streets edged with whitewashed cottages. Bougainvillea in flamboyant red, orange and purple rioted over the walls, and hundreds of plants in pots brightened windowsills, balconies, verandas and even doorsteps. It was a wonder how some people got in and out of their homes.

Near the top of the ridge, Nick drew the car to a stop outside a rundown house on a side street. "Wait in car," he said, taking a package from the glove box.

He knocked on the door, but no one came to answer it. Eventually, he yelled *"E! Kostas!"* and a middle-aged, denim-clad man appeared round the side of the house. Gina resigned herself to another session of male bonding, but Kostas stopped short of hugging distance. Her knowledge of Greek didn't extend beyond "hello" and "thank you," but she didn't need to understand the words to know, from Nick's escalating voice and gestures, that something was wrong.

She waited for Kostas to leave before asking, "What's the matter?"

He climbed into the driver's seat and started the engine, his face suffused with red. "New problem. Many people—er—sick. I go to Parga."

"Oh, good. I've never been to Parga."

Nick shook his head. "You not come. I take you back to *taverna*."

"Wait, wait, what *taverna*?"

"You see boat?" he said, pointing down the hill to the port. "*Taverna* there. Owner is my friend. I return two hours."

"Don't bother. If I have two hours, I can walk it, thanks." She climbed out of the car and slammed the door with a satisfying *thunk.*

She watched him drive away. Another two hours to wait to deliver her news. The *taverna* could be a good place to tell him, with other customers around. But she would still have to go back to the island on the boat with him, alone.

Before finding the whip, she would never have contemplated walking out on someone without saying a word; it seemed such a cowardly thing to do. Now...now, she wished she had begged a headache and stayed on the island and asked Monika for a lift instead. She chided herself for not thinking of it.

Perhaps she could find Dimitri, or some other fisherman, to take her back to the island. But what if they were Nick's friends, like the policeman? They might ring and tell him before she was safely away.

She started down the hill. More than once, she had to hop up on someone's front step to let a car go by on the narrow street. About halfway down, she had to sidestep to avoid a gaggle of tourists too, led by a tour guide with a flag. Out of curiosity, she joined them, and found herself climbing again, this time towards the castle on the promontory. The group stopped at a café and she followed suit, her stomach reminding her she hadn't had breakfast. While the group dithered over the menu, she ordered some yogurt with fruit and a coffee.

She felt a sudden urge for a friendly voice. Ordinarily, she never phoned her family from the Continent except in dire circumstances because the roaming fees were astronomical. This counted as dire circumstances.

She fished in her bag for her phone—and went on fishing. *Bugger.* In her rush, she'd left it behind. She wouldn't be able to call them from the island, either. There was no signal there at all. Another lifeline cut.

Leaving the café, she noticed a souvenir shop with dusty carousels of postcards out the front, and another idea struck her.

"*Kalimera*," she said to the stooped, gray-haired man behind the counter. "Do you know, how can I get to Athens? Or Thessaloniki?"

The man looked thoughtful. "Perhaps Giorgios can take you. He goes to see his mother in Thessaloniki on Fridays."

"There's no bus?"

"You could take the bus to Parga, then from Parga to Preveza, then there is a bus to Athens. It is about seven hours I think."

Seven hours! "When's the next bus to Parga?"

He looked at his watch. "You have missed it. The next one is tomorrow at ten o'clock."

"*Efharisto.*"

Deflated, she left the shop. The village was so tiny, she was probably lucky it had a bus service at all. She would have to spend another night on the island...

She gave herself a mental slap. There would be a way, she just had to work it out.

She would ask Alex. No, he'd be upset at her for dumping his brother. She would ask Monika. All she needed was permission to sleep in their villa tonight. She would tell Nick after dinner, then beat a hasty retreat. She could always wedge a chair under the door handle.

She returned to the shop to buy a few postcards and fell in behind the straggle of tourists walking towards the castle.

The last section was a stiff climb, but the scene at the top of the cliff was worth the effort. Where she'd anticipated a jumble of ruins, people had built their houses inside the crumbling fortress walls. Two majestic stone arches remained standing at the edge of the cliff. Perfectly framed in the far one was the island. She put a hand in her bag and discovered she'd forgotten her camera as well as her phone. *Damn.* She found a comfortable flat rock where she could admire the view and write her postcards.

The tour guide waved her flag, calling her flock to move on to the next sight on their itinerary. Gina ought to start moving too; she didn't want to anger Nick further by being late. Reluctant to repeat the same route, she looked around for another way back.

On the other side of the castle, a steep flight of stone steps led through cypress trees to the breakwater. She could walk down to the sea and along the waterfront promenade to the port. A perfect shortcut.

She took the steps down to the winding path through the trees. At the bottom, the sudden shade caught her unawares and she stopped to remove her sunglasses and put them in her tote. When she looked up, a stout, uniformed figure stood by the path, under a tree. Nick's policeman friend?

"*Kalimera,*" she said.

He didn't reply. She couldn't see his face. The trees seemed to close in around her. She had seen no one else on the way down from the castle.

He stepped onto the path. As he left the deep shadow, she made out his expression. His mouth was twisted in a one-sided smile, hungry eyes running up and down her body. She stepped back. Her toe touched the ground but her heel sank. Unbalanced, she flailed her arms, but it was no good. She crashed backwards, landing hard at the base of a tree. The fall knocked the wind out of her.

He was in front of her before she had a chance to

recover. His hand, big and beefy, encircled her arm easily with thick, strong fingers. He hauled her upright and said something in Greek.

She tried to pull her arm free, to no avail. "I must go. Nick's waiting for me."

He snorted, gripping her tighter, and replied in English. "Nick is in Parga."

Gina forced herself to stay calm and assess her opponent. He wasn't tall, but he was solid. If he got hold of her properly, she wouldn't be able to fight him off. She had one chance. If she could startle him, he might loosen his hold.

She screamed, "Let me go!" Throwing her body forward, she thrust her free hand at his face, her fingers two stiff, deadly prongs aimed straight at his eyes.

He blinked and reared back, releasing her to raise his hands in front of his face.

She ran, flying up the steps to the castle in her flat gladiator sandals. She had no idea how close he was, but she resisted the urge to glance behind. It would only slow her down, and she might trip. Lungs searing, leg muscles screaming, she kept running through the castle grounds, over the broken stones, down the street towards the harbor. She didn't stop until she reached Dimitri's boat.

There was no one on board. She stood for a moment, catching her breath, before turning towards the *taverna*. At least there would be people there. With shaky hands, she raked through her hair and brushed the dust from her shorts.

As she found a seat at an outside table under the vine-covered pergola, her body started to tremble with the reaction. God, that had been close. She closed her eyes and practiced her deep breathing ritual.

The familiar routine soothed her, bringing her heart rate a little closer to normal. The surroundings helped, too. At several of the other tables sat crinkle-faced old men. Their presence calmed her, reminding her of the kindly Italian pensioners she'd met in Sydney cafés, reminiscing about the old days in Calabria. Even if Stelios caught up with her, surely he wouldn't dare try anything in front of so many locals.

Tender spots suggested a bruise on her butt where she'd landed on the tree root, and maybe on her wrist where Stelios had grabbed her, but nothing more. She'd shown him, the fat pig! She bit back a bubble of triumphant laughter, imagining Stelios somewhere up at the castle, chest heaving, red-faced from the effort of chasing her. Serve him right if he'd had a heart attack.

The two-finger prong attack had worked well. She'd never had to use it in real life before. The self-defense lessons had been Dad's way of keeping her safe while they traveled the shows, yet she'd never needed them there. She had never expected to need them in a sleepy little village.

Where was Nick? Surely he should have been here by now. She raised her wrist to read her watch, but it was gone. The strap must have broken when she wrenched her arm free.

Where was her bag? She must have dropped it when she tripped. In her panic, she hadn't noticed. *Shit.* Her purse was in it. And perhaps, she thought with dismay, her passport too.

The waiter approached and asked what she would like to order.

"*Ohi, efharisto,*" she said, but that was the limit of

her Greek. "I'm waiting for a friend."

He gave a slight bow and walked away.

The attack had frightened her, but she had escaped, and she was unhurt. All she had to do was picture Stelios as a podgy, beetroot-faced piggie and her jitters subsided. Her bag was a different matter.

How stupid of her to leave her passport in the tote! Normally when traveling, she was careful to carry only what she needed for the day, and no more. But she could picture her passport in the inside zip pocket, and she couldn't remember taking it out.

The door to the *taverna* opened and Nick entered.

Gina hurried over to meet him. "I'm so glad you're here. I lost my bag, Your friend attacked me."

"My friend?"

"You know, the policeman. Stelios. And I dropped my bag and—

Nick grabbed her arm. "Did he fuck you?"

"What? No—no, he didn't. What—" Gina broke off, confused, but she didn't have time to decide what to make of his question. What mattered was getting her purse back. "I dropped my bag, it's still up there. I think my passport's in it. I was in the park up at the castle. Could we go and look for it, please? "

She took a step towards the road, but Nick didn't move. Instead, he pulled out his phone and made a call.

"Better Dimitri and his son search. They come now," he said when he hung up. "I take you to boat, clean up."

"But—"

"They know place better than you. They search well. No worry." He pointed to her left leg. "You need clean up."

She lifted her leg and for the first time, saw the blood streaming down the length of it, from her calf to her heel. "Oh!"

Next moment he had swept her off her feet and was carrying her back to the marina. She had never felt more uncomfortable in a man's arms, but she kept quiet, worrying about her leg. Two men passed them, coming the other way. The older man smiled at Gina and touched the peak of his gray hat. Dimitri. She had seen his bulbous nose and snowy mustache before, when he came to pick up his wife Clara from the island. The younger man, with a neatly trimmed black beard, must be his son.

Nick deposited her on the leather seat in the cockpit of his boat. He disappeared into the cabin, returning a moment later with soap, towel and a packet of band-aids. Gina raised the lid on the wet bar and, with some difficulty, managed to get her leg under the faucet of the tiny sink.

Once the blood was washed off, the damage wasn't nearly as bad as she'd feared. A nasty purpling bruise and a small cut, which she wouldn't have believed could cause so much mess.

She unhooked her leg from the sink. "I'd really like to go and look for my bag. I'm sure Dimitri is doing a good job, but it's so important. Losing my passport..."

"Sorry, not possible," he said, pointing northwards. "I go to Kavos now."

He was already climbing into the driver's seat, not waiting for her response. After a moment's hesitation, she sat down. She wasn't brave enough to set off for the castle on her own, not with the policeman out there somewhere. If Nick wouldn't come with her, she would have to trust Dimitri to find her lost bag. He seemed a kindly soul. She felt sure he would try his best.

"Clara gone already; you need keys," Nick said as they docked at the island. She waited while he worked them off his key ring. "I back dinnertime."

She took the key and stepped on to the jetty. "But if they can't find the bag, I need to know, so I can report my passport."

"Tomorrow," he said, and gunned the engine.

"Thanks for your concern," she shouted as he sped off to the north.

Running her fingers through her curls, she turned and entered the house. How long did it take to replace credit cards? How could she leave now, with no money and no passport? What a mess…

Chapter Six

Alex heard the knock on his bedroom door and sat up, wondering who it could be. He had gone back to bed early because Monika had gone to Juliette's and planned to stay the night. She'd been worried about leaving him alone for so long, but he had everything he needed. Pitcher of water, bedpan, remote control...not so very different from every other day for the last six months. Now he'd had a taste of the outside world, though, it felt claustrophobic—but worth it to give Monika her space.

"Hello?" he said.

Gina sidled into the room, her face even paler than usual, her eyes downcast.

"Are you all right?"

She took her time to reply, leaning back on the door to close it. "Yes. Yes, I'm fine. A bit shaken, but I'm fine."

He didn't feel reassured. "What happened?"

"I was attacked."

"Where? Is there someone on the island?" Alex's muscles stiffened again in automatic readiness to meet the threat, then released as the futility of it struck him. Much good he would be against an intruder.

"No, I was in Venetiko."

"Are you hurt?"

She rubbed her wrist. "I cut my leg. A few bruises.

That's all. Nothing for you to be concerned about."

"Come here, sit down. Take a deep breath and tell me what happened." He poured a glass of water while she perched on the edge of the bed. "Take your time."

She accepted the glass but didn't drink. "Nick took me to the mainland this morning. A man tried to grab me while I was sightseeing at the castle. I got away but I dropped my bag. It had my passport, credit cards, money, everything."

"Where was Nick?"

She waved a dismissive hand. "Off doing some business deal."

Business deal? What the f... He would think about that later. "At least you're all right. Did you report the attack?"

"No!" She looked horrified. "I can't. He's the one I'd have to report to. He's the local policeman."

"I see. In that case, we need to report it to someone higher up. We can find out where the regional headquarters are—"

Gina shuddered, screwing up her face. "No, I'd rather not. I just want to forget it. Anyway, it's my bag I'm worried about. Nick has some guys looking for it, but I'll have to get a new passport and cancel all my cards if they don't find it."

"Where's Nick now?"

"He's gone to Kavos, wherever that is."

How typical of Nick to leave her high and dry at a time like this.

"If they don't find your bag, I'll ask Monika to help you sort it all out tomorrow," he said. "In the meantime, try not to worry."

She looked doubtful. He searched for something to

divert her. "What about a workout? Nothing like a good class to take your mind off things."

Her smile reappeared, at full wattage. "Do you mean it? Oh, that would be wonderful if you could. Nick won't be back till dinnertime, so we have time."

He had meant she could do her own workout, but her face was so transformed that he didn't have the heart to disappoint her. "If you can give me a hand…"

Am I crazy?

He hadn't spoken to Nick about teaching her. And how was he going to get out of bed? Too late to change his mind— she was already bringing the chair around, that shining look still on her face.

What the hell, it was only one class, and if Nick had gone to Kavos, they'd be done long before he returned.

He threw back the covers and saw the shock on her face. His pajamas were cut off at the knee, exposing the metal frames and the gouged flesh. "I'm held together with titanium and screws. They love me at airports," he said. Anything to break her focus on their ugliness.

"I didn't mean to stare. I didn't know what your injuries were, I wasn't expecting—"

"They're called external fixators. They're not permanent." He didn't want to discuss it. "Let's go."

He swung his legs around, trying not to flinch. He didn't want to ask Gina to help—she was shorter and slighter than Monika and might not be able to support him. But he had only practiced getting himself into the wheelchair once, yesterday. "Pass me the crutches."

She leaned close to put the crutches in his hands. He could smell the familiar backstage perfume of warm sweat and woman. It was a seductive mixture and he felt the first stirrings of arousal.

"Bring the wheelchair as close as you can. Closer. Left a bit – that's it."

Alex visualized the moves in his head. This was it—he would either make it into the chair or wind up in a humiliating heap on the floor. He positioned the crutches one ahead of the other and pushed upright. A moment to recover, a small adjustment to line up with the chair, and sit. As he lowered himself, the chair slid away from him. He'd forgotten to tell her to apply the brake.

She lunged forward and grabbed him around the waist. The crutches clattered to the ground as he threw his arms round her shoulders. They stood together for a moment while she steadied herself against his weight. His heart was pounding, and not just because he had almost crashed to the floor. Her skin was so soft. He could feel the slickness of sweat on her neck, the silkiness of her curls tickling his face.

"Can you manage a couple of steps backwards?" Her voice was unsteady. Was he too heavy?

He straightened, finding his balance. Her head was practically on his chest now. Her breasts were pressed against him. "I'm ready."

Boy, am I ready. He moved his hips away from her, hoping she couldn't feel the rising heat in his groin. Together, they shuffled back until his heel made contact with the chair.

"Wait," he said. "The brake's still off. Can you reach to hold it steady?"

Gina bent her knees to reach under his arm and grab the chair. He watched her head start to slide down his body, and had far too clear a vision of her getting down on her knees and…

He was almost grateful for the spearing pain of the fixator in his left calf as she lowered him into the chair. He tucked the blanket over his lap.

She opened the bedroom door and he quickly set the wheelchair in motion, so she wouldn't offer to push. He didn't want her to think he was completely helpless.

In the entrance hall, Clara stopped them. "You are okay, Mr. Alex?"

"I'm fine, thank you Clara," he said. "Thank you for staying late."

"Miss Gina will be dining with you?" Clara looked uncertainly at Gina.

Her question made Alex realize how much had changed. Thanks to his own reclusiveness and Monika's hostility, Nick's girlfriends had always been kept at arm's length. Now Alex had stopped hiding in his bedroom, there was nothing to stop them eating together. "Yes, Gina and Nick will be—"

"—will be eating in our villa as usual, thanks Clara," Gina broke in.

Clara bustled back to her kitchen. Gina made no comment, turning to step out onto the deck. Alex followed. The sea breeze buffeted him with its salty, fresh smell. What the hell had he been thinking, turning away from all this?

They entered the studio. The last time he'd been in a studio was the final rehearsal with Louise. The image of the accident reared up in front of him and he raised his hand, as if to fend it off.

"Are you okay?"

He forced his hand back down to the armrest. "Yes, I'm fine. Are you sure you don't want to get cleaned up first? Change your clothes?"

Gina looked down at herself. "Why bother? I'm only going to get sweatier."

Because I'm not sure I can handle you dancing in those shorts, that's why not. Alex said nothing.

Gina opened the cupboard, pulled out her soft ballet slippers and folded gracefully onto the floor to put them on. Only a dancer would sit like that, one leg casually stretched full-length while she bent over her other foot to pull on the shoe.

What am I doing here?

She set up the music and looked at him expectantly.

After a moment he said, "Just…do your usual warm-up."

While she limbered, his mind see-sawed. The studio, the floor, the music, even the way she put her damn shoes on, everything conspired to remind him of what he'd lost. His need to close his eyes and make it all go away, warred with his desire to watch every detail of Gina's body as she bent and stretched at the barre.

The calm, dispassionate cadence of the familiar exercises gradually steadied him. By about half-way through, he had composed himself enough to make some attempt to analyze her dancing. Her flexibility was wonderful—he had to stop himself from embroidering on that thought—and her technique was sound, though she tended to arch her back too much. She had excellent turnout, not from the knees but from the thighs. Bare thighs. Powerful muscles visibly working under the soft flesh. How would they feel, wrapped around him? He stifled a groan. How was he supposed to survive an hour of this?

He had to shift his brain into gear, to set the *enchainements* for *adagio* and *allegro*. It helped. He even managed some corrections. At the end, Gina asked if he would watch her audition piece, a solo from Giselle.

If he had ever doubted she had the soul of a dancer, he didn't now. He knew the rapt expression on her face, understood the passion behind it. It was beyond drugs, beyond sex, beyond anything, a place where the rest of the world disappeared and there was only the body and the music, their power and energy fused together in a glorious whole. The best high in the world. One that he would never, ever feel again. He couldn't bear to watch.

When the music stopped, she turned to him, hopeful for his verdict, obviously unaware he hadn't seen half of it. Even so, he didn't need to see her dance to know what her chances were. He debated what to say, unwilling to upset her.

"I can see you love the Romantic style, but it doesn't show you at your best," he said, eventually. "Let me think about it."

Think about how to break it to her gently. Ballet companies were rigid places. No matter how well she danced, he couldn't think of a single major company that would employ a female dancer of her height, shape and style.

He declined her offer to put him back into bed, saying Monika would be back to take care of him. He didn't trust himself to go through that again, even if it meant staying up the whole night.

"Thanks for the class," she said at the entrance to his villa. Her eyes were sparkling and her cheeks glowing like a kid at Christmas. Her smile would have lit up the whole tree. "Can I get you anything?"

"Thank you, I'm fine."

"Thanks again," she said, leaning to peck him on the cheek. He gripped the arms of the wheelchair so as not to put his arms around her. If he had, he would have wanted to pull her to him and kiss her properly.

He admired her rear view as she swayed off. Nick was a lucky man, but it wouldn't last if he treated her so casually. If Alex's girlfriend had been attacked, he wouldn't have abandoned her, no matter how urgent his business was. Which raised another question. Nick hadn't worked a day in the last eight years; how could he possibly run a business?

Alex lingered on the deck to gaze across the water at the town. Such a tiny place, he couldn't imagine anyone finding much to make money from. Apart from the odd bus tour to the castle, tourists ignored Venetiko. No hotels, no trendy restaurants, no deckchairs for hire…but it did have a dodgy local policeman, no customs officials and a fairly short run to the Albanian border. Surely Nick wouldn't…

"Erm…?"

Alex turned his head. Gina had returned, her face serious. "I was enjoying the class so much, I wasn't thinking. I have a favor to ask." She looked down at her hands, playing with a fingernail. "The reason I didn't want to have dinner with you is—I'm going to break up with Nick tonight."

Yes! Nick doesn't deserve her. Alex had to suppress a smile. No doubt she expected him to be upset on Nick's behalf. If only she knew.

She spoke again before he had worked out an

appropriate platitude. "I wondered if you'd mind if I slept in your villa, just for tonight?"

He said nothing as the implications of her decision sank in. Poor Nick, having to spend the evening next door to the woman who just dumped him. And knowing Nick's temper, it wouldn't be a pleasant experience for any of them—least of all Gina.

"Don't you think it will be awkward being on the island?" he said.

"Well, yes, but I've got no money for a hotel and I don't even think there is one in Venetiko."

"Maybe not, but I have an idea. Why don't you go and pack up, and I'll see what I can do?"

As Gina disappeared into Nick's villa, Alex went to his kitchen and asked Clara to give him the satellite phone. He had to take it out to the deck and change position several times, but eventually he found a signal, pulled a slip of paper from his pocket, and called Juliette's landline. As he'd hoped, Monika answered.

After the call, he stayed on the deck, enjoying the sea breeze and sun he'd hidden from for so many months. It might have been half an hour before Gina came out to join him, two frosted glasses in her hands. "I thought you might like one."

He took one of the glasses from her. "All packed?"

"Except my PJ's and toiletries." She leaned against one of wicker chairs. "I'll move it all into your place, if that's all right with you."

"It's fine, but I have a better idea. I called Monika. Her friend Juliette has a villa in Venetiko, and she has a spare room. Monika will take you there after dinner, so you will be ready for an early start tomorrow."

Gina frowned. "Monika? I don't want to put her to

any trouble."

Alex held up his hand. "Please. I don't know why you're splitting with Nick and I don't want to know, but if my brother has messed you around, it is the least we can do."

She took a sip of her drink. "Thanks. I'm very grateful to both of you."

He had managed to make her happy for a while, but she looked miserable now. He longed to comfort her, but all he could do was sit and try to commit every inch of her to memory as she stared out to sea, her curls blowing across her face.

****

A few hours later, Gina fidgeted on the sofa in Nick's kitchen, still marveling at Monika's new, friendly attitude. Whatever the reason, the change was very welcome. Monika had even helped her stow her luggage in the runabout, ready to go as soon as she'd talked to Nick.

The thrum of the cruiser drifted through the open kitchen door. Nick would walk in any moment. It was a relief to know she could sleep at Juliette's tonight, safely away from Nick, but she had an ordeal to get through first.

She rose from the sofa as he entered, then gasped as he barged past her. He took a bottle of vodka and a glass from the shelf by the fridge and knocked back a shot. He poured a second shot and headed for the door, glass in hand. "Get dinner," he said.

"What about my—" she said, but he had left the room.

On the brink of marching after him, she checked herself and went back to retrieve his meal from the fridge and put it in the microwave. He would be mad enough when she told him—she didn't want him angry before she even opened her mouth.

He returned a few minutes later with a hold-all bag which he threw down in the hall. She placed his dinner on the breakfast bar between them. He dragged the plate towards him and wolfed down the food. She had been about to microwave her own meal, but since it appeared he wasn't going to wait for her, she decided against it.

"Nick, what happened with my bag?"

"Beer," he said, with his mouth full.

She was about to tell him to get it himself but stopped herself in time. Best to humor him, for now. She brought a beer from the fridge.

He took a long slug. "Your bag is lost."

This was unbelievable. Didn't he understand what a big deal it was to lose a passport? Didn't he care? "I had everything in that bag. Are you positive they searched everywhere?"

His brow beetled farther. "Yes, I am sure. I have no time. I leave now, back next week."

Where did that leave her? "When next week?"

He shrugged. "Friday. Maybe Saturday. You go home now. I fetch you when I get back."

What on earth was he talking about? "Fetch me from where?"

"Take bus to Parga tomorrow, you get bus to Thessaloniki there." He opened his wallet and dropped a wad of notes on the counter.

"But I don't live in..." She didn't finish the sentence, her brain racing through their conversations over the past month. Yes, she had talked about England, plenty of times. If he'd taken the slightest bit of interest in her life, he would know she lived there, not Thessaloniki. He had always seemed so attentive. Hadn't he listened to a word she'd said?

He walked around the breakfast bar to pull her to him. He squeezed her breast, slid his hand down her side, grabbed her butt cheek and mashed her mouth with an aggressive kiss. He let her go. "Goodbye."

The word sounded final. She stared at the money. For services rendered? She felt sick.

By the time she turned around, he had picked up his hold-all and left.

Moments later, Monika entered the kitchen. Alex stopped in the doorway behind her.

"We heard the boat," she said. "What happened?"

Gina threw her hands up. "I didn't even get a chance to tell him. He's gone. He won't be back till next Friday."

"Where has he gone to?" Alex asked.

"He didn't explain the details. These trips he's had recently—he says people are sick and he has to cover for them."

Monika broke the silence by clinking the runabout keys in her fingers. "I suppose we should get going."

Gina looked at Alex. One last, long look, trying to drink him in before she never saw him again.

"I wonder if you'd mind staying," he said.

Gina wasn't sure if she'd heard him, or if it was her own wishful thinking. But Monika paused in mid-turn.

"I'm sure Juliette's spare room would be more comfortable than our couch, but it's been quite a day for both of you," Alex continued. "With Nick gone, there's no real reason for you to leave, Gina, and it would save Monika the trip to the mainland and back."

Couch? Why would she need to sleep on the couch? Before Gina could ask, Monika spoke. "Suits me," she said. "I can still take you over to Venetiko first thing in the morning, to fix up your cards. Would you mind staying?"

Would she mind another evening with Alex? Gina had to restrain a little dance of glee. "Of course I'll stay. It is much more sensible. I'll get my things from the boat."

"Great." Monika dropped the keys on the breakfast bar. "You didn't eat with Nick? We can all eat together, in that case. See you in the other kitchen in five."

Gina walked calmly across the beach, then pirouetted to the end of the jetty to get her things from the runabout. One more evening with Alex. What joy.

Chapter Seven

Promptly at eight o'clock, Gina climbed into the runabout with Monika. The morning air was so sharp and clear it almost fizzed, and the sky dazzled with blue. It was hard to feel down about anything. She had no regrets about Nick. She'd made a mistake. At least she'd discovered it early, no harm done. And if she hadn't met Nick, she would never have met Alex. Her missing passport and cards were mere fleabites in the scheme of things.

"How did you come to meet Nick?" Monika said, raising her voice over the hum of the runabout's motor and the buffeting of the breeze.

"I was teaching at a dance camp in Thessaloniki and he was at a cocktail party."

"So you're a ballet teacher?"

"God, no!" Gina pulled a face. "If there's one thing six weeks of summer camp has taught me, it's that I never want to teach another teenager ever again. No, that was just a fill-in job."

"What do you normally do?"

Good question. "Up till December last year, I was working in musical theatre in London. Then my boyfriend and I split, and I decided to have another crack at getting into a ballet company. I've spent this year traveling around Europe, doing master classes and auditioning as much as I can."

Monika shot her a sideways glance. "I guess you haven't had much luck, if you ended up working at the dance camp?"

"No, it's been frustrating. I'm not sure what I'll do next. I could go back to musical theatre in London easily, but my dream was always to be a proper classical dancer, not just a hoofer," she said, not expecting Monika to understand the distinction.

"Oh, I can relate to that. I was a dancer too, once, and I had the same dream. Eventually, I had to accept I was too damn tall, and the best I could do was be a Bluebell girl at the *Folies Bergere*."

Monika eased the runabout into a mooring at the marina, and Gina hopped out to fix the mooring rope. Gina's stomach fluttered slightly as she stepped onto the dock, but she refused to let anxiety get the better of her. She and Monika would be more than a match for that old roly-poly of a policeman, if they happened to run into him.

Monika pointed out Juliette's place, high on a promontory to the south of the town. "We could walk, but it's quite a hike. My car's over there." She indicated a Fiat Panda parked next to the *taverna*.

Progress through the narrow streets was slow thanks to the early morning traffic. "How did you meet Alex?" Gina asked her.

"That was way back at the start, when he first came to London from Russia." Monika's face blossomed into a smile. "He was only nineteen, but we all knew he was going to be great. And of course, I fell madly in love with him, like everyone else."

The answer was not what Gina had expected, but she recovered quickly. "I was twelve, but I remember seeing him on TV, in *Bayadère*. He was absolutely amazing."

"You're a died-in-the-wool fan, then?"

"Oh, yes. I saw him dance in London several times. Plus his movies, of course."

Monika rolled her eyes. "Don't let him hear you say that! He says the movies were fantastic for his bank balance but terrible for his artistic reputation. He hates them both."

She stopped in front of a building which looked like all the other village houses—whitewashed with bright splashes of color in pots on the step. Juliette herself turned out to be a willowy brunette, easily as tall as Monika. Gina wished she'd worn heels, not that they would've helped much.

"Breakfast first, or phone calls?" Juliette asked as she ushered them into the traditional, blue-and-white kitchen.

"Breakfast," Monika said, before Gina could reply. "The consulate won't be open yet, anyway."

Gina had planned to phone the bank immediately, but the fragrance of fresh coffee and the panoramic view from the kitchen table made her waver. It wouldn't take long to demolish a croissant or two, anyway.

She ate as quickly as she decently could, and left Juliette and Monika chatting while she went through to the hall to use the phone.

Canceling her credit cards was easy. The passport was more difficult. Gina had to ring the embassy, and it wasn't good news.

She found both women still sitting at the table. "How do I get to Athens?"

"Athens?" Juliette said. "Why would you need to go there?"

"It's the only way to get my passport replaced. I have to make an appointment and present myself in person, then they'll give me some kind of emergency replacement."

"What a nuisance. Anyway, the quickest way is to fly from Corfu."

"Corfu? That's an island!"

"It is, but it's very close and it's our nearest airport." Monika pointed through the window, northwards out to sea. Gina could just make out the hazy landmass. "I can drive you to the ferry, it's only half an hour from here."

"If you're really sure it won't put you out, a lift to the ferry would be great," Gina said. "But I have to pay for it, and the flight. Oh, *shit*! They won't let me on the flight, will they? I've got no ID!"

"Don't worry, we'll find a way."

Just then, Gina remembered the souvenir shop. "There is a bus."

"A bus? You have to be kidding."

"A shopkeeper in town told me. I can get a bus to…Preveza? Then there's a bus to Athens from there."

"That'll take hours. Tell you what, I'll drive you as far as Preveza. Juliette and I can make a day of it." Monika smiled at Juliette. "I'll take you to see Ali Pasha's fortress!"

"That's really kind of you," Gina said. "I don't know how to thank you."

Monika paused. "There is one way to thank me. You could stay here a bit longer."

"Stay?" Did she mean stay with Juliette or—Gina's

heart skipped a beat—stay with Alex?

Monika set down her coffee cup. "Look, I'm going to declare self-interest here. I don't want you to leave. You've worked magic on Alex and I don't want to risk losing the progress he's made. When he told me you were using the studio, I thought the music would make him worse, being reminded of what he'd lost. Well, I was wrong. He's behaving as if he believes he has a future again. It would be great if you could stay on the island, at least for a few days. It's so good for him. And a few master classes with Alex might help you with your auditions."

Gina's could hardly breathe.

"Besides," Monika continued. "Juliette's my best friend and I haven't seen her for six months. I'd love to spend more time with her while she's here. If you're with Alex, I'm free to do that. I'm not asking you to do anything for him, it's just good to know someone's around. If you're sure you can put up with that couch for a few more days, that is."

"Oh, I don't mind."

Pants on fire, Gina. You don't mind, indeed. You can't wait to get him to yourself, and you mustn't. This is his girlfriend you're talking to!

"Take your time to decide how long you want to stay," Monika said. "Discuss it with Alex. There's no rush for you to leave."

No rush. She could have a whole week learning from Alex before Nick returned. It was almost too good to be true.

****

They arrived back at the island just as Dimitri, having delivered Clara, was preparing to leave. He gave them a friendly wave. Gina turned to walk up the beach with a smile on her face.

"Something funny?" Monika asked.

Gina shook her head. "I'm relieved. I thought Nick might have told Dimitri to make sure I went home, but he didn't seem worried to see me still here."

"To be fair, he wouldn't expect you to be gone already, surely."

"Oh yes, he would. Nick told me to be on the bus to Parga this morning."

"For goodness sake, how ridiculous! You couldn't just hop on a bus, you've got too much to organize."

"Yes, but Nick doesn't know that. He thinks I live in Thessaloniki, where we met—even though I'm sure I spoke about England many times." Gina sighed. "It makes me wonder how much he really understood. He does struggle with English."

"Maybe he didn't understand, or maybe he wasn't listening. I think I'd put my money on the second one," Monika said, pausing in the hallway. "Anyway, are you up for class this afternoon? Say, three o'clock?"

"I'd *love* to! I don't know how to thank you both."

Monika waved away her thanks. "No need. Like I said, you're the one doing *me* a favor. You're part of my evil plan to get Alex back on his feet."

Finally, a chance to answer the question which had been nagging at Gina since that first meeting. "How likely is that?"

"There's no way of telling until those cages come off, I'm afraid. He might walk with a limp. Or he might spend the rest of his life shuffling around with a walking frame. Monika bit her lip. "The thing is, even if it's the worst-case scenario, there's no reason he can't be independent. The challenge is to persuade him that's a good enough target to aim for. When it happened, I think he felt that if he couldn't dance, nothing else was worth the effort."

Shuffling on a walking frame. Gina could hardly bear to imagine it. "I can understand that."

"I think he's adjusting. He got himself out of bed this morning and he insisted on trying to shower and dress himself." Monika consulted her watch. "Except it's almost afternoon now—I'd better go and give him a hand, or Clara will be serving lunch while he's still half-dressed!"

Gina declined lunch. Monika might have changed, but Gina didn't want to test the friendship by intruding on her time with Alex. Besides, a heavy meal would weigh her down in class. She made a sandwich instead and went for a swim. Floating on her back, flipping her hands lazily, she thought of the days ahead. Sun, sea, sand, and the personal attention of one of the best dancers in the world.

Lost passport or not, could paradise be any better than this?

****

She walked into the studio at three o'clock to find Alex sitting tall in his wheelchair near the door. His head turned as she entered, and she had an image of him standing on stage, with his head and shoulders in exactly that pose. It was such a tragedy he couldn't dance.

"I appreciate this so much," she said.

Alex shook his head. "It's my pleasure. If you hadn't come along, I'd still be staring at the wall in that bedroom, feeling sorry for myself. I owe you for that."

Gina liked to exercise in the afternoon: she was always at her most limber late in the day. She was delighted when Alex began calling instructions and making corrections, right from the start. He set some fiendish barre exercises that challenged her strength, and the center work was fast and demanding. By the time they got to the *enchainements*, she was dripping sweat.

"No, no, no! What's happening to your alignment? Keep that hip in place! Wait." He wheeled over to her, then cursed out loud as he struggled to maneuver the chair closer to her.

His hands settled on her hipbones, gentle but firm. Even though she was ready for it, the pressure of his fingers sent a tremor through her. "Now, lift your leg without twisting your hips."

She tried it, not very well, feeling the heat of his hands through her leotard. She suppressed a moan as his thumb pressed into the soft flesh in front of her hipbone.

"No. Get your starting position right. Where's your neutral spine? What's this?" His hand brushed her belly reprovingly. Her stomach contracted, partly to correct her posture but partly in response to the electric tingle of his touch.

She practiced her Pilates breathing with studied determination. It was the only way to steady her racing heartbeat.

"Better, much better." He let go of her, backed the wheelchair away a little, and held his hand out. "Now, let's have a *posé* into a *penchée* and keep everything the same. Use my arm for support."

She stepped forward onto her toe and bent forward

into the deep arabesque, her leg rising high behind her, reaching for his hand. His arm was still strong. He would have been so special to dance with.

"Come on, leg higher." Her face was level with his, and she was looking into his blue, mesmerizing eyes. She lost her balance and landed in a heap on the floor.

She got back on her feet, feeling silly.

"You're tired, I'm pushing you too hard," he said. "Why don't we call it a day?"

Half her mind told her to run away before she embarrassed herself any further, but the other half wanted very much to stay. Her mouth opened to say "I'm fine," but she noticed how pale his face was. She checked the clock. They'd been going for almost two hours!

"Yes, I think you're right. It's been amazing, thank you." She hesitated. He was officially her teacher now, so a kiss, even a peck on the cheek, no longer seemed appropriate.

She smiled, turned and went over to the sound system to turn off the music. Behind her back, she heard him leave the studio.

She took a deep breath and exhaled.

The arabesque had brought back the memory of helping him into his chair, far too vividly. When he'd thrown his hands around her neck, his raised arms had lifted his pajama top, so her hands came to rest on the cool, bare skin of his back. His arms were warm on her neck, his peppermint breath on her brow. She remembered looking at the strong curve of his jaw and the way tendrils of his long hair licked around his ear. She'd had an absurd urge to brush them away and take his ear lobe between her teeth.

Then he'd straightened up and she was looking at his chest, as if they were about to tango. She had wanted to rest her head on it and close her eyes…

Stop.

She was treading into dangerous territory. Having a crush on Alex was one thing. He wasn't the sort of man you'd want to actually fall in love with—she had known that, even as a teenager. Every time she'd picked up a magazine, there was some new, eager woman clinging to him, but none of them had ever lasted. He was a classic commitment-phobe, a lover and leaver, a sure pathway to a broken heart.

Worse, it looked as though Monika had been in love with him all those years, while he played the field. It would be cruel and unfair to even imagine stealing Alex from her. Gina had seen how her mother suffered, after her father's betrayal. She would never put another woman through that. Never.

Alex could be her teacher, her mentor, her friend. But a lover?

No. Never, except in her dreams.

Chapter Eight

Within a couple of days, Gina's body clock slipped naturally back into dancer's time— late to bed and late to rise, in spite of the bright sunlight that battered through the sheer blind on the lounge room window. It would have felt wrong, somehow, to sleep in Nick's bedroom.

She had been surprised, at first, to be offered the sofa bed in Alex's lounge instead of the upstairs bedroom, which she'd assumed would be empty. Discovering otherwise had led to a surge of hope— maybe Alex and Monika weren't such a close couple after all—until she worked out the obvious reason why they didn't share a bed. The fixators were large, clumsy and heavy, and could injure Monika if Alex moved in his sleep. Of course she needed her own room.

The sofa bed wasn't so bad, anyway, and she couldn't bring herself to sleep in Nick's room. The only slight inconvenience was having to shower in Nick's bathroom so as not to invade Alex's or Monika's space.

At around ten, she made her way to Alex's kitchen, expecting them to have finished breakfast. To her surprise, Monika was setting up a tray.

"I thought you'd be up and off ages ago," Gina said.

"Alex takes forever to get ready, now he's doing everything himself." Monika placed the coffee pot on the tray. "I'm not complaining. It's great to see him trying so hard. Thanks to you."

Gina didn't know what to say. The idea that Alex was doing it for her gave her a warm glow in her chest, swiftly followed by a feeling of guilt. *Don't let it go to your head, Gina. He's Monika's.*

"I was about to take this out to Alex, he's on the deck," Monika said. "Would you mind doing it? I'm running late for Juliette."

"No, of course I don't mind." Breakfast with Alex, what was there to mind?

"Oh, you're a darling, thanks. There's enough coffee for two, just add whatever you want for breakfast. Must dash."

Gina found some yogurt for herself and carried the tray out to the table on the deck.

"Good morning!"

The happiness in his eyes made her heart turn over.

As she set down the tray, he pulled out the chair beside him. "Sit here. We can both enjoy the view."

The chair was close enough that when she sat, their elbows almost touched. The hairs on her arm stood on end, as if an electric charge flowed between them. Could he feel it too? She could sense him watching her as she poured the coffee. The spout of the coffee pot clinked on the rims of the cups.

Alex spread dollops of honey on pieces of toast and handed her one. They ate quietly for a while, Gina unable to think of anything but the acute proximity of his body. She kept her gaze firmly on the horizon, afraid to look at his face in case she felt tempted to lean over and kiss him on the mouth.

"I'd like to talk about what we'll work on," he said.

She turned to face him cautiously, telling herself to keep her focus on professional matters. "I explained, I'd like to develop my audition pieces."

"I know, but I do not believe that would be the best use of your time. I'd like to forget about classical choreography and concentrate on balance and strength."

"Why?"

His eyes slid away from her. Her heart sank.

"You are a born performer. When you dance, you radiate joy. No one can teach you that, it's a gift."

There was a "but" coming, she could feel it.

"This is going to sound harsh, and I'm sorry," he continued. "but if I'm going to help you, I have to be honest."

Gina busied herself with tidying the table, her vision blurring. She mustn't cry, he would think she was pathetic.

He rested his hand on hers, forcing her to stop stacking the plates. "No major ballet company is going to recruit you as a soloist, even if I recommend you. You don't have the experience."

Her breath caught. Harsh was right. "I'd be happy in the *corps de ballet*," she managed.

Alex shook his head. "Dancers join the *corps de ballet* at eighteen. If a company hires you for the *corps* now, you have nowhere to go because by the time you're experienced enough to be promoted, you'll be too old. It's not worth the company's investment. Surely you know that."

A tear escaped her eye and trickled down her cheek. Yes, she knew. It was exactly what she'd been thinking when she'd accepted the job at the dance camp. For nine months, she had tried everything—at the cost of most of her savings—to get her big break in ballet. And failed. She'd known all along she was running out of time.

It still hurt to hear it from Alex.

"You can still have a career," Alex said. "You're on the wrong path, that's all. Tell me, am I right in thinking most of your training was in gymnastics?"

Blinking away tears, she looked at him in surprise. "Is it that obvious?"

"Yes. It's not a bad thing, but it is one of the things that has held you back. You don't have conventional classical lines. But it could be an advantage elsewhere. Have you thought of trying for a show like *Cirque?*"

As a bubble of hysteria welled up, she laughed. She could hardly believe it. All that work for the last ten years and he was telling her to try for the *circus?*

"I don't want to work in a circus," she snapped.

Alex removed his hand. "It's up to you."

He had grasped the wheel rims, ready to move away. She grabbed his arm to stop him. "No, I'm sorry. I appreciate your advice, I really do. The thing is…my parents are circus people. My mother retired when she had children, but my dad has always been obsessed with it. He can do anything—juggling knives, knocking a cigarette out of a lady's mouth with a bullwhip. He started teaching me as soon as I could walk. In the summer, we'd travel with him and be part of his act."

She stared into nothingness, remembering those sun-washed summers, balancing on her brothers' shoulders.

Alex frowned. "I don't see the problem. Why did you switch to ballet?"

"All the time we were traveling, my father was

having it off with his pretty assistants. He ran off with one of them when I was fifteen, leaving my mother to bring up three kids on her own. I've wanted nothing to do with circuses ever since."

"I'm sorry to hear that, but why let your father ruin your career?" Alex paused. "You're a good ballet dancer. I am sure you're a good gymnast. We both know that's not enough. But put them together, and you have an edge. If you can leverage that point of difference, you have a chance to achieve something."

She could see the logic of his argument, but it was hard to let the resentment go.

"Think about it," he said. "I can teach what you want, but our time is limited. I don't want to waste it."

His eyes were fixed on her face. Gazing into their blue depths, she no longer cared what he taught her, so long as she could be with him.

Only she couldn't be with him, except for these few precious days.

****

Alex massaged his neck and gazed through the lounge room window. The first stripes of pink and lavender shaded the sky. He must have fallen asleep in his wheelchair after his class with Gina and had a crick in his neck to show for it.

He wheeled through to the hallway, grateful that Gina had remembered to leave the doors open for him. His inability to go beyond the deck was beginning to irritate him, but at least he could move freely between the villas.

No sign of her in the kitchen, nor out on the deck or on the beach. He moved on, across the connecting deck, into Nick's villa, conscious it was the first time he'd been there since the renovation works, all those months ago. When he could still walk.

Gina was in the lounge, sitting with her back to him in the big cream armchair. She didn't react as he entered, seeming transfixed by the scene on the television. A delicate woman in a pale blue, Greek-style tunic and a bare-chested man in blue tights danced on an unadorned stage. Alex recognized the *pas de deux*, from a gala event in New York.

On the screen, Svetlana took three small steps towards him. He bent his knees, took hold of her inner thigh with one hand and her waist with the other, and hoisted her high above his head. A burst of applause as he paraded her around the stage. A final arabesque, then he lowered her, and they both ran offstage.

A moment's pause in the darkness of the wings, a few precious seconds to focus all his energy, then Alex exploded from the wings, already in mid-air. Two more prodigious split jumps and he had crossed the floor. He remembered that moment; he had misjudged the size of the stage, and the final leap took him perilously close to the edge.

A muscle in his cheek twitched as he watched himself in action. The only sign of effort was the sweat glistening on his chest. That was the goal, to make it look effortless. In reality it took a huge amount of muscle power—he felt his thigh muscles bunching instinctively—but when the music was thundering and the audience applauding, it really had felt like flying. Never again. His throat constricted.

On the screen, he saw himself move around the stage in long twirling jumps, seeming to hang in the air on every turn. He heard Gina gasp at his final mid-air twist. He couldn't watch any more. He backed the wheelchair away and cursed as the right wheel bashed into the sideboard.

The music stopped.

He looked up at the screen. It was blank, and Gina was staring at him.

"I see you found my performance recordings," he said, making a fair attempt at a light-hearted tone. "I hadn't seen that one myself. It was in New York, just before—" His voice failed him for a moment.

"I'm sorry, I shouldn't have—" Gina gestured to the television.

Snap out of it. "It's fine. Watch as many as you like. I came to find out if you'd eaten yet."

Gina stood with a smile that gladdened his heart. "Not yet. I was waiting for you."

She was dressed in a disappointingly baggy dance pants and long-sleeved t-shirt, but the thin shirt revealed the shape of her bra-less breasts, peaking with a hint of nipple each side of the central valley.

He hit the sideboard again as he attempted to turn, but he waved away Gina's offer of help. He followed her to his kitchen. Squeezing past the breakfast bar and avoiding the legs of the glass table posed more challenges. He would have liked to help lay the table and serve the food, but the kitchen had not been designed for a wheelchair, and he didn't want to risk dropping a plate or breaking a bottle in front of her.

"Don't bother with that one," he said as Gina reached for the bottle of wine on the kitchen benchtop. "You'll find better wines in the store. I collect—rather, used to collect—wine on my travels. It's the door at the back there."

Gina opened the door at the back of the room. Her head disappeared into the blackness for a moment, then she turned with a bottle in her hand. "Will this one do? It's *Côtes du Roussillon*."

"Good choice. It's made by friends of mine, Oscar and Jeanne. Both ex-dancers. They have a beautiful vineyard in the south of France. Unlike me, they had an alternative career planned for when they stopped dancing." He gave a mirthless laugh. "I don't know why I thought I was immortal. It only takes a small injury to end our career—an achilles tendon, a ruptured patellar tendon in the knee—but I still thought it would not happen to me."

She placed the bottle and two glasses on the table. "Dancers are superstitious. If we don't think about having to retire, we won't have to retire. Silly, really."

"I am not superstitious," he said. "I didn't think about life after ballet because I couldn't imagine it. I have never known anything else. I entered the Academy when I was ten, and from then on, my whole life was the ballet. Even in the vacations, I stayed with a teacher, because I had no family to go to."

"No family at all?" Gina paused with a frying pan in her hand. "What happened to your parents? And what about Nick?"

"Our parents died just before I started at the school. I had a legal guardian—whom I never saw—but Nick was adopted by another family." Alex felt surprised Nick hadn't mentioned it to her. But he wouldn't have wanted to explain the missing years.

"Didn't you ever get to see him?"

Alex shook his head. "I had no idea where he was, and no idea how to find out. I didn't even know his new surname. He found me eventually, about eight years ago, when I became successful. He saw my name in the newspapers…"

"…and you've been together ever since?" Gina finished for him. "What a lovely ending."

Yes and no. Alex would never forget the joy he'd felt at being reunited with his long-lost baby brother, but there was no denying that Nick had been a headache ever since.

Gina took a plastic container from the fridge and tipped something into the pan on the stove. "This won't take a minute. Clara decided to trust me to cook the lamb for the salad, it's much nicer warm."

The aromas of garlic and rosemary filled the kitchen. He sipped his wine, enjoying the sight of Gina moving around the kitchen, her curly ponytail bouncing on top of her head.

Only a few minutes later, she put the bowl of salad on the table and sat beside him, close enough to touch.

He felt at a loss for words. All he could think of was the smell of her scent and the closeness of her body. He applied himself to his salad. The longer the silence continued, the less able he felt to break it.

When they had finished, Gina stood and removed the plates. It was like breaking a spell. "We were talking about life after ballet," he said.

"Right. You could teach."

"I don't know. Watching someone else do what I can't—it's almost worse." Seeing her face fall, he added hastily, "That's not entirely true. I enjoy coaching you. It gives me a purpose. I just don't think I would like to make a career of it."

"Me neither. I taught at a summer school in

Thessaloniki—that's how I met Nick—and that was enough to know I couldn't do it full-time. But it's a shame, because you're a good teacher. It's such a crime that you can't dance—I mean, that jump, to have that taken away is so unfair."

He didn't want her pity. God knows he'd spent too long pitying himself over the last six months.

Monika saved him by walking through the door, bringing a waft of cool, salty air with her. "Hello darling!" she warbled. "What's this? Entertaining another woman? You treacherous dog!"

Alex ducked as she aimed a mock slap at his head.

"I'd better go," Gina said. Her face was pink.

"No, no!" said Monika. "There's no rush. I'm early. I can come back later."

But Gina had already slid off her chair and was on her way out.

As soon as she was gone, Monika apologized. "I'm sorry if I screwed something up there."

"Be reasonable, Mo. You know it's not as simple as that."

Monika's matchmaking raised the question. Did he seriously contemplate making a move on his brother's ex-girlfriend? He looked down at the blanket covering his legs. Besides the thorny question of Nick's involvement, he was making a massive assumption. If he read her right, Gina still harbored a teenage crush for the strong, fearless dancer he used to be. That didn't mean she was interested in the man he had become.

Chapter Nine

On the way to the studio, Alex paused on the deck to watch Gina swim. Their week together had flown by. This time tomorrow, Monika would be driving Gina to Preveza to catch the bus, and who knew when he might see her again?

Why did she have to be Nick's girlfriend? Alex was angry at him for treating Gina badly, but the fact remained that Nick was the only family he had left. He couldn't let a woman drive them apart.

Could he?

Everything was academic, anyway. It would be at least six months before he could walk. If at all. In that time, his feelings might change. Perhaps, with hindsight, he'd realize Gina wasn't the most amazing woman he'd ever met. Or perhaps she'd be snapped up by someone else.

God, I hope not.

The last few days had been an odd mixture of pleasure and pain, having her so close yet so out of reach. He enjoyed his new mobility, even if it was on wheels. He had originally aimed to use the crutches, but he had quickly changed his mind. For short trips, like getting out of bed to go to the bathroom, they worked. But any task that required him to use his hands became a perilous exercise in balance, and thanks to the bulky fixators, the crutches were just as clumsy as the wheelchair. Besides, he hated putting his scarred legs on display, and no trousers in the world were wide enough to fit over the fixators.

The runabout drew up to the jetty. Monika strode up the beach, an envelope in her hand.

"You're back early," Alex said, accepting the letter from her.

"I'm not staying. I'm not seeing Juliette till four, so I might as well grab a late lunch here. Enjoy your class!" With a wave, she turned and entered the villa.

Alex knew what the envelope contained—he recognized the realtor's logo. The contract for the sale of the island. There was no doubt in his mind about selling. He had no desire to continue living here. While he was in the wheelchair, and even on crutches, the soft sand surrounding the villas might as well be a moat. He needed somewhere he could get around by himself. The question was, where?

As Monika kept reminding him, his Hackney terrace house was comfortable, had a small bedroom on the ground floor, and was close to several good rehab clinics. All he had to do was give a month's notice to the tenants.

But returning to the London suburb would mean the paparazzi would find him and start up again with melodramatic headlines about a career cut short. Photos of him being helped out of wheelchairs or struggling with crutches would flood the media rags. Speculation. Sympathy. Pity. That was the whole reason he'd fled London in the first place. No, going home would have to wait. He would step back into the limelight if he could do it on his own two feet, not before.

The island wasn't practical, but Hackney was not

the answer, either. He had a couple of options in mind, but neither of them was in England.

Every time he saw Gina, he questioned his decision. She had decided to return to London. If he was in England, he would be close to her. But he'd gone over this time and time again. Nick would still be an immovable obstacle. There was no sense in rehashing it.

They'd been getting on well, and sometimes he read a message in Gina's eyes that said she was attracted to him. But then she would say something sympathetic about his injury. He didn't want her to be with him through some kind of misplaced mothering instinct, a desire to care for the poor helpless cripple. His skin crawled at the thought. He didn't want her pity. Even if...

She came out of the sea, picked her towel up from the sand and sashayed up the beach towards him.

...even if she was Venus in a red bikini.

****

The hours seemed to fly. Before he knew it, it was afternoon and already, half their ballet class was over. Gina moved to the center of the room. "Where do you want me?"

Where do I want her? Let me count the ways. The mangled quotation made Alex smile. *Don't even think about it.*

"Let's try that *adagio* we were working on. Start with the second arabesque. No, no, no, what have I told you about your alignment?"

He wheeled over to correct her. He'd had to give up on his resolve to stay back and coach from the sidelines – he simply couldn't get across to her what he meant. Since he couldn't get up and show her, the only alternative was to push her into place. That might mean holding her wrist to reposition her arm—or supporting her thigh so she could correct her turnout. He might gently push her hip into alignment or put his hand on her back to improve the arch. It was much more satisfying to teach hands-on. Professionally, that is.

Bullshit. He touched her because he couldn't sit and watch her for two hours without aching to feel the softness of her, and the way her body shivered under his fingers.

The studio door opened.

Two men entered. One was mid-twenties, tanned, black hair slicked back. The other was older, graying, stooped. Officials of some kind—they were dressed in suits but lacked the polish of business types. They stopped, just inside the door, their eyes on Alex's wheelchair.

He wheeled forward to meet them. "How can I help you?"

The two men exchanged glances. They looked embarrassed. Alex held his breath. He had a feeling he didn't want to hear what they had to tell him.

The stooped man spoke in a thick Greek accent. "I am Inspector Ioannis Antoniou. This is my colleague, Sergeant Panagiotis Vlahos. I have to ask, Mr. Korolev, if you are aware of the activities of your brother, Nick Rostov."

"What's happened?"

"Mr. Rostov was arrested last night," Antoniou said. "He has been charged with the trafficking of drugs and alcohol. We are also investigating his involvement in the attempted strangulation of a woman."

Alex closed his eyes. *Shit*. Behind him he heard Gina's gasp.

"To be honest, sir, we came to take you in for questioning," Antoniou said. "But…"

Alex stiffened. "As you can see, unless you feel like carrying me across the sand, that would be difficult."

"Yes, sir. We can interview you here."

The detective was calling him sir. That had to be a good sign.

Gina stepped forward. "I'll be in the villa next door. In the kitchen."

"We will need to speak to you too," the inspector said. "Miss…?"

She didn't answer, already on her way out, glancing at Alex as she left. Her face was pale, but he couldn't read the expression in her eyes.

The sergeant collected two chairs from the corner and placed them in front of Alex.

"When did you last see Mr. Rostov?" said the inspector.

Alex had to think. It had been the morning he met Gina. "Monday morning."

"I have to ask you, were you aware of the activities of your brother?"

"No, I was not!" Alex caught himself. Showing his annoyance would only antagonize the inspector. He tried to adopt a more normal tone. "For the last six months I've been confined to a bed. It was only in the last few days that I've been more active. I've had no awareness of anything outside my bedroom. My PA can vouch for that."

"Your PA?"

"Personal assistant."

"She lives here?"

"Yes. Monika Adler. She's on the mainland at the moment."

The inspector said something in Greek to his sergeant, who scribbled in his notebook, then turned back to Alex. "Why does your brother use the name Rostov?"

"It's his name." *Don't antagonize the inspector,* he told himself. "We were separated as children after our parents died and he was adopted by the Rostovs. What has he done, exactly?"

"We found a large amount of a prohibited substance in Mr. Rostov's car. Also flagons of dangerous alcohol."

The evidence sounded damning. Alex had hoped there would be some doubt.

"Are you aware of any previous criminal activities? Smuggling, perhaps?" the detective continued.

Alex opened his mouth to say, "No" but thought better of it. They would check. No point in being caught out in a lie. "He got into some kind of trouble when he was a teenager, in Russia. I don't know the details. But he was only a boy, I'm sure it was nothing serious."

The policemen asked a few more questions, but they seemed satisfied Alex could not help them. They left the studio still calling him "sir." He followed them as far as the corner of the deck and watched them enter the villa to speak to Gina.

He blamed himself for what had happened. He had been so busy feeling sorry for himself after the accident, he had stopped paying attention to what Nick was doing. Eight years of good work undone by six

Marisa Wright

months of inattention.

The policemen's voices brought Alex back to the present. They emerged from the villa, deep in conversation, and walked to their launch which waited at the jetty. Alex headed for the kitchen. Gina didn't appear to notice him as he entered. She sat hugging her knees on the couch, staring into space.

He managed to wheel around the breakfast bar to the kitchen cabinet. With one hand on the counter, he raised himself out of the wheelchair enough to retrieve the vodka. He poured two shots. Gina accepted one, still with a dazed look on her face.

"Drink up," he said.

Her eyes finally focused on him. "Did you know?" she whispered.

Did I know? He hesitated.

Anger distorted her face, her voice escalating up the scale. "Why didn't you tell me?"

"I didn't know anything for sure."

"But he's a criminal! He's violent! He has a bullwhip, Alex, those things can kill. What if..." She stood, spilling the vodka from her glass, and tried to push past the wheelchair towards the door.

He caught her arm. "Gina, wait, please! Please! Let me explain."

He could sense the tension vibrating through her, but she stopped, her gaze averted.

"I don't know what the police told you, but I swear, I did not know he was smuggling."

She gave a scornful laugh. "How could you not? That flashy boat, the car, the suits..."

"The boat and the car are mine, and I pay him a generous allowance."

She turned to stare at him. "Are you saying all Nick's money comes from you?"

"Yes." He paused, taking in the bewildered look on her face. "Nick didn't tell you, did he?"

Gina sank onto the nearest sofa. "I don't get it. Why bother with all this racketeering if he didn't need the money?"

"Fear?" He gazed into his vodka glass. She might as well know the whole story. "I told you Nick was adopted. I did not tell you he ran away when he was eleven and lived on the streets. He won't talk about how he survived but it was obvious. When he came to find me in Stuttgart, I took him to buy clothes—he shoplifted the cuff links. We ate dinner at a restaurant, he took the cutlery. Once he understood I could buy him anything he wanted, he stopped stealing." He sighed. "In the last six months, I've done nothing but warn him that the money could run out. Maybe I've driven him back to it."

He waited for her to walk away. She didn't.

"You're wrong," she said eventually. "You should've seen him in Thessaloniki. The five-star hotel, all that fine dining, the champagne, the gifts…that's not a man afraid the money will run out. He didn't care if he bankrupted you, because he knew he had drug money to fall back on."

"That's—"

"No, Alex, don't defend him. I know you don't want to believe it, but I think Nick's been taking advantage of you for a long time. He fooled me. I think he fooled you, too."

Her mouth lifted slightly at the corners. Not her megawatt smile, but it was a beginning.

He knew exactly what would lift her mood. "Why don't we finish that class? We can do some of those romantic pieces you enjoy. It'll take your mind off this."

Her smile widened and she started towards the door. Alex lagged behind, having to negotiate round the island. By the time he reached the studio, she was at the barre with the music ready to go.

****

Gina found it hard to concentrate at first. She kept remembering Nick's face while he brandished the belt. In hindsight, the look in his eyes took on even more menace. That intensity should have warned her it wasn't a game for him. What would have happened if Alex and Monika hadn't been on the island? The thought chilled her.

Gradually, the routine of dance class steadied her nerves. Her brain became absorbed in the rhythm of the steps: *assemblé - changement - temps levé - pas de bourrée.* When she sat on the floor to change into her pointe shoes an hour later, she realized she'd achieved a better perspective.

There was no point in dwelling on the danger Nick's sexual preferences had posed. That was in the past. He was safely locked up now and couldn't do her any harm. At last, she could enjoy her time on the island—the little that was left—without worrying that he might return for her.

Alex must have been thinking along similar lines. He wheeled over beside her. She swiveled to look up at him, her legs tucked under her to one side. "You know, now, that Nick isn't coming back, you don't have to go home tomorrow."

"But I've booked my flight," she protested. "It's all arranged. The consulate is expecting me to pick up my temporary passport."

"Change the flight. I'll pay," he said. "You're making such good progress."

Warmed by his praise, her breath caught. "Am I?"

He nodded.

She felt light-headed. Was it the vodka making her head buzz, or was it the thought of spending more time with Alex? But the longer she stayed, the harder it would be to leave him. "I'd love to. But I really do need to get home. I have to make a living, you know."

"I'm going to miss you."

I'm going to miss you. She hugged the words to her as she tucked her shoe ribbons into place and took her position in the center of the studio.

"The first time you used the studio, you played something from *La Sylphide,*" Alex said. "Was that for practice, or do you know the solo?"

"I know it," Gina said. "It was one of my first solos, at the Performing Arts school."

"In that case, you remember what it was about."

"Yes, James is sleeping and the Sylph is dancing around his chair." *His chair.* "Yes, I'd love to do it."

Alex positioned his chair upstage left. Gina found the music and got ready to make her entrance. "You're cheating," she called. "James is *asleep* in his chair."

"How can I enjoy this, if I can't see you?"

As the music played, she began to lose herself in the character. She was a Sylph, a fairy creature, no longer wearing leggings and a cut-off top. Her hair was adorned with flowers, and her white chiffon dress swirled and floated as she moved. In love with a mortal man, she had sneaked into his house, and found him asleep by the fire. She knew they could never be together, but she could dance for him, and he would see her forever in his dreams.

The Sylph danced around him, aching to touch him, trailing her arm across the back of his chair then whirling away. Again and again, she returned and retreated, torturing herself with his nearness, lamenting the fact that she could not be with him.

The music was coming to an end, and the Sylph would have to leave him forever. Unable to bear the thought, she ran back to him. Closing her eyes, she bent to kiss him. If only it could be more than a chaste peck on the forehead…

Her lips met lips. Alex's fingers threaded through her hair, locking her mouth to his. The rush of longing, the salty-sweet taste of him, were too much to resist. Her lips parted, welcoming his tongue, answering with hers. He groaned and kissed her harder. His arm snaked round her waist, to pull her onto his lap.

"Alex!" She broke away, shocked back to reality. She'd promised herself never to do this. And how could he betray Monika after all she'd done for him?

"I'm sorry," he said.

Sorry? He had set the trap and she had fallen into it. She fled the studio, not even bothering to take off her pointe shoes.

Chapter Ten

Alex went to his bedroom, pondering what to do about Gina. The kiss had been a moment of weakness. He couldn't blame her for being annoyed, but her reaction had been stronger than that. Why had it upset her so much?

Anticipating a cooler evening, he opened a dresser drawer to look for a sweater. Should he find her and apologize? No, he should let her have her privacy. Besides, she would be more ready to listen when she'd had a chance to calm down. He could wait until dinner.

Footsteps behind him. Before he could grab the rims to turn, the wheelchair jerked sharply and he was whirled around to face the door.

To face his brother.

"You've been fucking my girlfriend, you bastard," Nick growled in Russian.

"What are you talking about? How did you get—"

"Dimitri told me she is here!"

"Yes, she's still here. That doesn't mean—"

"He has seen you together, every morning. I not a fool."

Alex had never seen Nick so agitated. "So, we have breakfast together. So what?"

Nick's lip curled. "And the rest."

"She's a guest in my house, what am I supposed to do, lock her in her room?" Alex said. "If you've been talking to Clara, yes, I spend some time with Gina in the afternoons. In the *studio.* She's a dancer, I'm coaching her. Strictly professional. I haven't laid a finger on her."

Not strictly true. His fingers tingled at the memory of her silky hair tumbling over them while he kissed her eager mouth. *Don't think about that.*

"Coaching?" Nick sneered, pacing the floor. "Coach her to suck cock, you mean."

"Come on, Nick, would I do that to you?" Alex struggled to keep his tone reasonable. Something was wrong. Why couldn't Nick stand still?

"Hah! She is not supposed to be here. I told her to go. I knew if I left her here with you, you'd have her. You always stole all the dancers for yourself, I never stood a chance."

"Oh for fuck's sake, Nick, that's crap and you know it! I never stole a woman from you in my life!"

"Every time I dated a dancer, in the end they were only seeing me to get near you. This time, I scored one, all on my own. She did not even know you were my brother." Nick loomed over the wheelchair, fists clenching, sweat beading his brow. "But you couldn't leave her alone. Don't sit there and pretend you are innocent. She's mine, and she will be sorry for betraying me. And so will you."

Nick grabbed Alex by the collar and hauled him out of the chair until they were face to face. Alex yanked at Nick's arm to release his grip, but he was too unbalanced to get leverage. He was close enough now to see Nick's eyes. Their customary blue was almost eclipsed by his pupils. Alex's blood chilled. He'd thought Nick was stupid to be trafficking drugs. He never thought he'd be stupid enough to take them himself.

"You fucked every ballerina you ever danced with, Sasha. Don't expect me to believe you didn't fuck Gina!" He threw Alex sideways, sending him crashing against the bed frame.

Alex tried to sit up, but something large and heavy slammed into his midriff and knocked all the breath out of him. Before he could recover, the tip of Nick's boot hammered into him again. He managed to fend off the next kick and lift himself on to one elbow, but Nick was not so easily discouraged. A third kick landed squarely on Alex's chest, throwing him backwards.

His head hit the wall with a crack. Blackness.

****

Gina finished drying off and pulled on a gray sweatshirt and pants.

At Nick's bathroom mirror, she attacked her curls with a comb, viciously enough to bring tears to her eyes. The long, drenching shower hadn't calmed her. She berated her reflection. *Stupid, stupid girl! What were you thinking? How could you do that to Monika?*

The bathroom door crashed open against the wall. Nick stood in the doorway. "Why you still here?"

Shock glued her feet to the floor. He was standing in front of her before she could move. He was breathing heavily, sweat covered his brow. "Why you here?"

He was supposed to be in jail, and he had the cheek to ask why *she* was on the island? "Why are *you* here? The police said—"

He grunted. "Police my friends. Now tell, why you not go with Dimitri like I told you."

"I couldn't go." She tensed her core to stop herself

101

trembling and kept her voice steady. "I can't leave the country until I've got my passport sorted out."

"What?"

She'd forgotten, he didn't know. "I live in London. I can't go home without my passport."

"Bah!" He leaned in, his face inches from hers. "How many times you fuck him?"

She registered the large, dark pupils. He was high on something. Her heart beat faster. "What do you mean?"

He grabbed a handful of hair, yanking her head back. "How. Many. Times. You. Fuck. Sasha?"

Fear surged through her body. "Never! Never, Nick, I swear! Let me go! You're hurting me!"

He stepped forward, forcing her back, pinning her against the bathroom wall. "Good. Is only beginning. You whore with my brother. Now you show me. No more 'no, Nick.' Now you do what I want. *Everything* I want."

****

Alex tried to find a less painful position, without much success. Vicious stabs of pain in his ribs came with every inhalation. Not so bad if he kept the breaths shallow. He tried sitting up, but his head spun so hard, he had to lie down again.

He stared at his hand for several minutes before working out that the red marks on the palm were blood. What had happened? He'd fallen, obviously. What time was it? The floor was hard and cold. Moving was too painful to contemplate. He closed his eyes, resigned to waiting it out until Clara or Monika found him.

A scream made him open them again. *Gina?*

He sat up, far too quickly. Pain sliced like a cleaver

through his ribs and head. He put his hand to the back of his skull. When he felt something wet and sticky, he looked at his fingers. More blood. He'd hit his head somehow.

Another scream. Some of the cogs in his brain slipped back into place. Nick. Gina. Dear God, if Nick could do this to his own brother, what the hell was he doing to her?

He had to get to the wheelchair. Where the hell had it gone? Nick had pushed it away, next to the television, out of reach. He twisted to look for his crutches and gasped at the agonizing effect on his ribs. When the pain abated, he scanned the room again, more slowly. No crutches in sight. Without them, he could only stand, not walk. He'd have to crawl.

He rolled onto all fours and tried moving his right leg forward. The circular fixator slid easily enough on the polished floor but getting his knee to the floor meant tipping them painfully. He couldn't see an alternative. He crawled.

He rested with his head on the footrest of the chair for a moment before trying to pull himself up. The wheelchair rolled away from him. *The brake, dammit. How the fuck did it work?* His head ached. He was thinking through molasses. He pushed the wheelchair up against the wall instead.

He had a few false starts. The fixators kept getting in the way and his spinning head didn't help his balance. Finally he got up on one knee, put one hand on the arm of the chair and one on the TV cabinet, and pushed until he was balanced on the edge of the seat. The effort made him breathe heavily. The effect on his ribs was excruciating.

He sagged back into the wheelchair, wincing as his shoulder hit the chair back. Sweat trickled into his eyes and pain scythed through his rib cage. It was all pointless. He'd been far too slow. Whatever Nick was doing to Gina, it was over by now and he'd done nothing to help. Useless. Useless.

****

Gina screamed again as Nick dragged her by her hair, towards the bed. She dug her heels in and tried to resist his pull, but he was too strong. She flailed with her fists, but he had her at arm's length and she couldn't land a blow. Her mind was a jumble, her self-defense moves had deserted her. All she could think of was that woman, with Nick's hands around her throat, struggling to breathe, afraid she would die—

Concentrate. What moves could she use at this angle? *Hands around her throat.* She fought the panic down. They were almost at the bed, it might be her last chance, she had to try something. He stepped sideways to haul her level with him. She threw all her weight into a kick to his knee. Her body jarred as her foot connected.

Nick staggered and released his hold on her hair. Her momentum was too great, and she toppled forward, landing face-first on the floor, her head almost striking the bedside cabinet. She threw her hands out to break her fall and the little finger of her right hand brushed against something. Lifting her head to check, she saw the bullwhip, coiled under the bed.

Behind her, Nick spat a vitriolic stream of Russian. His fingers hooked into the back of her collar. She knew how much a whip could hurt—if she could manage to use it. There was no time to think of anything better. The edge of her collar was cutting into her windpipe as Nick hauled on it. She moved her right hand over the handle and wrapped her fingers firmly around it.

She deliberately slumped against the collar, even though it made her choke. Her dead weight would slow Nick down, and she needed time to visualize the move she had to make.

Almost there, he had lifted her far enough that she could bring her right knee up and plant her foot on the ground. She powered upwards, twisting with her right elbow high behind her, aiming for his chin. Her elbow caught his throat—even better!—and he reared back, losing his grip on her collar.

She turned to face him, legs in a wide stance, whip at the ready. Her chest heaved as the adrenaline coursed through her veins. She was ready to fight.

He stood between her and the door, clutching his throat. His lips parted into a sneer as she backed up towards the wall. He thought she was retreating, but he had a surprise coming. She was getting in range. Too close, and the end would wrap around his neck or body. That might not disable him, and if it failed, he'd be able to pull the whip out of her hand. She had to be far enough away to strike with the tip.

Her father's instructions echoed in her head. *"Palm forward, Gina. Keep it relaxed. The whip will go where your thumb is pointing. Form the loop first. You must form the loop first."*

She launched a sidearm flick that went wrong. There was no crack, but the swish startled Nick, and he stepped back. Gina advanced, flailing the whip right-left-right-left in a continuous motion, as fast as she could, but he kept backing away, just beyond her reach. He might catch the tail if she slowed, but how long could she keep up this speed?

His foot hit the door jamb and his eyes flicked down. Now was her chance—the whip cracked and found its mark. He yelled and clapped his hand to his eye. An underarm crack struck his nose on the way back. He staggered and crumpled into the corridor, mewling, both hands covering his face.

Gina jumped over him, flew down the stairs and out of the villa, and sprinted for the jetty. Taking the mooring rope with her, she leapt onto the stern of the cruiser and dived for the ignition. The engine whined and bellowed as she pushed the throttle to full, but she didn't care.

As the boat shot forwards, she looked back. Nick was at the generator shed, hauling at the tarpaulin covering the dinghy, but he'd told her it wouldn't start. She swung the cruiser in an arc away from Venetiko, silently blessing her grandparents for making her help with their boat business.

Chapter Eleven

Alex couldn't give up. Even if Nick had gone, Gina might be lying, hurt, somewhere.

Gritting his teeth, he pushed on the rims, and immediately faced his first problem. Who was he trying to kid, thinking he could be any help to anyone? He couldn't even work out how to open a fucking door. How the fuck do you open a door towards you when you're sitting in a fucking wheelchair and the fucking wheels are in the way and...

For Christ's sake, pull yourself together.

He took a deep breath—bad idea—and set out to maneuver the chair in order to get the door open. Too many little movements, far too much stretching, but he made himself do it.

He had to repeat the exercise all over again at the front door. The salt breeze wafted into the villa. The jetty was empty. Alex tried to think. He never heard Nick arrive. Either he came on his cruiser—or Dimitri dropped him off. All this was too hard to work out.

Thankfully, the door into the other villa was open. He wheeled through it and along the passageway. The ground floor was empty. He called out, but there was no reply from upstairs. Nick had gone. And he'd taken Gina with him.

He was too late, much too late.

With difficulty, Alex turned the wheelchair around

and went back to his kitchen and the satellite phone. At first, he couldn't understand why he couldn't get the damn thing to work, then remembered he had to be clear of the house in order to get reception.

Back into the hall, moving very slowly now due to the pain that seemed to stretch from here to beyond. Finally he was out on the deck. Even thumbing Juliette's number took effort. *Please, please be home.*

He couldn't seem to catch a deep breath, but managed to say, "Hello? Monika?"

"Alex?" She didn't sound sure; did his voice sound so strange?

"Nick—" Too hard to explain. "Accident."

"Alex, are you hurt?"

"Yes."

"Okay. Keep still, rest. I'll get help. Hold on, Alex, I'm coming."

After he hung up, he let the phone drop. Nothing to do now but wait. He had no strength to move any further.

Nick had spent his childhood on the streets. Why had Alex ever imagined he could change him? Why had he persisted in believing that Nick was capable of stealing and gambling, but never maiming or—God forbid—killing? He berated himself for not facing up to the truth. Everything that had happened to Gina was his fault.

If he ever found her, he would make it up to her. If she was alive. Nick might have put her on his boat, but where would he take her? Alex looked at the expanse of water and his heart contracted.

****

Although she hadn't considered where to go—

other than avoiding Venetiko, because Nick had too many friends there—Gina held her course, north toward Corfu. She had no idea what lay south, except the island. Something, a sound maybe, made her turn her head to look back—and gasped. Nick had lied about the dinghy. It was a smart modern powerboat, in full working order, and he was driving it straight at her.

She opened the throttle and was gratified at how eagerly the cruiser responded—but she had no idea whether it could outrun Nick. The cruiser had powerful engines, but the snub-nosed little powerboat was lightweight and unencumbered, planing fast over the water.

With Corfu in sight, she barreled toward a cluster of whitewashed houses on the southern tip. The marina offered an obvious refuge; but in the time it would take her to dock, Nick would catch up. She didn't see a soul at the marina. With no one to help her, Nick would bundle her back onto the boat and take her God knows where.

At the last minute, she yanked the wheel left and instantly regretted it, expecting the boat to slew out of control—but to her amazement, the cruiser turned like a lamb, with only a small loss of speed. She patted the polished wood. "Well done, you. I'm impressed."

Her smile died as she looked over her shoulder. Nick had changed course to cut the corner, and he was far too close. She pushed the throttle lever forward and prayed.

Her speed topped out at thirty-seven knots. She swiveled around on the white leather seat to check on Nick. He hadn't given up, but it was only a matter of time. He must have noticed the gap widening between them. She throttled back slightly as there was no point in wasting fuel.

She contemplated her options. If she turned for the coastline in any direction, Nick would intercept her. Perhaps he wouldn't even need to catch her: the detective had said the smuggling network stretched all the way from Albania as far south as Patras. Once Nick knew where she intended to land, he could notify his contacts.

Another glance at Nick told her he wasn't trying to catch up. His boat bobbed and swayed in the rolling swell of the open water. Either he'd run out of fuel—she couldn't be that lucky—or he'd come to the same conclusion as she had and was waiting for her to turn back. She reduced her speed and adjusted the trim.

In the center of the console was a GPS screen. Her grandparents' budget hadn't stretched for something that elaborate, so she wasn't entirely sure she could operate it. She switched it on anyway, and a familiar outline appeared on the screen.

Italy. Could it really be that close? She checked the distance to the nearest landfall: only one hundred and fifty kilometers! The question was whether she had enough fuel, especially after her mad dash to escape Nick. The calculation was beyond her—too many variables, not enough information about the cruiser's performance. But the gauge indicated the tank was close to full. In theory, a cruiser like this should have the range.

While she considered her options, she continued to motor west, checking occasionally to make sure Nick hadn't resumed his pursuit. Or now had reinforcements.

Making for Italy was risky, but what choice did she

have? Until Nick was out of sight, she couldn't turn back. She might as well go forward—to Italy, the land of her forefathers. She spoke the language, more or less, and she had a right to hold an Italian passport. If the authorities gave her trouble, she had a network of relatives on whom she could call for help—provided she could remember their names and addresses. She would feel safer there.

She set a course for the heel of Italy's boot.

****

An hour or so later, with no signs of pursuit, she was almost enjoying herself. The sea swells weren't uncomfortable and the sky was clear. There was a brisk breeze however and she wore little more than a velour tracksuit.

She figured Nick must have wet-weather gear stowed somewhere. It wouldn't offer much warmth, but better than nothing. She took the three steps down into the cabin and paused, astonished at the shambles. Clothing, squashed beer cans and empty food wrappers were strewn across every surface—floor, bench seats, cupboards. She picked her way through the debris, the floor sticky under her bare feet.

She used the head and set about looking for anything useful. She had collected a mug, a reasonably clean sweater and a light rain jacket, when a stentorian blast sent her scampering back on deck.

From the north, a monstrous ship bore down on her. She froze, staring up at its huge bow, unable to breathe or think or move. The cruiser felt as tiny and useless as a rowboat. Snapping back to her senses, she grabbed for the controls and opened the throttle. The cruiser surged, out of the path of the juggernaut.

At a safe distance, she throttled back and slumped forward on the dashboard, waiting for her heart to stop pounding. Viewed from the side, the ship wasn't nearly as frightening. Only a car ferry, and it hadn't been as close as she'd thought. But it was still big enough to have destroyed the cruiser. If the crew hadn't spotted her and sounded a warning, she would've stayed below until it was too late.

She cursed herself for making such a rookie mistake. She should have known better. Whether it was delayed shock from Nick's attack or a lack of food, she wasn't thinking straight. She filled the mug at the sink and gulped the water. The sweater and jacket reached to her knees, and she had to roll up yards of sleeve. They also smelled of Nick, which made her wrinkle her nose, but she had no other way to stay warm.

Thinking of him made her think of the island, and Alex. She hadn't even been able to say goodbye. What would he make of her disappearance? Would he report her missing when Clara found all her belongings still in Nick's room? Would he care enough to worry?

The sky shaded to pink-tinged blue. She had never been to sea at night before. She'd heard her grandmother talk about how dark it got, so far from streetlights and houses. She wished she'd had time to look for a life jacket and a torch. Lights would help. She tried one of the switches on the console and jumped when the bright beam of a headlight stabbed out from the bow. She flicked it off. Until she got closer to land, seeing a few feet of water in front of the boat wasn't much use.

Another switch turned on lights inside the cockpit—reassuring, but they would ruin her night vision. The glow from the GPS and the tiny light illuminating the compass was all she needed. Finally, she found the button for the red and green navigation lights, which should ensure nearby boats would see her.

The horizon became a broiling orange. Soon, she wouldn't be able to see where she was going, but she was in the open sea, so obstacles should be rare. She could keep moving forward. The wind had dropped completely away with the sunset, and the sea had only a moderate chop. The cruiser hummed steadily forward as the darkness settled. The stars appeared. Gina gasped as the sky became black velvet, densely embroidered with silver sequins in swirling patterns. But when she lowered her eyes to the darkened sea, the blackness seemed to close in on her, flowing over the rail, enveloping her head, suffocating her, she couldn't breathe—

A flash of blue-green light caught her peripheral vision. And another. Leaping alongside the boat were three dolphins, creating scintillating trails of phosphorescence as they swam. There was a touch of hysteria in her laughter as the dolphins took turns to cut the surface, weaving in and out, jumping and splashing into the water.

"Thank you, guys," she shouted. "Thank you. Don't leave me!"

The dolphins skimmed along, close to the hull. She could do this. The cruiser was a solid ocean-going vessel, and she'd proved she could drive it as well as any man—and better than Nick.

As the night wore on, she managed to avoid passing close to any other vessels. A couple of times, large ships, lit up like skyscrapers, loomed high in the distance, but she changed course in order to give them a wide berth.

She deliberately avoided looking at the fuel indicator. There was nothing she could do about it, anyway. All she could do was pray the fuel would last and her vessel would carry her to safety.

Chapter Twelve

In the early hours of the morning, the coast appeared sooner than Gina expected. The GPS told her she had arrived at her destination. She motored slowly into the harbor mouth. Two fishing boats sailed out past her, lights gleaming on their rigging, but otherwise the only things moving were the seagulls.

The town looked too small—she needed somewhere with transport links and a proper police station. But her fuel was almost exhausted, and so was she. She could barely keep her eyes open; her body ached; and her stomach rumbled.

No doubt you were supposed to have a booking to moor in the marina, but she'd broken all kinds of regulations already. The marina office was hardly likely to be open. She peered into the gloom, trying to see if there was a night-time security guard.

What was she worried about, she thought with a laugh. Getting caught was probably the quickest way to make contact with the local police. Unlike in Greece, she knew enough of the language to explain herself.

Even in the dark, mooring was easy in the wide berths of the marina. After reversing in, slowly, carefully, she secured the lines. With nothing more to do until morning, she stepped down into the cabin, discarded the jacket and sweater, and got down on her hands and knees to inspect the space under the cockpit.

There was barely enough height to sit upright under there, but it had been set up as a sleeping area. It reminded her of her favorite hidey-hole in one of her grandfather's boats. How she and her brother Matt had giggled as they squeezed into the little cavern. Granddad would pretend he hadn't noticed the young stowaways, reacting with astonishment when they ran on deck shouting, "Boo!"

A jumble of quilt and pillows lay on top of the thin mattress. Gina pulled the quilt aside, uncovering a red messenger bag. She chucked it out into the main cabin, then arranged the pillows to her satisfaction, crawled onto the mattress, and fell instantly asleep.

****

A cacophony of seagulls woke her. The cabin was light. Stretching her arms over her head, she wondered whether to get up or try to go back to sleep. Apart from her rumbling stomach, she had no need to rush. The chances of Nick finding her must be remote. Even if he guessed she had made for Italy and alerted some of his cronies, they would look first in Leuca, the closest landfall on the point of Italy's heel. That was why she had chosen Torre Vado, just around the corner. By the time they gave up on Leuca and started checking other towns, she would be long gone.

The seagulls' continued squawking made sleep impossible. She crawled out of her cocoon to visit the head, then surveyed the cabin, considering her next move. She quailed at the thought of dealing with the petty bureaucrats in the marina office. Much better to avoid any connection between herself and the boat, she decided to go straight to the police station under her own steam.

Depending on where the location of the police station, she might need money for a bus or taxi. Nick had a habit of leaving coins scattered around the villa, why not on the boat?

The cabin had a surprising number of drawers and cubbyholes. By the time she checked each one, she'd collected almost thirty euros. Turning her attention to the discarded clothes, she found a one hundred euro note in the pocket of a pair of jeans. Riches, compared to where she had been a moment ago.

The coins would weigh her pockets down—but the messenger bag she'd discarded earlier could hold everything. She picked it up, noticing for the first time that it wasn't empty. Inside was a plastic bag containing slim red, green, blue and black booklets. She knew what they were before she opened the bag. As suspicion formed in her mind, she tipped the passports out on the floor and began checking the blue ones.

Sure enough, the fourth passport was her own. Nick had lied. Perhaps Dimitri had found the bag, or perhaps Stelios had taken it. Either way, the reason was obvious. Passports had value on the black market.

All the more reason not to go to the marina office. If they checked the boat, they might not believe she had nothing to do with the stolen passports, and she didn't want to throw them away. The true owners deserved to get them back.

Leaving the other passports on the floor, she stuffed her own, the money and the waterproof jacket into the messenger bag, pulled on the sweater and went up on deck. The clear sky promised a beautiful day, but the air was still cool. A seagull scuttled out of the way as she hurried along the short jetty.

A promenade ran along the waterfront. All she saw to her right was a road and an ancient circular tower. To her left, the promenade was lined with low whitewashed houses, but a Ferris wheel in the distance gave her hope of finding a livelier area further on. She turned left. Slowly, the houses gave way to small hotels, shops and kiosks, and the concrete of the marina became a pleasant, sandy beach. Gina was glad the town was a beach resort—no one would see anything odd about someone in sweats and bare feet.

Everything was boarded up and silent. She saw more shops farther along the street, so kept walking. During the day it would be a prosperous, bustling little place, but even the joggers were not up and about yet. Street signs proclaimed the way to hotels, camping sites and restaurants, but no police station.

The bus stop was so insignificant, she almost missed it. The sign was nailed halfway down a metal pole at the entrance to a hotel parking lot. Above the sign was a map, headed "*Salentoinbus*," but the place names meant nothing to her. Except for the final stop on the list: Lecce.

The name recalled one of her less-fond memories of her childhood visits to Italy. A farmhouse with endless olive trees and a very large pig. A cousin whose name she couldn't remember, who put spiders down her shirt. The one bright spot in the whole vacation had been a blissful ice cream in a *gelateria* in Lecce. She pictured the tall, elegant buildings around the café, the busy traffic, the line of stores where her mother had paused to window-shop. And the station, where they'd caught the train to Rome.

The bus timetable ran down the side of the map.

The first bus was due just after seven. With no watch on her wrist, or a clock in sight, she didn't know the exact time—but it couldn't be far off.

Why did she want to go to the police anyway? This morning, when she'd thought she had no money and no passport, they had been her only option. Now she had both, there wasn't much more the police could offer her. They certainly wouldn't pay her air fare home to London. She couldn't see the point of making a complaint against Nick to Italian police, who would have no jurisdiction over him. She settled on the low sandstone wall to wait.

In this backwater, she had expected a beat-up jalopy, but the bus that eventually drew up was a smart, modern coach. She paid the driver and settled herself in the almost-empty bus for the two-hour trip.

It seemed only moments later that the driver was tapping her shoulder and telling her to get off. Still foggy from sleep, she got to her feet and stumbled off the bus. Diesel fumes tainted the air. A dull roar of traffic was punctuated by the honking of car horns, the eggbeater buzz of scooters and the occasional growl of a departing coach.

The bus stood in an enormous parking lot in the middle of a huge roundabout, surrounded by large office blocks. A woman approached the bus and gave her a frank top-to-bottom stare. Gina looked down at herself, remembering what an odd figure she must present. Having grown up in Australia, running barefoot to and from the beach, she hadn't given a thought to walking shoe-less in Torre Vado. Now she wished she had stayed in the town until the shops opened, so she could buy a pair of shoes. Even a cheap pair of flip-flops would have been better than nothing. She would look for a shoe shop en route to the station.

Her tracksuit might not be usual Italian street wear, but at least it was designer label. She pulled off the shapeless sweater she'd found and dumped it in a bin as she walked to the bus terminus, a low building at the edge of the lot.

Aromas of brewing coffee made her forget all else. She followed the scent to a kiosk at the end of the building. She ordered at the counter, devouring half of her first *cornetto* before she even sat down at an outside table. Two *cornettos* and a second coffee later, she felt ready to face any challenge.

On her way to the *bigletteria* to ask directions to the station, the departure board caught her eye. A bus to Rome, leaving in fifteen minutes. It would mean sacrificing her shoe-buying expedition, but the opportunity seemed too good to miss—especially as the trip would take eight hours. The train might be slightly faster, but she would lose time finding the station, and the train ticket would be more expensive. It would be awful to get all the way to the station and find she couldn't afford the fare. She joined the line at the ticket office.

Climbing onto the coach ten minutes later, she was all too aware of the stares of other passengers. She found a seat on her own, right at the back. She would be in Rome in eight hours, and she didn't have to consider what her next step should be.

In her family, Rome meant only one person: a tall woman wearing a riot of old lace, faded velvet and rose-printed silk. Battered red cowboy boots on her feet and a fraying, wide-brimmed straw hat on her head. A fat pink tapestry bag her constant companion, full of all kinds of treasures irresistible to a small child.

"Crazy Teresy" as Gina's brothers called her. Aunt Teresa had led an unconventional life herself and wouldn't be fazed by her niece arriving on her doorstep, barefoot and unannounced. More importantly, she knew how to keep a secret. She wouldn't insist on calling the police, or go off blabbing to her sister, Gina's mother.

She leaned her head on the window and smiled.

****

Gina had hoped the bus terminus in Rome would be somewhere central, so she could at least buy some shoes, but it was in an outlying suburb. The few shops nearby were already closed by the time they arrived. She went to the taxi rank and bent her head to consult one of the drivers through his car window. *"Mi scusi, quanto verrà a costare per andare alla Valle Aurelia?"*

The figure he quoted was more reasonable than she'd feared, and she had enough to cover it. She climbed into the taxi, relieved not to have to take the Metro so late at night. Aunt Teresa's home was only a short distance from Valle Aurelia station, but at night the ancient roadway with its looming stone walls and wooded banks was no place to walk alone.

By the time they reached Aunt Teresa's neighborhood, it was very late and pitch black. Gina had to direct the driver, since she couldn't remember the name of Aunt Teresa's street. As the taxi bumped along the cobbles, she prayed her aunt would be home.

"A sinistra, per favore," she said, recognizing the turnoff at the last moment.

As the taxi drew to a stop, she paid the driver and climbed out, greeted by a frenzy of howls and barks.

"Ssshh, you'll wake everyone." Gina hurried over to calm the excited black Labrador retriever. He had jammed his face hard against the bars of his prison, offering his nose for her to pat. "I've got nothing for you, but I'll bring you a treat for you tomorrow, promise," she said, reaching through the bars to rub his head. "Though if my aunt's not home, I'll be back to keep you company for the rest of the night."

She turned down the next driveway, her bare feet slapping on the cobblestones. Pressing the bell marked Reception, she heard the ding-dong somewhere behind the imposing double-leafed door. Eventually, the door was opened by a tall, rumpled figure with a shock of unruly dark hair. The frown on his face cleared as he looked at Gina.

"My God, you're Teresa's niece, aren't you?" he said. "What brings you here at this time of night?"

"It's a long story, Lorenzo," Gina said, the tension in her shoulders easing as she recognized the building owner's son. "Is Aunt Teresa home?"

"As far as I know, she is. Saw her this morning. You'd better come in. I'll give you a hand with your luggage." Lorenzo took a step over the threshold and stopped, obviously confused at the absence of baggage.

"No need, I haven't got any."

He stepped back, frowning, and ushered her into the reception area. "You're lucky I was here. The office closes at five. I only came over because one of the guests had a blown fuse."

They emerged into the inner courtyard. Four stories of windows looked down on them from all sides, their wrought iron balconies with brightly colored flowers cascading down the pale stucco walls. There was no light in Aunt Teresa's second floor window. Gina thanked Lorenzo, promising to explain everything tomorrow, and ran towards the stairs.

She reached Teresa's door and knocked. Nothing. She hated to disturb the neighbors, but she could hardly sit on the landing all night. "*Zia* Teresa?" she called, her lips close to the door.

The door opened a crack and closed again. The rattle of a chain, the door flung wide, and Aunt Teresa's arms were around Gina, enveloping her in acres of cashmere shawl and the scent of patchouli.

"Come in, come in." Teresa said, bustling her into the apartment and closing the door. "It's so good to see you, but what are you doing here?"

Gina burst into tears.

Teresa shepherded her over to the couch, wrapped a patchwork shawl round her shoulders and offered a handkerchief. Gina blew her nose and sniffed. "I'm sorry, but you sounded so like Mum…"

"Never mind, never mind, *cara.* Whatever it is that's brought you here, I can see you're too worn out to talk about it tonight. Let's get you to bed and you can tell me everything in the morning."

Gina nodded, a sense of relief washing over her. She didn't have to deal with everything on her own anymore. Aunt Teresa's cozy apartment might not be her real home, but it felt like home.

She felt safe at last.

Chapter Thirteen

Alerted by the rumble and thump of Dimitri's boat, Alex raised his head from his book. Through the lounge room window, he watched Clara disembark. A tall vision in a cream linen suit followed her, stepping delicately onto the jetty. Placing a slim briefcase under one arm, he straightened the collar of his pink open-neck shirt, tugged on the lapels of his suit and hesitated at the edge of the sand, obviously fearing for his burnished leather shoes.

Alex grinned. His theatrical agent belonged on Mayfair streets, not Greek beaches.

Anthony Redmayne crossed the beach on tiptoe, his shoulders relaxing visibly when he made it to the safety of the deck. It irked Alex that he couldn't wheel out to greet his guest, but his fractured ribs were still too painful. Clara would show Anthony the way.

"Alex!" Anthony swept into the room. "My dear, how are you? What a dreadful business this is!"

"Improving." Alex had no desire to discuss his injuries. "I hope your trip wasn't too tedious?"

The agent shuddered. "If I need to visit you again, I may have to charter a helicopter. The ferry was ghastly enough, but that fishing boat…"

"No fear of that," Alex said. "I'm selling the island."

Anthony lowered himself gracefully into the plush

armchair opposite and placed his soft leather briefcase on the table. "Thank the Lord for that. It will make my job *so* much easier to have you in London again. Alterra is keen to do another TV campaign. And I—"

"No."

Anthony looked up with questioning eyebrows, frozen in the act of removing a diary from his briefcase.

"I'm not moving to London. I have arranged to stay at Oscar's vineyard. And I'm not doing any ads. I need to get out of *this* first." Alex slapped his palms on the armrests of the wheelchair to emphasize his point.

"But they're happy to work with you. They can shoot you from the waist up—"

"No. The paparazzi will be all over me and you know it. The only way you will get me in a TV studio is when I can walk into one. I'll stay at Oscar's until I've completed my rehab."

"Well, at least I won't have to take a smelly fishing boat to visit you there. And France is *so* much more civilized than Greece." Anthony set the diary on top of the briefcase, lining up the edges. "I understand you need some time to recover from this latest—er—setback, but I do hope you'll reconsider. You do realize, the longer you delay, the harder it will be to get you back in circulation? People forget, you know."

"It's a risk I'll have to take."

After a knock on the door, Clara entered, carrying a tray with a bottle of champagne, one champagne flute and a tall glass of water decorated with lemon and mint sprigs.

"Can you stay for dinner?" Alex asked, as Clara put the tray on the table, then poured the champagne.

"'Fraid not. I thought I'd kill two birds and visit

Nathaniel in Corfu while I'm here, but rather rashly I promised I'd be there in time for supper. I forgot to allow for the primitive modes of transport around here."

"Thank you," Alex said, accepting the tall glass from Clara. She left the room.

Anthony took a sip of champagne. "Have you taken the pledge, dear boy?"

"No. Monika won't let me drink alcohol yet. Concussion."

"I do not know how you can possibly stay here after what happened," Anthony said. "My nerves would be in absolute shreds."

Alex shrugged, then wished he hadn't. *Damn ribs*. "I would move to *Bonséjour* tomorrow, but the cottages are all occupied. I've got a security guard stationed here, and Monika has a bodyguard with her at all times. Besides, I doubt Nick will be back. While I was in hospital, he, or someone, came and packed up all his belongings."

Whoever it was, they had taken all of Gina's things, too. It was one of the reasons he couldn't count on the police to help find her. They didn't believe him.

"Mr. Korolev, be assured we will charge Mr. Rostov with assault when we find him," the inspector had said. "But kidnapping? There are no signs of a struggle in their room. The evidence suggests they packed their bags calmly and left in Mr. Rostov's boat. That does not look like a woman being taken against her will. We have spoken to witnesses on the mainland who say they were a happy couple. We have no reason to look for her."

Reliving what the pompous officer said reminded Alex of the other reason he'd agreed to meet Anthony.

"I'm not sure how much Monika told you, but there's someone else involved…"

"She did mention a girlfriend of Nick's who'd gone missing."

"She's a dancer and she worked in London, in musical theater mainly. I thought you might be able to help find her, with your contacts in the industry."

Anthony's eyebrows furrowed again, a sure sign he was adding two and two together. "A lot of effort for a stranger."

"She's an innocent bystander in all this." Alex knew Anthony wouldn't be so easily fooled, but he didn't feel like baring his soul. "I'm concerned that Nick kidnapped her. It would be a weight off my mind if I could find her."

"I see. Well, if she was dancing in London, I should be able to find her. What's her name?"

"That's the problem. Her first name is Gina. Neither of us can remember her last name." Alex paused. Anthony must think him mad to even attempt a search, with so little to go on. "She's Australian, though her accent didn't sound Australian to me."

"Leave it with me. The dance world is a small one. I should be able to track her down."

But what if he didn't? Alex gazed out at the sea, sparkling blue, so serene and innocent yet able to hide so much.

"So, Alex." Anthony's brisk tone brought him back to the present. "About our original discussion. How long before you're ready to start work, do you think? When should I start putting out feelers?"

That was the question. "Maybe never" was the answer, depending how well his rehab went, but Alex didn't want to think about that. "I'll keep you up to date with my progress, but I expect around six months. I'm looking for a full-time therapist to work with."

Anthony winced theatrically. "It's a long time, Alex. It would make so much more sense to make a start now. Stay at the vineyard, by all means, it's very picturesque there. *Paris Match* would love to do a shoot. Your recovery would make a great human interest story."

Alex grimaced. "A sob story in some women's magazine is exactly what I don't want!"

Anthony raised both hands in mock surrender. "I can't pretend I'm happy to have one of my most valuable clients *hors de combat*, but it's your decision. I must say, I was worried about you. But you have that old glint of determination in your eye again. It's good to see, even though I know it means I can't win the argument. I wish you well."

"Thank you."

"Enough business. I have all *kinds* of goss to share. I don't suppose you know a *thing* about the goings-on in the ballet world while you've been away. You'll never *believe* what happened to Stephanie Price at the premiere of…"

Alex's mind drifted as Anthony regaled him with the latest news, most of which interested him not one jot. Thinking of all he must do to prepare for the move, he listened with half an ear in case Anthony should mention someone he cared about.

It frustrated him that he had to depend on Monika so much. The reception on the satellite phone was unpredictable and patchy, and it was easier to ask her to make the calls when she was on the mainland—but it meant all he could do was sit in the villa and wait for answers. He couldn't wait to move to the vineyard.

****

Late in the afternoon, Gina stood on the balcony of her aunt's apartment, removing the last of the shirts off the clothes rack. The clothes had dried well in the sun. Hearing footsteps, she leaned over the railing and saw Teresa enter the courtyard below, her pink tapestry bag in one hand and two shopping bags in the other. Teresa glanced up and gave her a wave and a smile. Gina stepped into the living room, put the pile of clothes on the sofa and checked on the pasta bubbling on the stove, taking care to keep her wafting medieval-style sleeves away from the gas flame. Wearing her aunt's clothes made her feel like a princess in a castle.

"I have quite the housekeeper," Teresa said as she came through the door. "Laundry done, dinner cooked, I did not think you were so domestic, *cara*!"

"A bit of housework is the least I can do." Gina opened the fridge. "I'm making *spaghetti alle vongole*. White wine?"

Teresa nodded, placing her carpet bag and purple *pashmina* on a side table and settling into a winged, velvet-upholstered chair. Gina opened the bottle and poured two glasses. "I rang Mum," she said, leaning against the kitchen bench. "I told her I lost my handbag on the ferry from Greece."

Better to let her mother think she was careless, than admit she'd been dating a psycho. "I'll book my flight this evening if I can use your card. I'll transfer the money as soon as I get home. Or I could ask Mum to repay you if you're in a hurry."

Teresa set her glass on the coffee table, her face

serious. "Are you sure going home is the right thing?"

"*Zia* Teresa, I'd love to stay longer, but it's time to move on. Alex is right. I've missed my chance. I'm too old for the ballet companies now. The dream is over, time to face reality."

"Too old at twenty-three! What is the world coming to? But if that is the case, what will you do in Australia?"

Gina shrugged, determined not to show the tide of sadness welling up inside her. "Maybe I'll just help Mum with the boat business for a while."

"You are not ready to stop performing, *cara*. It is in your blood. The Tarascos topped the bill as acrobats, you know." Teresa went to the bookshelf. "Did I show you our album?"

Of course she had, several times, but Gina never tired of looking at it. She took the scrapbook from Teresa and perched on the arm of the sofa, leafing through the pages. Leaning over Gina's shoulder, Teresa pointed to a picture of Gina's mother in a backbend, her head tucked between her legs, grinning at the camera. "Your mother was always the star."

"What a pity she gave it up."

"She had no hesitation. You and your brothers came first." Teresa smiled. "Your father didn't understand."

"I never really understood that. I mean, Dad wasn't real circus people, he'd just decided to take it up as a career. But he was the one who wanted to carry on the tradition, not Mum."

"Ah, but that was the reason, *cara*. Your mother grew up in the circus. She knew what a hard life it was for families. She knew how children's education suffered, how difficult it was to make ends meet. She wanted a safe, stable life for her children. Your father never quite forgave her, I think."

Gina wondered if that had been the beginning of the end of her parents' marriage. Her father had loved the circus with a blind passion. It must have been hard to give it up and go back to working in his parents' boat business in Australia. No wonder he had been so obsessive about finding gigs at shows and carnivals.

"You say Alex was right about the ballet," Teresa said. "Could it be, he is right about the circus, too?"

Gina slapped the album closed and stood up. "Oh, *Zia*, not you, too!"

"It would make your mother very happy."

"Do you think so?"

"She always said you had the talent." Teresa stepped around the sofa and took the album from her niece's hands. "I think she was a little sad when you switched to ballet."

The thought had never occurred to Gina. "But it's too late to go back now. I haven't done so much as a handstand in years."

"Your mother and I were old school. The new circuses need more than just acrobatics. They need artists who can dance and act, too. Your cousin Fabrizio would jump at the chance to hire someone like you."

Gina shook her head. "I'm too rusty. It would take me months to get back up to standard."

"I disagree. You have maintained your strength and flexibility through your dance training. You have the aptitude. I know you will be very successful."

Gina frowned at her aunt, eyes narrowed. "*Will* be? What have you been up to?"

"Fabrizio will love you. I told him so this afternoon." Teresa picked up her wine glass and took a sip. "You start on Monday, at eleven."

****

By eleven o'clock on Monday morning, Gina was still searching for the *Circo Mirabile* rehearsal venue. She retraced her steps along a deserted, litter-strewn street. All she could see were old warehouses and industrial buildings. She checked the street sign for the third time. Yes, the address was correct. The circus headquarters had to be here somewhere. It had taken her nearly an hour to reach this outer suburb of Rome, and now she'd wasted another twenty minutes hunting for the stupid place.

Following the sounds of music, she identified the source as a window in one of the buildings. She tried the handle of the nearest door. It turned, and she stepped inside.

At first glance, the vast open space looked like a working factory, with its mass of metal gantries and scaffolding—but in a factory, the framework wouldn't have had men and women hanging from it in graceful attitudes on hoops and ribbons.

On the other side of the scaffolding, a smartly dressed woman stood beside a short man with a head like a bowling-ball. He wore jeans, an expensive leather jacket and a scarf that had quite possibly taken two hours to arrange. The woman's vigorous nodding and frantic scribbling on her clipboard suggested he was the boss.

Gina congratulated herself on her understanding of Italians. If this had been a British circus, she'd have turned up for work in her track suit, but that would never do in Italy. It had meant borrowing money from Teresa, but she was glad of her new designer jeans and smart jacket. She approached the boss.

He noticed her before she had a chance to speak. "You must be Gina!" He surprised her by speaking in English, though with a mangled Italian American accent.

"Yes, and you must be cousin Fabrizio."

"Yes indeed, but please don't ask how we're related, I can't keep track." He took her by the elbow and steered her towards the nearest gantry. "I am frantic right now so I'm going to leave you with Sophie to learn the ropes. Later on, Ludmilla will come back and get all your details, fix up your pay, etcetera. Sophie will show you where to get changed. *Sophie!*"

The last word was bellowed towards the roof and a lithe, dark figure descended in response, sliding smoothly down a thick rope that dangled to the floor. "Sophie, this is the new girl I told you about, Gina Tarasco. Get her started, I gotta rush."

Automatically, Gina opened her mouth to correct the surname, and stopped herself just in time. She liked her new stage name: a tribute to her mother and a fresh start. As a bonus, if Nick came looking for her, he wouldn't find her real name on any billboards.

"He's a bit of a shock to the sustem, aye?" Sophie asked.

Gina's brain took a moment to unscramble the tortured vowels and the black pattern tattooed on Sophie's chin and finally arrived at the answer. She laughed. "You're a New Zealander!"

Sophie nodded. "Maori through and through. You did good, most people guess Aussie."

"I wouldn't make that mistake. I'm an Aussie myself."

Sophie's braids bounced as she did a little jig. "Ace, we'll be the Australasian gang!"

"It'll be nice to have someone to speak English to."

"Oh, don't worry, everybody here speaks English. We have so many nationalities, English is the only language we all understand." Sophie paused. "I'd better show you the changing room, then you can get on the track."

"Track?"

"Sorry, it's the jargon they use here," Sophie explained as she led Gina to a box-like structure at the back of the rehearsal space. "Nobody here has just one part, we all cover for each other. You'll start out on the chorus track, with me. Once you've been here a while, you'll be given another track, meaning, you'll learn someone else's part so you can understudy them. We can all play at least one other role, and some of us can do three or four."

"Sounds complicated. A lot to remember, too."

"Yes, but it's important," Sophie said. "It's the circus. You know how common injuries are. If we all know each other's parts, management can juggle us all around at the last minute if someone gets hurt."

Sophie opened the door to a stuffy, windowless room lit by a row of fluorescent lights suspended from the ceiling. Gina saw no benches or mirrors, just chairs scattered against the walls. No one sat in them. One woman sat cross-legged on the floor, eating a sandwich. Another lay on her back, legs splayed wide against the wall, reading a book. Among the litter of bags, shoes and clothing, the arm of a fluffy sweater moved to reveal a smiling face, inches from the floor. Its owner sat up, legs still in a wide split, and looked at Sophie.

"Guys, meet Gina," Sophie said. "She's new today on my track. Gina, meet Jazmin, Larissa and Elena."

"Hi!" The word was a chorus, but not an enthusiastic one. Each went back to what they'd been doing.

"I'll head back out, come and join me after you've changed," Sophie said, and left.

Unsettled, Gina unzipped her jeans slowly. How could she start a job with no paperwork? She didn't even know what her pay would be. Judging by Sophie's description, she would be starting at the bottom. And Sophie had just reminded her how much more hazardous an acrobat's life was, compared to a dancer's. What had she got herself into?

The first thing she saw when she emerged from the windowless changing room was Sophie tumbling across the mat in a series of somersaults and rolls. Gina's confidence hit rock-bottom. If that was part of the choreography, she was sunk.

"Ready?"

Sophie's bright inquiry was the last straw. Gina felt a tear escape down her cheek. She batted it away with her hand, but Sophie had noticed.

"What's wrong?" she asked.

Gina sniffed. "I'm a fraud, that's what's wrong. I shouldn't even be here. Fabrizio's my fifth cousin ten times removed, or something like that. He only gave me the job because my auntie told him to. I'm a dancer; I haven't done acrobatics for years. There's no way I can do what you just did."

"Oh, don't worry about that. That's me practising

for another track. The chorus doesn't get to do much tumbling. We might outshine the stars, eh?" Sophie put an arm around her shoulders. "So you have done some acrobatics, right?"

"Yeah. I switched to ballet when I was fifteen. But that's a long time ago."

"You'll be fine, in that case. It's all in the muscle memory, you just have to wake it up. Come on, let's get you warmed up and practice some somersaults before Enzo gets here."

"Who's Enzo?"

"He's our captain, he's supposed to teach you the numbers. But since there's only one of you, I suspect he'll leave it to me."

Gina followed Sophie onto the practice floor and began to limber up. "I wondered about that. Where's the rest of the chorus?"

"They're all in Bolzano, or Macau, or Las Vegas, depending on which show they're in," Sophie said, sliding into the splits. "This place is just for new recruits and people developing new routines. You'll be here for two or three weeks, then you'll join a show. I'm off to Bolzano at the end of next week."

Gina's heart sank again. No sooner had she found an ally than she was going to lose her.

"Chin up, I'm pretty sure you'll end up on the European tour, too. Have a word with your mate Fabrizio." Sophie grinned. "Or get your auntie to sort him out."

Gina laughed. Knowing Aunt Teresa, she could rely on her to "sort him out." Perhaps things would work out after all.

Chapter Fourteen

Near Toulouse, Southern France

Monika turned the van into the vineyard's pebbled driveway. Alex couldn't see much from his seat in the back of the van, but he knew the view so well, he could picture it clearly. Immediately ahead, three white-painted houses sat at angles to each other on a gentle rise, partly obscured by trees and manicured hedges. Behind the elegant homes, dark green conifer forests rolled up a slope into the distance.

Oscar was waiting as they drew to a halt on the driveway in front of the main house. Based on talent alone, he should have been a *premier danseur*, but for the fact that he barely reached Alex's shoulder. What he lacked in stature, he'd made up for in vitality. At forty that restless energy still vibrated from his trim body.

"You've been busy," Alex said as Oscar unloaded the wheelchair and helped him out of the van. "The estate is looking good."

Oscar laughed. "It all looks good from the outside. Some of the insides have a long way to go. We're still living in chaos in the main house."

"Those are *gîtes*?" Monika studied the two houses to their left. "I thought that meant a holiday cottage. Those look more like full-scale homes."

"They are a good size," Oscar said. "We had a

party of ten in that far one last month. I've put you in the closer one because it's level access, and there's a bedroom on the ground floor."

Since Alex's ribs were still too sore for him to comfortably maneuver the wheelchair, he allowed Oscar to push him to the *gîte*. He held his crutches and one carry-on tote in his lap, while Monika strode ahead trundling the two wheeled cases. As they entered the cottage through the French doors, he admired the airy living area with its beamed ceiling and massive stone fireplace. Monika took her suitcase upstairs.

"I'll leave you to it," Oscar said. "There's sandwiches in the kitchen, and fresh coffee. When the candidates arrive for your interviews, they can wait in the main house. We'll send them up as you call for them."

"Thank you, but Oscar," Alex put his hand on the man's arm to stop him, "I appreciate this. You know I'll pay you the full rent, with interest, as soon as I've sold my property."

"Don't worry, Alex, there's no rush. We'd never have got started here without your loan. And forget the interest, you wouldn't take any from us, so we won't take any from you."

Alex opened his mouth to protest, but Oscar cut him off. "No. We mean it."

How he hated owing a friend. If only the island would sell. It was all very well for the leasing agent to say, "Wait till summer to get the best price," but he needed the cash flow now. In the long run, did it really matter if the sale went for two million—or two and a half?

Monika came down the stairs. "All set?"

"There are sandwiches in the kitchen," Alex said. "We'd better eat now. The first candidate is due any minute."

"I don't know why you had to arrange the interviews this afternoon," she grumbled on the way to the kitchen. "Another day wouldn't have hurt, would it? You're still recovering, you need to pace yourself."

"I don't want to waste another day. I have already wasted too many months."

There were four candidates to be interviewed for the position of physical therapist. Oscar had found two locally. Monika found another two via contacts in England. By five-thirty in the afternoon, Alex was bringing the last interview to a close. "Thank you, Madame Martineau," he said. "I'll be in touch."

As she stalked out of the cottage, he almost heaved a sigh, but stopped himself in time, thinking of his ribs. Thank God that was over. As he considered the four people he'd just interviewed, he contemplated the lovely gardens through the wide French doors. The flower beds were almost bare, but the leaves of the trees glowed against the sky, in every shade from yellow to deep red. Moving to the vineyard had been a good decision.

Monika approached up the path and entered through the French doors. "I saw the last one leaving. How did it go?"

"I am not hiring Madame Martineau, that's for sure. I know I want a hard taskmaster, but she's terrifying."

"She's also local, so she'd save you the cost of accommodation. And she's well-qualified." Monika said, making herself comfortable among the chocolate velour cushions of the armchair.

"Cost is not an issue," Alex said, mentally crossing his fingers that the island would sell soon. "I'm going to see this person every day for the next six months, it has to be someone I can work with."

"Well, if not the martinet, who's your pick?"

Alex ran his eyes across the papers on the table. At one time, his choice would have been Coralie, the pretty blonde with the high breasts and gym-toned glutes, but he was facing six months of hard work— best to avoid personal entanglements. That left Peter, the ex-tennis pro, or Suzanne, the former hockey player. Both had impressive qualifications and experience with his type of injury.

"You talked to all three of them while they were waiting," he said. "What do you think?"

"They're all nice people." She played with the hem of her skirt, avoiding his eyes. "I thought Suzanne seemed very easy to get on with."

Was that a blush on Mo's cheeks?

"Is she single?" Alex asked.

"What does that have to do with it?"

Monika's face was bright crimson. *Bullseye.*

"I meant, do you think she's likely to get homesick and run back to the boyfriend?" he said.

"That is a sexist remark!"

He found Suzanne's application on the table and reread it. "Actually, I like her because I think she's more likely to stay for the whole six months. Whereas Peter might be tempted away if he gets a shot at a tennis job, and Coralie…"

"Coralie is local, which is an advantage. But if you ask me, she's hoping to take care of more than just your legs," Monika said tartly. "I think you're right about Suzanne. She wants to move here to be near her parents in Toulouse. That's a strong incentive to stay."

"Yes. I think that settles it." Gratified by Monika's look of delight, he couldn't resist another tease. "Do you mind sharing upstairs, or should I book the other *gite* for her?"

She went pink again. "For goodness' sake, there are two bedrooms upstairs, and you should see the size of the bathroom. Besides, I'll be off back to England soon. Once those ribs have healed, you won't need me anymore."

Alex frowned. Monika had raised the matter of her future role once before, but he had managed to avoid discussing it. "I can't imagine not needing you. You're part of the furniture."

"I could take offense at that," she said with a smile. "but I won't. When I was your PA, that's what I was always striving for: for everything to run so seamlessly, you'd hardly notice I was there."

"Believe me, I noticed. Everything *was* seamless, but I always knew it was thanks to you."

"Thank you. But the thing is, there's nothing for me to organize while you're here, is there? Once your ribs are healed you won't need a caretaker, and you won't need a PA either." Monika rose from the armchair and approached the desk. "Even once you've done your rehab and get back to work, you'll be able to manage your own schedule."

"You have more confidence in me than I do."

"Don't be silly. It's just common sense. Before, you juggled a full-time career in dance with movie and TV commitments, charity events, photo shoots, and goodness knows what else. Now…"

"Now, even if I go back to being a celebrity, I have no dancing career," Alex finished. The words still caused him pain.

"I'm sorry, Alex, I didn't mean to upset you."

He shook his head. "No, I'm fine. I have no idea what I'll do, but one thing is certain: it won't be my old life. It will be far less—" he groped for the right word, "—intense. You may be right, perhaps I will not need help. But I will miss you."

"I'll miss you, too." She reached across the desk and squeezed his hand. "But I'm not going yet. You need a driver if nothing else. That's a good enough excuse for me, for another week or two, if you're okay with that."

Alex didn't bother to hide his grin of relief. "Very much okay."

After she turned and left the cottage, Alex picked up his new mobile phone and checked his emails. Nearly a month, and still nothing from Anthony. Every day of silence made him more anxious that he would never find Gina. He hoped—prayed—that he'd been wrong about where she lived, or that she'd landed a contract in Timbuktu, or decided to emigrate to Canada. Anything other than the possibility he most feared.

He had stopped Nick's allowance, of course. Would his brother have the balls to come and ask for money, after what he'd done? Knowing Nick, he was just self-centered enough to think it was all Alex's fault, that Alex had made him do it, that he didn't deserve to be cut off.

Alex almost hoped Nick would come back. Not yet though. Not until Alex was out of his wheelchair and strong enough to pin him to the wall. Then he'd beat the shit out of him until Nick told him what had happened to Gina.

A new email dropped into his inbox. Confirmation for a visit to his specialist in London. He should be itching to have the fixators removed, but the email gave him a sick feeling in the pit of his stomach. Of course he looked forward to getting rid of the irksome things. But while the frames were still in place, he could hope for the best possible outcome.

Once they were gone, there would be no more doubt about where he stood—or didn't stand. He almost didn't want to know.

****

From the wings, Gina watched in admiration as Sophie hooked one leg around the hoop hanging high above the stage and dropped backwards into an upside-down attitude. Lyra aerials were Sophie's specialty and her expertise showed, outshining Elena and Judith on either side of her. Her promotion to feature spot was well-deserved.

If only Gina deserved her own promotion—but she knew otherwise. She'd been thrilled when Tony had picked her from the chorus to replace Andrea, his injured partner, and she hadn't questioned why he picked her. After all, she was one of the few cast members who could dance *en pointe*, which the act required. She had felt flattered Tony thought she was good enough to master the aerial section in such a short time.

But that was before their first practice session. Tony had rounded on her the minute she came through the door. "Jazmin just told me you can't do aerials," he said. "That you could hardly do a bloody somersault when you arrived. Is that true?"

As he loomed over her, she barely came up to his smoothly waxed chest and was forced to take a step back to see his scowling face. "I—I was out of practice. I've been doing ballet for the last few years. But I've been training really hard every day—"

"Jesus! How did you get this job?" Tony turned and threw his towel on the floor, his biceps bulging. "Have you ever done slings?"

Gina had a feeling that "what are slings?" would not be a wise response. If she could stop panicking for a minute, of course she knew what they were. Slings were long loops of silk, suspended above the stage. As she pictured Tony and Andrea spinning and twirling on them, the anxiety welled again. Why had she ever thought she could learn that in a week?

"No. No, I haven't," she managed. "I did some trapeze work though."

"Years ago, I suppose."

She nodded.

"Shit. Well, I suppose I'll have to do my best. Nobody else is short enough."

So he wasn't going to fire her—but what exactly did he mean? "Short enough?"

"Yeah." Tony splayed both hands on his hips. "Why do you think you got the part? If I start throwing around one of those other great galumphing girls, I'll give myself a hernia. I'm not bloody Hercules. Besides, Andrea's costume will fit you. I'll just have to modify the routine."

Gina blinked hard, determined not to cry.

Since that day, she'd spent hours every day

working on the routine with Tony. Though her arms had strengthened in the four weeks since she joined the circus, they were still a ballet dancer's arms, not an acrobat's. Her shoulders ached and her fingers felt like sausages.

Tony cursed and modified the tricks, again. And again. Too soon, they ran out of time. Andrea's understudy couldn't stay any longer. She was flying back to Hong Kong for her sister's wedding, then joining the Macau show.

Tony kept insisted Gina wasn't ready, but in the end, he had no choice. If he didn't let her perform, the act would be cut from the show.

Now she wondered about the wisdom of that decision, but it was too late. The lights dimmed as the previous act left the stage. Gina sensed Tony towering behind her. He rested one hand on her shoulder. Her cue, ready or not.

The first half of the act was easy, a flowing contemporary ballet, no acrobatics or props involved. Dancing *en pointe* was second nature. Some of the lifts might appear challenging to the audience, but they weren't so very different from the ones she'd become accustomed to doing as a dancer. With Tony's strength and her balance, they were able to pull them off with ease, and she could focus on her character's motivation. She had been hazy about that at first, and Tony had been no help. That was the difference between them, she supposed. For an acrobat, the priority was the precision of the moves. For a dancer, interpreting the music came first.

The choreography called for her to cling to Tony one moment, yet in the next bar, try to escape his grasp, over and over again. Gina made sense of it by deciding she wanted him desperately, but in her heart, she knew he was a heartless cad—which nicely explained his rather wooden expression. The haunting music helped her sink into character and feel her heartbreak. At the end of the first section, she pushed him away and curled into a ball on the floor, center stage.

She didn't look up, but she knew the orange silk slings had descended from the fly loft and Tony climbed into them, making them swing and twirl as he executed his tricks. She counted the bars, waiting for the moment when he was flying above her Superman-style, supported by the slings at his neck and thigh. She rolled to one side and stood up. In one movement, he released his feet, flipped around so one sling was under his armpits, and scooped her up into his arms.

None of their movements was explicitly sexual, but somehow, as their bodies flowed over and around each other, and the music rose in an ecstatic crescendo, they managed to convey the sense that she had surrendered herself to him.

Although they were circling well above the stage, Gina didn't feel afraid. Tony had modified the routine so she could use her legs and feet instead of her arms to support herself. Most of the time, he kept her in close contact anyway and he was so strong, she had no fear he would drop her. Her fears were all for what the audience would think of her novice-level tricks, which Tony so disdained.

She felt relieved when the slings descended. Tony slowed the spin, lowered her until her feet touched the ground, and released her. The slings rose again, this time even higher, carrying her lover up into the sky.

Gina blew him a last, desperate kiss and reached out to him, but he did not respond—and then he was gone. The lights faded to black as she collapsed in despair to the floor. Applause.

She reached the wings to find Sophie waiting for her. "You were aces!"

"I got through it, but only because Tony cut out most of the tricks," Gina said as they headed to the dressing room together.

"Pshaw! The audience didn't know that. Did you hear the applause? You could've heard a pin drop when you were dancing. They were so caught up in the story, they didn't care about tricks. You did good."

Before she could respond, Tony appeared beside them. He wasn't smiling. Biting her lip, Gina waited for his verdict. "Not bad, but it's still beginner's stuff," he said. "We've got to improve on that if we want to hold the spot."

"Surely they wouldn't cut the act?" Gina asked. "I'm only covering for a week or two."

Tony gave a short laugh. "Didn't you hear the news? Andrea's knee's worse than she thought. She needs an operation. She's going to be out for weeks. You're all I've got."

Gina's mind whirled. She couldn't decide whether to feel sorry for Andrea, elated at keeping her place in the act, or daunted at the thought of mastering all Andrea's tricks.

Tony slapped her on the back. "See you tomorrow morning, eleven o'clock, as usual."

Sophie grinned. "It's your big break, Gina. You're on your way!"

On her way.

Maybe, but where to? Circus stardom or a busted knee, like Andrea? Could she really learn to control those damn slings? She turned to her friend. "Come on, Sophie. I need a stiff drink"

Chapter Fifteen

Lying on an examination table at the private hospital, Alex braced himself for an ordeal.

The bizarre feeling as the bolts in his leg were unscrewed, then removed, was both worse, and better, than he'd expected—a gruesome sensation deep in his bones that he couldn't describe.

His right leg looked naked and vulnerable without its metal framework. Blood, deep burgundy and viscous, oozed from the holes left by the bolts. The male nurse, gloved and safety-spectacled, cheerfully mopped at the syrupy fluid with gauze sponges.

"You want to try it?" Mr. Mansfield asked, one grey eyebrow rising above his round wire spectacles.

Alex stared at the surgeon "You mean, walk on it?"

Mansfield held out his crutches. "Yes."

Did the man actually expect this to work, or was it a test to assess how bad things were? Leaning on the crutches, Alex slid off the bed and placed both feet on the floor. With crutches, he wouldn't fall flat on his face, but he still hesitated to put all his weight on his right leg.

He took a step—and laughed with delight. It worked! His foot worked! The leg felt weak, and he was grateful for the support of the crutches, but he could take a normal step forward. And another. And another. Heel, toe, heel, toe. Normal. Easy.

Hope surged. They'd said he might not ever walk again. Here he was, able to bear weight before he'd even started therapy. If he could walk so soon, maybe they were wrong about the dancing, too.

He swung around and returned to the bed, grinning.

"You've healed well," surgeon Mansfield said. "You should make an appointment to come back in a fortnight to remove the other fixator."

With freedom so close, Alex couldn't bear to wait any longer. "What? Can't you do it now?"

The surgeon hesitated.

Alex thought of an argument. "At the moment I'm living in France with friends. As it's remote, out in the country, it's not easy for me to keep flying back and forth to London like this."

"Normally," Maxwell explained, "I'd prefer a patient to get used to bearing weight on that leg first. Removal of the fixator effects your balance, and I'm sure you noticed how weak the leg is. With both fixators gone, you'll find it hard to stand unaided and more physically taxing to get around. You may have to use your wheelchair more often."

Alex had to know if his other leg had healed, and how well. "I don't care. I'd like it gone."

Mansfield capitulated. Lying on the bed again, Alex experienced the same strange sensation when the bolts were unscrewed, then removed.

He was free.

He could stand, though most of his weight was taken by his arms in the crutches. One step with the right leg. Fine. Now for the left. He smiled, ready for a whoop of joy.

But something was wrong.

As he lifted his left leg, the toes did not follow. His foot hung uselessly from the ankle. To take a step forward, he had to either drag his toes along the ground or bend at the knee, raising the leg high, as if he was about to climb a stair.

He tried a few more steps. Step—drag—step—drag.

The discovery crushed him; the same sickening horror he'd felt the day, six months before, when the surgeon delivered the bad news. He recalled sitting up in the hospital bed, head filled with plans for his recovery. Then the surgeon spoke.

And Alex's world tumbled around him.

For a few minutes, he had dared hope he could rebuild that whole world again, based on nothing more than being able to walk on one foot. Knowing how foolish that was did nothing to lessen the impact of the disappointment. If he'd been alone, he would have collapsed on the floor and wept.

After several moments, Mansfield spoke. "You have a condition called drop foot. Don't worry, we'll get you fitted with an orthotic brace before you leave today. It will slip into your shoe, holding the foot in place so you can walk more-or-less normally. If you'd like to sit down, we'll get those wounds dressed."

Alex told himself he had nothing to complain about. The outcome was better than he'd feared when he entered the hospital that morning. It was churlish of him to feel cheated now because one foot didn't work as it should.

As the nurse attended to the holes left by the bolts, Mansfield continued delivering his prognosis. "Your left foot may well improve with time, so I suggest we do nothing for now. In a year's time, if there's insufficient improvement, we can try a tendon transfer. That involves cutting the tendon which runs to the bottom of your foot here—" he ran a finger along Alex's sole, "—and attaching it to the one that runs across the top of the foot."

"What are the chances of success?"

"Very good, in fact. Before you get too excited, the result won't be a "normal" foot as you understand it. The operation will remove the need for an external support, but the mechanics of your foot will be completely changed."

Alex sighed. He had to keep reminding himself. *This is better than I expected. This is better than I expected.* "When do I see you again?"

"That's up to you. You could consider having a procedure to tidy up the scars and skin grafts on your calves. It's a minor operation, recovery takes about two weeks. Other than that, I don't need to see you again unless you decide on the tendon transfer." Mansfield patted him on the shoulder. "Just book in with my secretary if you want the procedure. Wait till those bolt holes have healed properly, though. Good luck with your recovery."

"Thank you."

Alex watched Mansfield leave the room, unsure whether to feel relief that he wasn't facing more operations or disappointed the surgeon could do no more for him.

He still had a long road ahead.

****

"What a perfect day!"

Gina threw up her arms and twirled along the wide

dirt path, the carrier bag in each hand angling outwards. She could see her breath on the crisp air, but the sun shone through the bare tree branches—and she was free from Tony's relentless supervision.

Though he still complained, he didn't browbeat her any longer. Not since the review in the *Corriere della Serra*. The critic had found the "little ballerina's" performance "touching and lyrical" and "a highlight of the show." No mention of her partner.

To be fair, she would never have received such a positive review without Tony. Thanks to his drive, she had recovered all her old skills and learned a few new ones, far quicker than she would ever have thought possible.

She'd be the first to admit she still had more to learn, but Tony couldn't get away with treating her like a "better-than-nothing" partner any more. She'd earned her place as his equal. And a day off. Life was good.

Sophie trudged along the path, laden with more bags than Gina. "It's freezing. And this park isn't as green as I expected."

Gina looked around at the threadbare lawns of the *Giardini Publici*. "It is a bit dusty, isn't it? Too many paths and not enough grass. It's still nice to have a park in the middle of the city. Oh look, there's the café."

Just ahead stood a square, flat-roofed building, surrounded by bright red umbrellas that shaded a collection of outdoor tables and chairs. "I'm not eating outside in this weather," Sophie said. "I still don't see why we couldn't have gone to Macca's."

"Sophie, you cannot be in Milan, the fashion capital of Italy, and eat hamburgers."

"Don't see why not. After buying this lot, it's all I

can afford." In spite of her objections, Sophie trailed after Gina as she walked around the side of the building, looking for the entrance. "Do you really want to do more shopping this afternoon?"

"We've only done the *Corso Buenos Aires* so far. We haven't seen any of the real—" Gina stopped dead at the corner of the building.

A man sat at an outdoor table, facing away from her. Broad-shouldered, biceps spoiling the line of his sleek Italian overcoat, crew cut blond hair... She backed away, turned and bustled Sophie along the wall, making her drop two of her shopping bags.

"What the—?"

"Shhhh!" Gina could hardly get the words out. "There's a man. A man. At the table. He's—"

"Wait." Sophie picked up her bags, surveyed the area, then took Gina's arm and pulled her into an alcove half-full of rubbish bins. "Now calm down and tell me properly."

Gina didn't want to waste time explaining. Every instinct told her to run, but the park was too open. She would be exposed the moment she left the shelter of the café. She closed her eyes, trying to do deep breathing exercises, calmed by Sophie's hand stroking her arm.

"There's this guy I dated. When I was in Greece. He's a psycho. I think he's here."

Sophie instantly drew her further into the alcove. "Is it that guy walking this way now?"

Gina shrank back, then peered around the edge of the wall in the direction of Sophie's pointing finger. The man in the Italian overcoat was indeed walking towards them, but he was clean-shaven and his face was nothing at all like Nick's.

Weak with relief, Gina slumped against the rubbish bins. "I'm sorry, Sophie, I'm jumping at shadows."

"I think what you need is some food and maybe a glass of wine," Sophie said, taking her arm to lead her back to the café. "Then you can tell me the whole story."

Gina was glad of the way Sophie dithered over her sandwich. She didn't want to have to tell "the whole story," if only because Alex had asked her not to tell people about his situation.

By the time they were settled at a table by the window, she had worked out how much to say. "It's embarrassing, really. I dated this guy in Greece. After I went to stay at his place, and I met his brother Alex."

"Say no more, it's all over your face. Alex was *gorgeous*, right?"

Gina bit into her *panino* and chewed, blinking hard. She didn't want to talk about how gorgeous, it upset her too much. She coped, most of the time, by refusing to think about him at all. But she couldn't control her dreams…

"So did you and this Alex…?"

"No, no." Gina swallowed the mouthful of food. "He just made me realize Nick wasn't the right man. Only when I tried to leave, I discovered Nick was this insanely jealous psycho. I had to leave everything behind and make a run for it."

Sophie's eyes widened and her eyebrows rose. "I can see why you don't want to meet the guy. D'you think he's still after you?"

"I don't think so. We didn't even know each other that long—it's not like we were engaged or married. But he's probably still mad that I stole his boat."

Sophie paused with a slice of onion halfway to her mouth. "You *stole* his boat?"

"That's how I got away. Gorgeous cruiser, it was. Handled beautifully." Gina sighed. "It wasn't even his boat, actually, it was Alex's, but—I made a fool of him. Nick's the kind of guy who would hold a grudge about something like that."

"Does he know where you are?"

"I doubt it. Honestly, I'm being ridiculous. He's wanted by the Greek police, so he's got bigger problems on his mind."

"He's *wanted*? Holy crap, how did you get mixed up with him?"

Gina shook her head. "You'd be surprised. He could be really charming. A bit like Tony—a sweetie in public but a real a-hole in private."

Sophie laughed. Gina lifted her face to the wintry sunlight pouring through the window. If she was totally honest with herself, this wasn't the first time she'd mistaken some stranger for Nick, even though she knew, logically, that he couldn't be hunting her. She had to get over it. There was so much to be thankful for.

She had made a great friend in Sophie and she was beginning to feel like part of the tribe. So what if Tony was a pain in the butt? Management liked the act and had signed them for the rest of the season, a better start to her circus career than she had ever imagined. Her only sorrow was Alex, but she didn't dare to have any contact with him, in case Nick was watching him. Besides, what would be the point? He belonged to Monika.

And Gina had to move on. Somehow.

Chapter Sixteen

March 2003

As Oscar rolled back the door of the bottling shed, Alex wiped the sweat from his face with a towel.

When he had first arrived at the winery, he had been surprised to see Oscar still looking as fit as he had in his dancing days. After living a relaxed life in the country, most dancers would have lost some tone. In the last six months, Alex had discovered the reason for his friend's still impressive physique. Harvesting and winemaking were both demanding and physical.

As soon as he felt he was strong enough after all the fixators were removed, Alex did as much as he could to help around the property, believing the exertion would be good for his rehab. But he had enjoyed it far more than he would have thought possible. Being part of transforming fat green grapes into delicate, fragrant wines was fascinating. He would miss it when it was time to move on.

The spring sun shone brightly, though there was no heat in it. Alex took his time walking back to his *gîte*, letting the fresh breeze cool his over-heated skin.

He had another reason to walk slowly; Ludevine Dubois would be waiting.

He had no idea whether she'd somehow heard of his presence at the vineyard, or her visit had been purely coincidental. Whatever the reason, her eagerness to resume their past relationship offered him welcome relief after almost a year of celibacy—but after three weeks, he was looking forward to her departure.

He pushed open the front door. Ludevine lay on the couch in the lounge room, nude, her long blonde hair tumbling over the cushions. "I thought you were flying back to Paris today," he said.

She swung her long legs off the couch and sauntered over to him, hips swaying. "My flight isn't until six. Why don't we take a shower?"

****

In his bedroom a few hours later, he opened his eyes to see her standing by the bed, wriggling into a pair of leggings. He propped himself up on one elbow. She dropped a shapeless tunic over her head, spoiling his view.

He rolled over and clipped on his new foot brace. He'd had it less than a week and was delighted with it. Little more than an L-shaped piece of carbon fiber with a cuff to secure it to his shin, it didn't embarrass him even when he was naked. Once dressed the leg of his trousers hid it and the plate that extended inside his shoe. He could even flex his ankle slightly.

He grabbed his cane and followed her into the lounge. She turned and smiled, running her fingers down his nude body. "It has been fun."

"I can visit you in Paris."

Her mouth made a *moue*. "You do not mean that, Alex, so do not pretend otherwise. It is clear, your heart is not with me. It is with the woman who owns the *pointe* shoes."

Pointe shoes?

Before he could react, Ludevine had slung her cardigan over her shoulder and glided through the front door.

How dare she look through his belongings? He stormed back to the bedroom and flung open the closet door, sending it crashing into the wall. The shoes were where he'd left them, in a mesh bag on the shelf.

He sat on the edge of the bed, waiting for his breathing to settle.

Clara had found the pair of Gina's toe shoes in the studio when they'd cleared out the villas in preparation for the sale. When he thought of Gina, that was where he always imagined her; in the studio, standing in the center after a routine, her beautiful eyes wide as she awaited his verdict—or sitting on the floor after class, legs akimbo, with that smile lighting her face.

After Anthony drew a blank trying to find her through his contacts in London, Alex hired a private investigator to track her down. Though they'd had no success, officially they were still on the case—only because Alex refused to terminate the contract. They had told him, more than once, that the search was futile.

Damn Ludevine for reminding him about Gina when he was doing his best to forget her.

Outside, a car horn tooted. Anthony must have arrived early. Abandoning his plans for a shower, Alex pulled on pants and a t-shirt, and hurried to the front of the main house.

A silver Peugeot stood in the driveway, Oscar and Anthony chatting beside it. Anthony's face broke into a grin as he saw Alex approach. "Good gracious, my dear, you're improving every time I visit."

"Never as quickly as I would like." Alex stepped

back as Anthony leaned in for his usual theatrical hug-and-air-kiss. "I'm filthy."

Anthony raised a wicked eyebrow. "Dear boy, there is absolutely *no* need to apologize for appearing before me looking hot, sweaty and in a t-shirt which is, if I may say so, one size too small for that chest. As for those biceps—you are doing my blood pressure no good at all." He rolled his eyes as he fanned himself with his hand.

Alex grinned, accustomed to Anthony's teasing.

Oscar coughed. "If you'd like to have your meeting on the veranda, you're welcome. It's such a beautiful afternoon."

"Perfect," said Anthony, and gestured for Oscar and Alex to lead the way.

Conscious of Anthony's eyes on him, Alex tried to walk as smoothly as possible. He negotiated the three steps up to the veranda without mishap. They took a seat at the long table looking out over the vines, while Oscar left to organize refreshments.

"Seriously, you're doing so well, Alex," Anthony said. "If your surgeon could see you now."

"He will. No amount of rehab is going to fix my left foot. If I'm going to get rid of this brace, I'll need more surgery."

"And when will that happen?" Anthony asked.

Oscar's wife arrived with a tray bearing a teapot, cups and a plate of delicacies on the table. Alex paused while she and Anthony shared cheek kisses and pleasantries. When she'd gone, he said, "I haven't decided about the surgery yet."

"I will need to know, Alex, so I can allow for it in my forward planning,"

"It won't be for another six months at least."

Anthony placed his briefcase on the table and extracted a sheaf of papers. "In that case, consider this."

Alex put down his glass and accepted the file. He read the first line and gasped. "*Spartacus* for the National? Is this an early April Fool's joke? I can't believe it."

"Believe it, my dear. They want you to stage it, and I think you'll be happy with the fee."

"I'm sure I will," Alex said. The money would be useful. Plus, after all that happened in the past couple years, the chance to stage his favorite ballet was reward in itself. He could hardly wait "When do I start?"

"End of April."

"End of April?" He felt the smile fade from his face. No one ever decided to mount a ballet at such short notice. "Be honest. Who was first choice?"

"Ratmansky. He had to pull out for health reasons, apparently, though the goss says something *entirely* different and *far* more fascinating. I'll tell you later." Anthony leaned forward. "Look, my dear, I know it's utterly galling to realize you're second banana, but you simply cannot afford to be precious about this—"

"No, no, that's not the issue." Alex paused. "Well, perhaps it is. But more important, I haven't finished rehab. I shouldn't cut it short."

"You'll have artistic freedom," Anthony said. "They're not expecting you to produce a carbon copy. They have choreologists who can do that, after all."

Before Alex could reply, Anthony looked beyond his shoulder. "Isn't that Ludevine Dubois?"

Alex didn't turn to look. "Yes. Oscar and Jeanne had a crowd of friends here a couple of weeks ago. She was one of them."

"Ooooh. Awkward."

"Not at all. Ludevine and I are…on good terms." Alex looked Anthony in the eye with as impassive a face as he could muster.

Anthony's eyebrows bobbed. "I seem to recall things got a tad nasty when you split up last time, but time heals, I suppose. She might still hold a grudge, though. Aren't you worried she'll go running to the press?"

"It hardly matters now. The wheelchair is gone, I'm walking…and if I take this London contract, I'm going to have to face the press soon anyway. A few weeks won't make much difference."

"In that case," Anthony said, pulling another piece of paper from his briefcase, "you might consider the *Paris Match* shoot after all?"

Alex laughed. "I walked into that one. Fine, I'll do it. The publicity for the vineyard will be good for Oscar and Jeanne, too."

"And the National…?"

"Where do I sign?"

Chapter Seventeen

Gina paused on the last landing of the six-story walkup. She shouldn't complain—they'd been lucky to find theatrical digs in London which offered a private bathroom *and* a tiny kitchen, so the climb was worthwhile. But after a full day of rehearsals, her legs barely carried her up the three flights to the attic room.

"It's only me!" she caroled as she dropped her gear bag and hurled herself onto the saggy brown corduroy couch.

Sophie's head, hair covered in cream, popped out of the bathroom. "Did you remember my mag?"

"Naturally."

Sophie stepped out of the bathroom in a too short towel and put her timer down on the coffee table. "Gotta leave this for fifteen minutes. Cuppa?"

"Yes, please. What color are you going this time?"

"It's just a treatment. My hair's like straw." Sophie unplugged the microwave so she could put the kettle on to boil.

Gina pulled her sweatshirt off and lounged back in her leotard and dance pants, leafing through the magazine she had bought for Sophie. She sat up. "Omigosh! Alex is coming to London!"

"Ace!" Sophie came to look over Gina's head to look at the magazine. After a moment, she gasped, "Wait, *that's* your Alex?"

Gina had forgotten she hadn't told her the whole of Alex's identity. "Yes."

Sophie slapped her shoulder. "Beeyatch! How could you not tell me? *The* Alex Korolev? Wow!"

"He didn't want anyone to know he was in Greece. I promised not to say."

"I *might* forgive you. You've got to promise to introduce me."

"That's if I get to see him. It says here he's staging a production of *Spartacus* for the National. He'll be busy."

One of the photos was the stock black-and-white image of him as Spartacus, the same poster she'd had on her wall. The camera had caught him, dagger in hand, in an aggressive stance. The gladiator's brief tunic displayed his lean, muscular physique—so different from when she had last seen him.

"I've never seen *Spartacus*," said Sophie.

"Productions are pretty rare because you need a big cast of strong, hunky men. How many ballet companies have that? The Australian Ballet does it really well."

"Strong, hunky men, eh? In tiny leather shorts?" Sophie moved back to the kitchen bench to pour the tea. "Hmm, sounds like my kinda ballet."

Gina traced her finger over the proud face, the defiant stare, the determined mouth. She could still feel that mouth kissing her, taste the alcohol on his lips, feel the thrill that melted her body. "It's very good news. It must mean he's feeling better."

Sophie said something.

"What?"

"Wake up, dream-weaver." Sophie put the two fat-bellied pottery mugs and a plate of cookies on the coffee table. "Where were you?"

"Thinking."

Sophie's dainty features looked impish as she curled herself onto the sofa. "About Alex?"

"No – well, yes, but there's no point."

"Why not? He's going to be in London."

"Yes, but maybe I didn't mention. He's got a girlfriend. She was on the island with us."

"Oh. Well, you never know. They might've broken up by now."

Gina sipped her tea and shook her head. "But that would be worse. He owes Monika. She's been devoted to him for years."

"Say what? Isn't Alex Korolev the one who used to be in the magazines with a new woman every five minutes?"

"He wasn't as bad as that." Gina said, though her indignation was half-hearted. Alex had indeed been bad enough when it came to women. "Anyway, that's what I can't quite work out. If she's been his girlfriend the whole time, she's tolerated an awful lot of screwing around, and it's not as if she could've avoided knowing about it."

Sophie finished her cookie. "If she's so spineless she'd let him shag everything in sight, she deserves everything she gets."

"Soph, don't be mean. I liked Monika. Hey, that's mine!" Gina grabbed the other cookie before Sophie could reach it. "Maybe she was in love with him for years, but he never gave her a second look until he needed a woman who could look after him. And if that's the case, it would be horrible if he dumped her because he doesn't need her now, wouldn't it?"

"I see what you mean. Honestly, even if he is gorgeous, it sounds like he's as much trouble as that brother of his. You're better off without the both of them."

Gina shivered at the mention of the phrase *that brother of his*. She'd been trying not to think about Nick.

Though logic said he would be too busy hiding from the police to chase her, she couldn't forget their last conversation, where she'd reminded him she lived in London. One of the first things she did, after arriving at Aunt Teresa's, was to contact all her London friends and acquaintances. She had told them a man might come asking about her and warned them to deny all knowledge of her existence.

By the time Fabrizio announced the circus's next tour would include London, she had convinced herself that after six months enough time had passed. But now she was back, on a public stage, with her face on the billboards. Perhaps she shouldn't have come to the UK.

But if she had declined the gig, she'd lose the whole tour. They'd send her to Asia or the States and maybe—since she'd let them down—send her back to the chorus. It had taken hard work to win her spot and she didn't want to lose it. It was ridiculous to think Nick would still be looking for her after all this time.

She closed the magazine with a shudder of doubt.

****

Though being back in London was bittersweet, Alex rapidly became too tired to think about it. Lucky that Monika wasn't there to fuss over how wrong he'd been about "orientation day." He'd been traipsed around the whole of National's headquarters for myriad meetings in offices and rehearsal rooms. The main studio, in the far reaches of the building, was the last stop. He followed the secretary down an endless corridor, conscious that his progress was flagging, leaning heavily on his ebony cane.

The secretary opened the door to the studio and stood back to let him enter. The room was impressive, a stage-sized space with a towering ceiling and a massive mirror along one wall. But his eyes were fixed on the woman by the piano. Thin as a reed in black dance pants and sweater, her flaxen head with its sleek chignon balanced gracefully on a long, elegant neck.

"Mr. Korolev, I think you know our chief *repetiteur*, Karen Renthe," said the secretary.

Karen swept forward, threw her arms around him and planted a hard, open-mouthed kiss square on his lips. "Oh yes, Alex and I know each other very well, don't we, darling?"

She continued to hold him while the secretary mumbled a farewell and shot out of the door. The assembled dancers looked on with interest.

"You're looking tired," Karen said. "Sit down and take a break. I finish in ten minutes. After that, you'll come and have dinner at my place."

Her body, muscle on bone and small hard breasts, pressed against him. She had aged but was still as stunning as ever. Her veiled invitation should have resulted in a quickening in his groin and an unqualified "yes." She'd been his first lover, and his best.

To his surprise, today was different. It wasn't hard to work out the reason, although it was utterly irrational. After all, he was single. Even the strictest prude couldn't accuse him of infidelity if he slept with

Karen. Yet Gina was so much on his mind now, it would feel like a betrayal if he did. He pushed her away, gently. "I'm afraid I've had it for today."

"Come along, don't be a bore. We'll go to my place—you can have a snooze on my couch." Her eyebrows made a completely different suggestion.

Karen hadn't changed a bit. Her hand traced the line of his jaw, then she was off to galvanize the dancers into action for their final *enchainement.*

Thankfully, her apartment was not far away. As soon as they entered, she threw off her coat, flung herself flat on a rose velvet couch and held out her arms in invitation.

"I'm sorry, Karen. It's been a long day already."

She came upright, rueful smile on her face, and pulled her legs beneath her. "Oh all right, sit down—I promise I won't attack you. You don't fool me, you know. You're a serial monogamist. All the women in the world but only one at a time. I never could persuade you to be unfaithful to your current squeeze. So who's the lucky lady?"

He sat down beside her, relieved to get off his feet at last. "No one."

"The great Alex Korolev without a girlfriend?" She squinted at him. "Don't tell me you're pining for someone. Not you."

"I pined over you."

She looked pleased. "Did you really?"

"You knew! How often did I call you?"

"Oh, yes! I thought that was just your hormones. You had quite a sex drive, I seem to remember. . . besides, I thought you knew it was just fun. Good heavens, how old were you? Nineteen? And me over—

nearly thirty already. You did my career a great deal of good, you know, but you were in Copenhagen for just one season." Small indentations formed above her eyebrows but didn't reach the center. "Were you really hoping it would last?"

"Yes, I was."

She gave his cheek an affectionate stroke. "But no more, hmmm? Broken hearts do heal, you see. So will this one."

Perhaps. It had taken a string of liaisons to heal his scars after Karen dumped him. Though, if he was honest, his bruised ego had needed healing as much as his heart. His feelings for Gina were different. Ludevine Dubois had proved that.

"Who is she?" Karen said.

He leaned back. "A girl I knew in Greece."

"And you can't forget her, hmm?" She smiled as he nodded his head. "You know, it's easy to romanticize about someone when there's no risk of ever meeting them again."

He didn't want to explain the whole sorry mess to Karen. "It's not that. She disappeared. I'm not even sure if she's still alive."

Thankfully, she didn't press him. "Do you have the energy to help me fix dinner?"

There was hardly room for them both in the steel-and-granite kitchen. He felt her watching him as he moved around, helping her prepare the meal and set the table.

"You remind me of the story of the Little Mermaid," said Karen. "She was offered the gift of legs, but the catch was that every step would cause her pain."

Too observant, as always. "At least I still have legs," he said quietly. "It was a close call. It's not so bad, except when I'm tired."

Karen shooed him to the table. "Then for goodness' sake, sit down and let me pamper you."

The meal was a vegetarian salad, and as usual, Karen hardly ate any. No wonder she was still so spectacularly thin. Less eating meant more chance to talk, of course. "Tell me about this girl."

"I'd rather not."

"You must've been very much in love."

"We weren't even together. That's what makes it worse. I could have helped her, and I let her down. Maybe she'd still be here today if – "

She put her hand on his. "If I know you, you did everything you could."

He shook his head. It was all he could manage.

"Is that what this job is about? Keeping busy? Keeping your mind off things? If that's the case, then we can help each other. I'm down to give some open classes at Pineapple in the run-up to the auditions and I just don't know where I'm going to find the time. It's only three classes. It'll give you something to do this week before you get started with *Spartacus*. How about it, darling?" she asked with a sly look. "If it won't tire you too much."

He smiled at her. "If I can't manage to teach a couple of classes, then there's no way I'm going to survive staging a ballet, is there? I'd be glad to do it."

"Good! I'll let the office know. Give me your phone."

Puzzled, he handed it over. She punched her number into the directory. "If you ever decide I can help you get over her, just call."

****

The buzz about Alex's master classes raced over London's dance community. With the chance to see him again too strong to resist, Gina managed to get a place in the second class.

The studio was packed, and there was no more room at the barre. She settled for a space on the floor, sat down and started her warm-up. There was a steady chatter and a certain amount of one-upmanship as the dancers eyed each other's moves and tried to outdo them. She spread her legs smugly into a sideways split and flattened herself to the floor—when it came to flexibility, she could beat the lot of them.

The door opened and a hush descended. She sat up, holding her breath.

Alex entered. He walked slowly towards the piano, followed by a young girl, presumably an assistant. Everyone recognized him, of course. A murmur hummed around the room—speculation about Karen Renthe's absence and, of course, his injury. The tabloids were never able to uncover the details, and there was very little sign of what she knew he'd been through.

He wore slim black jeans, so the fixators must be gone. He used a cane and he limped ever so slightly on a stiff left leg. The muscled chest and arms, revealed by a close-fitting black t-shirt, was very different from the Alex she had seen in his bedroom all those months ago. Compensating for the loss of strength in his legs, she supposed. He looked fit and well. And gorgeous.

"Good morning. I'm Alex Korolev, I'll be taking this class today instead of Karen Renthe. Will everyone take their positions please?" He turned to speak to the pianist.

The stretching dancers removed their legs from the barre to make space for the others. Gina found a good spot, but then a tall, broad-shouldered male dancer took the place in front of her, obscuring her view of him.

The barre work began. She could hear Alex's voice—and wished she could see his face.

Then she did. The dancer in front of her stayed in his forward bend, while Gina straightened. Alex's eyes looked directly at her across the length of the room. He staggered back a step and grabbed the piano for support. The assistant touched him on the shoulder, looking anxious, and asked him a question. At his nod, she went back to the music deck.

He turned briefly to the pianist, then back to face the class. "Let's move to the diagonal now, please."

His *enchaînements* were complicated and the pace challenged her because her concentration wasn't what it should have been. All she could think of was being able to talk to him at the end of the class. It was so good to see him again. She could hardly wait to—to what?

She faltered in the middle of her *chaîné* turns and the girl behind almost cannoned into her. She straightened up and finished the traverse, then stood in the far corner of the studio pretending to fiddle with her shoe ribbon while she thought it over. She'd come to class because she was curious to know how well he had recovered, nothing more. She had not come with any intention of getting involved with a two-timing womanizer.

"Next combination—waltz please, Amy."

He named the steps, merely sketching them with

his hands, but the dancers all understood and were ready to throw themselves across the room at his signal. Gina took her place in line with the rest. Normally she would enjoy this part of the class when the static exercises were over and there was freedom to really dance. Today, the time seemed to drag.

Finally, class ended. As the other students applauded, she grabbed her shoes and left the studio at a run before she had a chance to weaken.

Chapter Eighteen

Tonight, the Crush Bar was well-named. Alex was forced to breathe in and lean back in order to let Karen reach the tray of champagne. On her other side, Anthony also picked up a glass, but Alex waved the waiter away.

"Not even one glass to celebrate?" Anthony teased.

Alex shook his head, not trusting his hand to hold a glass steady. He hadn't quite recovered from the unexpected emotions brought on by the curtain calls. Opening night had been a huge success. After the cast took their bows and the principals received their bouquets, it was his turn to walk out on stage.

The audience rose in a standing ovation. He hit his mark center stage, the same place he'd stood so often in the past. He bowed to the stalls, a second to acknowledge the upper levels, then one more to the minor princess seated in the Royal Box.

Within minutes, the stage was littered with long-stemmed roses, thrown by members of the adoring crowd. He bent to pick one up to present it to his ballerina—and was shocked to find she wasn't by his side. For a moment, he had been transported back in time, imagining himself in the leather tunic of *Spartacus* instead of a dinner suit.

But another man wore that costume now. As Alex took two steps to hand the flower to the ballerina, he

174

felt insanely and unreasonably jealous of her partner who was still able to fly and leap across this familiar stage, while he …

Not the end. The start of a new chapter. He had to keep telling himself that.

****

The after-party was too crowded, the room was too stuffy and the babble of voices seeming to grow louder by the minute. He had been tired enough before the show, wrung out from the long hours of rehearsals and the stress of the tight staging schedule. Now he felt exhausted.

"Perhaps you should call it a night," Karen said. "You've been pushing yourself pretty hard these last few weeks."

"Don't you start on me. I get enough nagging emails from Suzanne. I'll—"

A loud clang silenced the whole room, followed by the musical tinkle of breaking glass. A waiter had dropped a tray. The crowd eddied away from the carnage, clearing a path to the other side of the room. One of the taller members of the *corps de ballet*—Adrian something or other?—stood next to a petite brunette

Gina.

She had put her hair up, with ringlets tumbling over her bare shoulders. Her short, plum-colored dress was body-hugging, the low-cut front accentuated with a white crisscross of fabric.

It had been a shock to see her again at the master class. Only professionalism prevented him interrupting the class to cross the floor and throw his arms around her. The ninety minutes had seemed like an eternity, waiting for the moment when he could hold her and weep on her shoulder from relief.

Then she'd left before he could reach her. He had called her name, but she hadn't heard.

Or she had chosen not to. The second interpretation seemed more likely now. Before the crowd closed in, she'd seen him—and her reaction was to grab Adrian and turn for the door.

He reached for a champagne from the waiter's tray. Cheap bubbles in a fancy glass—for which he found a sudden need.

"Was that her?" Karen said. She had always been too perceptive.

His voice was steadier than he expected. "Yes. Looks like her boyfriend's in the cast."

Anthony leaned over. "My, my! I'm sorry, Alex, but I think you're mistaken. I've seen that young man before. He couldn't possibly be interested in her."

"What makes you say that?"

"I'm never wrong."

Alex couldn't resist. "You were wrong about me."

"That was wishful thinking!" his agent said indignantly.

"And this isn't?"

"No. You were nineteen at the time, and a perfectly beautiful young boy, you could hardly blame me for the mistake." Anthony adopted his most martyred look. "I will selflessly sacrifice myself to prove that young man is no threat to you and trust you'll appreciate my devotion to duty."

Alex and Karen were laughing by now.

"Forget it, Anthony," Alex said. "She was at one of the classes when I covered for Karen, and she took off.

She doesn't want anything to do with me."

Anthony grabbed Alex's arm. "Darling, do you think I could care less? This is the best excuse I'm likely to get for you to introduce me to that *scrumptious* young man!"

Alex allowed himself to be dragged in search of the couple. They hadn't moved far. Gina had her back to Alex, gesticulating at Adrian, whose mouth was set in a mulish expression.

As the two men drew closer, Adrian's mouth gaped. He prodded Gina on the shoulder and pointed past her at the approaching men. "See?" he hissed. "I told you we shouldn't leave."

Shaken by the dismay in her eyes, Alex kept his focus on Adrian. "Adrian, Gina, I'd like you to meet Anthony, my agent, He's one of the best in town. You should talk to him. He did a great deal for my career."

"Thank you, appreciate it," said Adrian, forsaking Gina to shake Alex's hand firmly.

There was a subtle softening in Adrian's demeanor as he turned to Anthony, and Alex was forced to admit Anthony's assessment was right. Adrian's eyes looked Anthony up and down as he extended his hand, almost as if he expected it to be kissed.

"Pleased to meet you, Anthony."

Anthony took Adrian's hand with relish, cutting across Alex to get closer to the young dancer, and launching immediately into conversation.

Alex and Gina were alone, and he couldn't think of a single sensible thing to say. She looked as though she wanted to be anywhere else but here. He should probably say something polite and withdraw.

But he didn't want to.

They spoke at once.

"It's been a long—"

"I'm relieved—"

They both stopped, both invited the other to speak, both broke off with an apology.

"I'm relieved to see you're okay," he said. "I was concerned. I didn't know what had happened to you."

She looked stricken. "I didn't think. I was frightened to contact you in case Nick found out and tracked me down. I felt bad because I still owe you for the air tickets you booked for me. Did you get a refund?"

So that was the reason. "Forget the tickets. I owe you more than that."

"You've done a wonderful job on *Spartacus*," she said.

"I simply re-staged another's choreography for an outstanding group of dancers. I can't take much credit."

"Nonsense. Especially those sword fights, they were amazing. I've never seen anything so realistic in a ballet."

"I can't take credit for that. I brought in a fight choreographer that I met on my second movie. All the swordplay was staged by him."

Gina leaned in earnestly, close enough to smell her perfume. "But it was still your idea."

He shrugged, pleased that she'd liked it. But the important thing was to find out what she was doing—to make sure he'd know where to find her the next time. "What are you doing now?"

"*Circo Mirabile*. It's an Italian circus."

"I'm pleased to hear it."

"You were right when you told me not to reject

circus work. I am enjoying it more than I expected. Getting back into acrobatics has been a challenge—I'm even doing *aerials*!—but it's a real buzz to be in that creative atmosphere. And yesterday I was given a solo spot, which is exciting."

"I'm sure you deserve it."

Her face colored. "I'm still not sure I do. My cousin's the owner, you see."

"If he's like other company owners, he puts profits before people. If he didn't believe in you, he would leave you in the chorus."

She sipped at the straw of her tall cocktail. Her lips were like a glossy plum, the light reflecting on her lower lip. "How's Monika?"

"Doing fine, I think. I haven't seen her since—"

As he spoke, Alex's attention was drawn to the curious sight of two black-clad arms stretched up in the air, not far behind Gina. Seemingly detached from a body, the arms were made jerking progress through the crowd, each hand holding aloft two champagne glasses. They moved fast. Too fast.

He reached to pull Gina out of the way, too late. The person cannoned into her and she fell into his arms. Her glass clashed with his chest, sending alcohol, ice and fruit cascading over his tux jacket and shirt. He put his cane arm round her waist to steady her. The sudden contact took his breath away. To be so close, after so long. No sweat or rosin this time, but the same jasmine scent. The same softness.

"I say, I'm most dreadfully sorry." A jowled face above a red Liberty cravat peered nervously up at them. The man was scarcely as tall as Gina.

"It's quite all right, accidents happen," she said,

fending off the handkerchief the man offered. "It's so crowded, isn't it?"

Alex willed him to go away.

Finally, the man walked off. Gina turned her eyes on Alex again and bit her lip. "You're soaked."

He picked a piece of strawberry off his lapel. "So are you."

She looked down. The white collar of her dress was splattered with pink splotches. "I don't think I can do anything with this. I better call it a night. I think I've lost Adrian anyway," she said, standing on tiptoe to scan the room.

He couldn't let her go. "I can't walk around with a pink shirt all evening either. Anyway, I've had a long day. Would you like to share a taxi?"

Her head started to shake "no."

"The company's paying. The taxi can drop me off and then take you home. It's no problem, really." He gestured towards the exit. After a moment's hesitation she stepped forward, following the direction of his arm.

His legs were beginning to betray him after the long day on his feet. Plus, he knew there was a flight of steps outside the restaurant. As he put his left foot on the first step, it slipped, tipping him sideways into her. She caught him with one hand on his chest and the other under his arm. Her face was so close, he could have kissed her. He got his weight back on both feet, but she didn't move away.

Her face was concerned—he must look as shaken as he felt. It wasn't because of the stumble. "Are you all right?" she asked.

He could feel the warmth of her hand through his shirt. "The steps are slippery."

"It's the rain. My shoes are sliding, too." Alex didn't believe it, but it was kind of her to pretend. "Hold onto me, we'll get down together."

He walked the rest of the way with his arm around her for support, his hand resting on the silky skin of her bare shoulder. Near the bottom of the stairs, he caught flashes out of the corner of his eye. Damn.

The first hint of *paparazzi* interest, and they had to snap him falling over.

****

Gina helped Alex into the taxi, then climbed in after him, trying to avoid letting her tight dress hitch up around her thighs. The cab driver had the heater on full and she felt sweat prickling her neck. She reached up to flick her hair away.

They were already moving fast, with little traffic to delay them. The late-night streets had a vacant look, no pedestrians in sight, no lights in the windows. Arabic music wailed from the cabbie's radio, the exotic melody muffled by the glass partition separating the driver from the passenger seats.

Alex propped his cane against the jump seat and leaned back, his arm stretched along the back of the seat between them. She was glad it was a wide, old-fashioned London cab. She wondered if he had dumped Monika, or she had dumped him. She hoped it had been Monika's choice. Either way, that meant Alex was free, but did that really change things?

"I'd really like to see you again."

His voice was gentle and sounded so sincere. She turned to face him. Even in the darkened cab, his blue eyes held a magnetic attraction that drew her towards him. His hand touched her shoulder as he slid closer to her on the bench seat.

"I've missed you," he murmured as he bent his head to kiss her.

The thought of those lips on hers was almost too much to resist. She wanted him so much she could have ripped the trousers off him, right there in the taxi. How her hand came to be on his chest, pushing him away, she wasn't sure, but she was grateful to her common sense for over-ruling her hormones. He tried to reach her, but she was back in control. She stiffened her arm to keep him at bay.

"No, Alex, please don't."

"I thought—"

"I'm not in the market for a casual fling."

"But—"

"Hear me out. I'm a fan, don't you think I know how many women you've made promises to over the years? I don't want my heart broken like all the others."

His mouth hardened. "That isn't fair. I never made any promises. If those women had broken hearts, it wasn't my doing. It's not my fault if some of them built a pleasant interlude into something it wasn't."

"Are you listening to yourself? What were they supposed to do, read your mind?" She couldn't contain her anger. "You made love to them, you bought them presents, you squired them at the best parties—did you actually *say* to them, remember you're just a quick fuck?"

"It wasn't like—" He broke off. His voice was quieter when he spoke again. "I never pretended feelings I didn't have. I've said 'I love you' to one woman in my whole life. I have never uttered those words to anyone else. Ever."

If he thought that would let him off the hook, he was wrong. "Was that Monika?"

He seemed genuinely confused. "Of course not."

"Why 'of course not'?"

"Because she's a friend, and an employee, not a—" Alex brow cleared. "You think she was my girlfriend?"

Friend? Employee? Had she got it all wrong?

"Monika was my personal assistant. After the accident, she took on the job of care giver and I will always be grateful for that. But there was nothing between us, ever."

"But Nick told me she was your girlfriend."

Alex brow cleared. "I suppose he was worried I might steal you away. Maybe he wanted you to think I was spoken for."

"You two seemed like such an old married couple."

Alex pulled his phone from his pocket and held it out to her. "If you don't believe me, call Mo. Suzanne might answer the phone. She's her partner."

Partner? She stared at the phone but didn't take it. Nick had lied about so many things, why not this?

She didn't have to call. She believed Alex.

The question was, how much difference did that make? It was a relief to know he hadn't used Monika, keeping her waiting in the wings while he played the field. But the fact remained that he *had* played the field. He had left broken hearts in his wake and from what he'd just said, it was clear he didn't believe he'd done anything wrong. To cap it all off, it was all over town that he and Karen Renthe had been bonking each other madly ever since he arrived. Could she, realistically, expect him to change after all this time?

Men didn't change. At least, they didn't change

just because women wanted them to. Her father certainly hadn't. "I don't know, Alex. I don't know." She glimpsed the red and blue sign for a train station. She tapped on the partition. "Driver, anywhere on the left is fine."

She practically leaped from the car. She didn't stop to check whether Alex followed. She saw a train at the platform and sprinted for it, jumping on at the last moment as the doors closed. Once she got her breath back, she discovered it was heading in the wrong direction.

Chapter Nineteen

Alex slammed the last glass onto the draining board and cursed as a shard flew off. He leaned on the edge of the sink and told himself to calm down. Gina's assessment had been brutal. He hadn't liked the picture she painted. For half the night, he'd fumed at the injustice of her accusation.

He'd spent the other half reaching the agonizing conclusion that she had a point.

He had never felt guilty about his season-long relationships. Provided both parties understood the rules at the outset, he saw nothing wrong with two adults enjoying each other for a few months, then saying goodbye with a warm hug and no regrets. He had always made it clear, upfront, that he was not interested in commitment.

But he should have known, from his own heartbreaking experience, that wasn't enough. All those years ago in Copenhagen, Karen had made plenty of comments about the fleeting nature of their relationship—but he, deep in infatuation, had dismissed them as jokes. So he, of all people, should have known there would be women who heard him say "no expectations," but secretly dreamed they'd be the one who could change him, the one who could shift his focus from his career to her, the one who would get the ring on her finger. And he was always too wrapped up in his work to notice. Then when the end came, there would be a row, recriminations, and a painful farewell.

It had happened far too often, but somehow he'd never admitted it, telling himself it was his lovers' problem if they chose to ignore his warnings. He'd been honest, it wasn't his fault, yadda yadda.

He had been a selfish prick.

The problem was, how to convince Gina it would be different with her. And what did he mean by different? Why did he want it to be different?

The scrunch of tires made him look up. Anthony's Porsche nosed into the parking spot next to the house. Alex dried his hands and opened the door to let his dapper agent sail in, brandishing a newspaper. "It's official, Alex, you're ba-ack!" he warbled, thrusting the morning's paper at him. It was open at a picture of Alex and Gina on the steps of the restaurant.

The article began, *"Alex Korolev is back in town, as always with a striking beauty on his arm. His brilliant staging of Spartacus has earned rave reviews. There will be a few hearts broken at the National this season, no doubt."*

"It's a lovely pic of the young lady, don't you think?" Anthony said, flitting around the apartment, tidying up as he moved. "How did it go? Is she still here? I waited till after lunch just in case."

"No."

Anthony stopped, open-mouthed for one of the few times in his life. "What happened?"

"Nothing." Alex put down the paper. "Will you stop cleaning up after me?"

"Darling, you know my OCD. I can't bear to see things lying around. Now, do give me the goss."

"There isn't any." He didn't want to discuss it. "What about you, Anthony? I'm not the only one who was chatting up a hot prospect at the party if I recall."

"Let's just say I had more luck than you, darling." Anthony drew his hand across his face with a theatrical flourish. "I will draw a veil. The details are far too x-rated, I'm happy to say."

"I'm pleased to hear it. And thanks for the paper."

"Now, darling, don't complain. It's good publicity." Anthony switched personalities suddenly, from camp socialite to slick, professional agent. The transformation always took Alex by surprise. "One paparazzo does not a campaign make, but it is a start. Keep getting coverage, and it will give me a better chance of reviving your endorsements."

"What did you have in mind?" Alex asked dryly.

"I'm very close with Alterra coffee, you have such a history with them. But you have been out of the headlines for almost a year. We need more coverage to persuade other prospects. See what you can do."

With that, Anthony straightened a pile of magazines on the marble coffee table, waved his farewell, and walked out.

Alex stared at Gina's picture in the paper, remembering her scent and her softness, how close he had been. She wouldn't appreciate being described as his "mystery new squeeze," but if he got Anthony to "leak" her name, the exposure could be good for her career. Best to ask her first, though—which would also give him an excuse to contact her.

He flicked to the entertainment pages and found the ad for *Circo Mirabile* and learned it was showing at the Roundhouse in Chalk Farm. He had a full day with the second cast to get through, but Saturday morning, he would pay a visit to a certain circus.

****

As usual, Gina was awake and out of bed before Sophie, keen to get to the theatre early to work on the finer points of her new act. In spite of the good reviews, she still felt some of her skills were too rusty.

She showered and dressed quietly, then crept around the kitchen to make breakfast. It was only as she carried her coffee cup and plate to the couch that she noticed Friday's newspaper on the coffee table. Sophie must have bought it. Gina knew it existed, having been teased by half the cast all day on Friday, but she hadn't managed to see the full-sized, printed photo. Perched on the edge of the sofa, crumpet in one hand and paper in the other, she scrutinized the image.

At least the photographer had managed to catch her at a flattering angle. He'd also caught the way Alex's head inclined toward hers. It was obvious it had nothing to do with his need for balance. A stranger would have said they were on the brink of a kiss, though she did not like being called a "squeeze."

Throwing down the paper, she gulped the rest of her coffee. No time to brood—she had to get to the theatre. She finished the crumpet, rinsed out her coffee cup and grabbed her dance bag.

Almost at the door, she stopped and looked back at the newspaper thoughtfully, then grabbed it and ripped out the photo. All the time she was pulling out her scrapbook and laying the photo carefully between the pages, she was telling herself it was a bad idea to keep it. She did anyway.

Sophie hadn't stirred.

Gina closed the front door behind her and set off at a brisk pace for the bus stop. The solid gray cloud cover and dark brick apartment blocks were depressing after the bright skies of Italy, but at least the rain had stayed away. She hurried along the quiet streets, 1960's social housing giving way to smarter Georgian terraces, which always made her think of *Upstairs Downstairs.* Behind their wrought-iron railings, stone steps led directly to their basements, where the servants would have toiled in the olden days.

As she passed one of the open gates, a hand closed around her arm. She opened her mouth as she turned her head, but the scream died in her throat as she stared into a pair of lagoon blue eyes.

"Alex…?"

He wrenched her through the gate and down the first few stone steps. Unable to find her feet, she cannoned into his chest, knocking the breath out of her. He rocked back on his feet but did not fall. Before she could recover, he had flipped her round, his free arm snaking round her neck. She reached up, clawing at his arm with both hands, trying to break the stranglehold, then nothing…

Chapter Twenty

Alex wanted to rush straight to the Roundhouse on Saturday morning, but he had obligations to the National to fix last minute glitches in preparing for the Saturday matinee. It wasn't until two o'clock that he managed to escape. He stepped through the front door of the theatre and turned immediately to his left, intent on getting to the Roundhouse, not wasting a glance at his surroundings.

As he turned a corner, an expanse of dense black fur blocked his way. He looked up, half-expecting a gorilla's face to stare down at him—but no, it was a man, in a shawl-collared fur coat. Alex smiled and moved to sidestep him politely—but another over-coated ape appeared at the man's shoulder.

The first man stepped back, opened the passenger door of a black car parked at the curb, and motioned him to enter. "Please, *Alexandr Mikhailovich*."

Alex didn't move. Only a Russian would use his first name and middle name like that. Come to think of it, only a Russian would wear a coat like that.

He studied the two men, assessing the massive shoulders and powerful arms straining the material of their coats. He might have tried to rush one, but he couldn't take on both. Running away would only delay the inevitable: if they were what he suspected, they'd be back, and probably less polite next time. He climbed into the back seat and was enveloped in the aroma of new leather and expensive cigar.

An older man sat on the other side, Gran Habano in hand. His mane of silver hair licked the collar of his cashmere coat. The two gorillas had climbed into the front seats. The silver-haired man waved his hand, fat gold rings and Rolex flashing.

Alex had been waiting ten years, ever since he arrived in the West, for an approach like this. Early in his career, he'd been warned by some ice hockey players from Moscow. Every successful Russian in the West could expect a visit from the *mafiya*, looking to take advantage of their influence or fame. But it had never happened to him, and he had always wondered why.

The car left the curb, slowly.

"Where are we going?" he spoke in English—a small gesture, to indicate he didn't intend to cooperate.

"Around the block only," the man replied in Russian.

The Russian *mafiya* liked to exploit weakness. Alex knew that much. The important thing was to keep calm and appear strong. Lucky for him acting was such an important part of his job.

"I'm surprised," he said, making a show of relaxing back in the black leather seat. "I was warned, years ago, that you might try to recruit me. I can't see why you are interested now. I am no longer so famous."

"Ah, Sasha," the man said. "I am not here to recruit you."

Alex frowned. No one but Nick had called him Sasha since he was a child, and this man had no right—but that was a clue. This man could have been a friend of the family. Perhaps even a relative. He searched the face, but saw no sign of familiarity.

Silverback smiled. "Every time I look at you, I see your mother, Alisa. You were so young when she died...do you remember her?"

Alisa? A man of Silverback's vintage would use his mother's first name and middle name. To call her only by her first name was disrespectful...unless they had been very close....

"Your father was vain and foolish, Sasha, but Alisa was a radiant woman. So beautiful. I wish there had been some other way. She did not deserve to die."

Her first name, again. Who the hell did this *thug* think he was? And what did he mean, his mother *did not deserve to die*? It had been an accident...hadn't it? So many questions crowded into Alex's mind. He had to fight to keep his expression impassive.

Silverback took his time lighting his cigar, teasing it lovingly with the lighter flame. The interior filled with the leathery scent of cigar smoke. "I must say, Alisa would be proud of you. She would be so pleased to know you have made a life outside the Family."

Wishing the old guy would stop using his mother's name, Alex struggled to absorb the implications of his words. *A life outside the Family*...he meant the *mafiya*, of course. Alex couldn't take it in. His parents, in the *mafiya*...

"As I said, I am not here to recruit you. I have a warning." Silverback took a puff of his cigar. "I have reason to believe your brother means you harm."

Alex's gut clenched with a deep sense of foreboding. He'd gotten used to the idea that Nick was mixed up in crime. But the *mafiya*? "Nick? What does he have to do with you?"

"Nikolai Mikhailovitch became a member of the *Solntsevskaya* as a child. Once a member, one never leaves. As a Russian, you are well aware of that."

Alex absorbed the implications. "Are you saying that all the time my brother was with me, he has been working for you?"

Silverback inclined his head.

Alex had always wondered how the teenage Nick found the money to get to Germany all those years ago. "Tell me one thing. Did he find me in Stuttgart of his own accord, or did you arrange it?"

Silverback raised his eyebrows, pursed his lips, and shrugged.

Alex swallowed. Now he understood why he had never been approached by the *mafiya* —they used his brother to shadow him. Nick had been by his side wherever he went, with access to the same places and the same people. He'd been able to use their world travels as cover for God-knows-what, while Alex paid for his flash suits and expensive habits.

Perhaps Nick's gambling debts, which Alex had paid off so willingly, were part of some money laundering scheme. Alex had done it all without question because Nick was his long-lost baby brother. He felt mortified at how easily he had been played, by the *mafiya* and by Nick.

"Do you know what he has planned?"

"That, I cannot help you with. It came to my attention because he failed to deliver an important consignment. My assistant's inquiries indicate that he is planning an operation of his own, against you, and his disappearance suggests to me that implementation is imminent." Silverback shook his head. "I am only sorry that I was not aware of this earlier. I would have put a stop to it."

"You have no idea where he is?"

"He was in London, so I assume he is still here. Other than that, no."

Nick in London. Had he seen the newspaper? Alex felt sick.

"My men are of course looking for him, and when we find him, I will ensure he is not in a position to threaten you again. In the meantime, you must be on your guard." The silver-haired man produced a card. "Do not lose this. You may need me again." Then, he leaned forward to tap his driver on the shoulder.

The car stopped, and one of the goons opened the car door for Alex to alight. As the car drove away, he looked at the card, hoping to discover Silverback's name, but it was blank except for a phone number.

He'd been tempted to ask for help to protect Gina, but he knew what a slippery slope that would be. The old man's affection for his mother hadn't stopped him exploiting Alex's relationship to his brother. To reveal another relationship might invite further exploitation.

If Nick had seen the photo in today's paper, he would know Gina was in London—which meant she was in danger. If Alex could have run to the Tube station, he would have. As it was, he could only walk, keeping an eye out for a black cab.

He almost crashed into a woman walking a poodle in the other direction. The fuss of apologizing, being recognized, and having to sign an autograph "for her daughter" almost drove him to screaming point, but it also gave him time to rethink his actions.

Nick would know his best chance of finding Gina was to trail Alex. He might even be following Alex already. He turned back towards the office. He would phone instead and insist on speaking to her. Even if she didn't want to see him, he could warn her.

When he finally got through to the theatre, they told him Gina hadn't arrived yet. No, they had no idea where she might be. Yes, she was due to perform at the matinee.

Damn it all to hell. He forgot caution and took a taxi to Chalk Farm anyway. The porter on the stage door wasn't someone he knew—but naturally, the man recognized Alex and had no qualms about letting him in to see the manager.

The manager flatly refused to provide Gina's address. Privacy regulations. Nothing Alex said would budge him, even the "do you know who I am?" card.

Leaving the office, Alex paused. The manager already had his head down over his paperwork and the porter was engaged with a visitor. Alex turned left and set off along the corridor. Mid-performance wasn't the best time to interrogate people, but he persevered, tapping on shoulders and stepping in front of hurrying cast members. None of them knew where Gina lived, or where she might be now. He was contemplating whether he dared enter the female dressing room when he heard his name.

"You're Alex!"

The woman in front of him was dressed in a breathtaking column of shimmering emerald from head to toe. The only visible skin was her face, and even that was adorned with a blaze of green eye make-up and a strange black pattern on her chin.

"Are you looking for Gina?"

"Yes. Do you know where she is?"

"She left as usual this morning but she's not here. She's not answering her phone either."

Alex absorbed the statement. *She left this morning.* "She lives with you, then?"

"We've got digs in Tufnell Park. She always comes in early to practice, but nobody's seen her." The woman looked at him with dark, troubled eyes. "She would've woken me and told me if she had to go somewhere. Besides, she's a trouper, she wouldn't miss a show."

He closed his eyes, fighting down his mounting panic. This was no time to lose it.

"You think Nick's got her?" she said.

"You know Nick?"

"Gina told me about him. She was always scared he'd find her."

Alex nodded. "I'm afraid she was right."

"Sophie, where've you been?" A young man with headphones and a clipboard appeared behind the woman, putting one hand on her shoulder and pulling her round. "You've got about two minutes to get on that stage."

She twisted her head around to look at Alex.

"Go," he said. "There's nothing you can do right now. I'll wait for you."

As she sprinted away, Alex pulled out his phone to ring the police.

Chapter Twenty-One

After Gina woke up, she kept her eyes shut. For one precious moment, she wanted to hold onto the hope it had all been a bad dream, that she lay safe under the cozy quilt at her place in Tuffnell Park.

Through the thin foam mattress, the metal frame of the camp bed dug into her hip and the single fleece blanket offered inadequate warmth. Yesterday's nightmare had been real—if it had been yesterday. She had no idea how much time had passed.

She'd been sure she wouldn't be able to sleep, but the hours of crying must have exhausted her. Her eyes felt swollen and gritty, her mouth dry. She couldn't summon the energy or the will to get up and look for a drink. Easier to stay curled into a ball in her fleece cocoon and shut out the world.

Her bladder had other ideas. Throwing off the blanket, she rolled over and sat up, taking a proper look at her prison for the first time. The dim glow of a single low-wattage bulb provided the only light in the windowless room. All four walls were painted in the same brooding shade of dark purple. Apart from the camp bed, the only other thing in the room was a large, red plastic bucket in the corner, a white lid propped against its side.

Lip curling in distaste, she walked over to the bucket, pulled down her dance pants and squatted.

Rumpled at her feet, her pants reminded her of how she'd woken up. She had no memory of anything between her kidnap on the steps of the house and awakening on the bed with her trousers around her ankles. She could imagine what had happened, but there was nothing to be gained by doing so.

She stood, scrubbing away the tears with her palms. *Enough.* She'd been crying for too long. Nick had told her she couldn't escape, but he might have missed something. She should check her surroundings.

A circuit of the room killed any hope. The door was solid wood, not a modern hollow core, with an old-fashioned keyhole. The walls were brickwork, roughly painted over.

She bent to look under the camp bed and found her dance bag She dropped to her knees to pull it out, and delved into the side pocket, but it was empty. Of course, Nick would have removed her phone. She checked the rest of the bag. He'd taken her make-up pouch, with its nail file and comb, and anything else she might have repurposed as a weapon, including her stainless-steel water bottle. He had left her dance shoes, two pairs of ballet tights, a leotard, a t-shirt and—hallelujah!—baby wipes.

Also under the bed was a cardboard box. She dragged it out. Inside lay several small bottles of water, three large blocks of chocolate and two jumbo packets of potato chips. Nick's idea of adequate nutrition. Well, she wouldn't die of thirst or starve. Provided he didn't leave her here too long…

She sat on the bed and pulled her knees up to her chest, wrapping herself in the fleece blanket again. When Nick came back, what could she do without a weapon? She made herself think about the kidnap, even though it made her stomach lurch. When she had looked into his eyes, she'd thought of Alex, not Nick. The likeness had thrown her off guard for vital seconds, otherwise she might have been able to shake him off. She should have had more sense. Why would Alex be lying in wait on her way to work?

No, she refused to blame herself. In that split second, her brain had made a natural mistake, because she'd seen Alex so recently, and Nick had been a distant memory.

On the other hand, if she hadn't been so stupid as to relax her guard and accept the London gig, Nick wouldn't have been able to find her…

Stop! This is not my fault.

She couldn't have stayed in hiding for the rest of her life. She had done her best. Wallowing in regrets wouldn't get her out of this place.

The details of the moments after Nick grabbed her were clouded. She could only suppose he had drugged her somehow—her head still ached. But if she concentrated, she would swear that Nick's body had felt thinner, and less muscular, than it used to be. That could mean she stood a chance of fighting him off when he returned.

If he did return.

She couldn't decide which she feared more—that Nick would come back, or that he never would.

****

Rubbing at his burning eyes, Alex pressed the button on the coffee machine. The aroma of espresso filled the kitchen but didn't revive him as it normally did. He felt as though he hadn't slept.

Contacting the police had been a waste of time. He and Sophie tried to explain that for a performer like Gina, not turning up for a matinee was a deadly sin. To the police, missing a show or two seemed hardly cause for alarm. He could only hope that now she'd been missing overnight, they might begin to take her disappearance more seriously.

She must have been snatched somewhere between Tufnell Park and the Roundhouse. It was a long shot, but perhaps if they knocked on the doors of people along her route, someone might have witnessed something. He was about to order a taxi to pick up Sophie when there was a knock on the door. Standing at the kitchen bench, he should have seen anyone approaching the house. Whoever it was must have sidled up to the front door.

He didn't need his walking stick to cover the short distance to the door, but he picked it up anyway. There was no spyhole or chain, something he had never worried about before. Hesitating at the door, he was about to call out when the door slammed open with a splintering sound and sent him flying.

As he rolled over onto his knees, Alex looked up to see Nick kick the door shut and pick up the cane. In his other hand, he held a gun. "I could break this stick of yours and you'd be helpless, yes?"

A voice in the back of Alex's mind told him to let Nick believe that. He stayed on the floor. His brother had spoken in Russian, as usual. Alex was not inclined to humor him by following suit. "What do you want?" he said, in English.

"I have come to see my dear brother." Taking a step back, Nick smirked. "I do not expect you to believe that. I do need money."

Alex breathed out. He should have known it would be about money. "And you need a gun for that?"

Nick shifted the cane and pulled a torn piece of newsprint from his suit pocket. A suit, Alex noticed, that hung loose from his shoulders instead of bulging with the strain of his muscles. His face looked thinner, too. "I saw your picture in the newspaper. How touching to see you with *my* girlfriend."

"She hasn't been your girlfriend for months."

"She was until you took her. I am willing to let you keep her. If you pay me a hundred thousand pounds."

The amount took Alex's breath away. "You know I don't have that kind of money. I couldn't find twenty thousand in ready cash, let alone a hundred."

"You'll find a way, if you want her."

Best not to admit that. "Why would I want her? She's a nice girl but…"

"So you'll let her die?"

Alex kept his expression impassive. If Nick knew just how much that statement clenched his heart, it would only make things worse. "No, of course not. She's a human being, Nick, that's murder."

"It is her own fault. If she hadn't seduced that stupid policeman, I would still be in Venetiko. I had good operation there."

"What are you talking about?"

"She led him on, the whore. So then I gave him a black eye to teach him a lesson, so he shopped me to the Ioannina police."

"And you've done all this to pay her back?"

"You think this is about revenge?" Nick laughed scornfully. "I had forgotten all about her until I saw the photograph. If I have to kill her, it will be a fitting punishment, but I do not care one way or the other. She is important only because she matters to you. I need a new identity, a new country. That does not come cheap."

So he wanted to leave the *mafiya* and start out on his own. Alex didn't like his chances, but if he wanted to try it... "I'll pay for that, whatever it costs, in exchange for Gina. That's as much as I can do."

"And then what do I live on?"

Work for a living, you lazy bastard.

Aloud, Alex said, "I can reinstate your allowance, if you tell me where to send it."

Nick's lip curled. "And you'll go on paying it, even after I hand her over? Sure."

One last attempt.

"Think about it. If you kill her, you have nothing. Let's compromise, please."

Nick shook his head. "How does it feel, Sasha? For years I had to dance to your tune. Now I'm in charge. You do what *I* say. You have two days to pay. I will tell you where. Do not think of calling the police, I have friends there."

He threw the cane at Alex and slammed the door behind him.

Alex stood up and crossed to the sink, where he'd left his phone. He'd dialed the first half Silverback's number before he thought better of it. No doubt his henchmen would act quickly to pick up Nick, but would they care whether Gina was hurt in the process?

What if they killed Nick before he revealed where she was held captive? Silverback might have promised his mother to look after Alex, but Gina would be little more than collateral damage.

Alex couldn't take the risk. He would have paid anything, but he'd told Nick the truth when he said he didn't have the cash. He owned his Hackney Terrace outright, but it would take time to raise a loan. The island had interested buyers, but no sale yet. He might be rich on paper, but he couldn't lay his hands on thousands of pounds in a hurry.

He would have to try.

Chapter Twenty-Two

Gina sat on the edge of the bed. Nick stood in front of her, gun in hand, a self-satisfied smile on his face.

In her prison there was no day, or night. She had no idea how long it had been—but it felt like days since Nick grabbed her. She had alternated between terror that he would come back, and fear that he wouldn't. Now that he was here, she could only hope she was too filthy for him to want anything to do with her.

"I speak to Alex," he said. "Soon, we find out how much he love you."

"Alex?"

"He will pay ransom. Or not."

Oh, no. She had thought this was some kind of revenge for her stealing his precious boat and that Nick would let her go after he felt she'd been humiliated enough—but he'd kidnapped her for money. Why did he think Alex would pay a ransom for her?

"We go," he said.

She stood. "Where to?"

With a wave of the gun, he pointed. As she walked past him, she was tempted to try tripping him or making a dash for it, but there might be locked doors ahead. Better to wait until she saw the actual exit.

As she stepped through the door, she stopped, confused. Since Nick had grabbed her on the steps of a basement flat, she'd assumed she'd been dragged downstairs into the cellar. Instead, she stood in a large open room with a scarred wooden floor and wide picture windows, most of which were boarded up.

A huge mahogany counter with a foot rail beneath stood against the far wall. Gina realized the place was a derelict pub with crude graffiti daubed across its peeling walls. Nick must have thrown her into a car and driven her somewhere, but she had no memory of the journey.

That created another hurdle. She knew the street where she'd been kidnapped, and she had thought about which way to run to reach shops and get help. Now, the odds that she'd recognize her location were slim. Though she had lived in London for a few years, her knowledge of the city was confined to her digs, the theaters, and the journey between the two. If she shook Nick off and ran, she wouldn't know where to go.

She had to try something. She was convinced Alex wouldn't pay. If she'd been his girlfriend, or his wife, then yes—but he hadn't even got beyond, "I'd like to see you again." He would go to the police, they'd advise him not to give in to a kidnapper, and she dreaded to think what would happen then.

Outside in the deserted street, the sunlight blinded her after so long in the gloomy storage room. Nick said, "Get in."

She blinked to clear her vision. At the curb stood a small car. He held the rear door open for her to climb in. As soon as he closed the door, she immediately tried the lever, but the child lock had been activated.

He was walking round the front of the car, unable to see her. This was her only chance. She lunged into the well between the front seats and pulled herself onto the passenger seat, reaching up to open the door as she did so and tumbled onto the sidewalk when he opened the driver's door.

He would have to run around the car to reach her, but she was already sprinting. She had no idea where she was. All she could do was keep running.

Within seconds, she heard the car, close on her heels. She spied a lane way on her left, too narrow for the car to follow, and ducked into it. It led into some kind of warehouse complex, through a maze of old sheds and machinery. The ground was strewn with papers, cans and broken metal, but she didn't have time to worry about what she might tread on. She ran past garbage cans and old carpets, then stopped at a line of tall fencing. Dead end.

She eyed the top of the fence. It looked impossibly high, but she had no choice. She backed up, took a run at it and leaped, but her fingers fell far short. She tried again, and this time managed to grab the top of the palings, her feet scrabbling for purchase on the smooth wood.

Nick's arms encircled her waist, hauling her off the fence. She screamed, adrenaline sending her heart rate off the scale, terror surging in her throat.

"I make you scream, bitch," he said, throwing her on the ground, face down.

All his weight was on her, and one of her arms was trapped beneath her body. She struggled, but he was too heavy. With her free hand, she tried to pull his hair or scratch his face, but he grabbed her wrist and twisted her arm behind her back.

He lifted his weight off her and wrenched her other arm behind her. Something hard and sharp-edged closed tightly around her wrists. He yanked her to her feet. One hand over her mouth, he frog-marched her back to the car, opened the boot and forced her into it.

He wasn't going to rape her. Even when the trunk slammed shut, plunging her into darkness, she felt so relieved that she started to laugh…and couldn't stop. She gulped in air, trying to calm her hysteria, barely noticing as the bouncing of the suspension racketed her around.

As the minutes passed, she regained control and began to think. If she could get her arms free, there must be a latch somewhere to open the trunk or release the rear seatbacks. She wriggled, testing to see whether she could break her bonds, or bring her hands under her bottom to the front. No luck.

She felt the car come to a stop. Several seconds passed before the trunk opened and Nick dragged her out, banging her head on the catch. The gun was in his hand again. He pushed her through an old warehouse to an empty parking lot, surrounded by tall, ramshackle concrete buildings with smashed windows. The tarmac was badly broken up and pot-holed, weeds breaking through everywhere. Their footsteps echoed around the walls.

She wondered how long it would take him to accept that Alex wasn't going to turn up. Then she heard footsteps approaching through the warehouse. Nick grabbed her waist and swung her round to face the new arrival.

Alex limped towards them, a black drawstring bag in his hand. She felt a leap of hope—which flickered out as she took in his limping walk and drooping shoulders. He looked more like the invalid she had first met in Greece than the man who had staged *Spartacus*. Leaning heavily on a crutch, he looked terrified.

Nick said something in Russian; Alex replied in a pleading, pathetic tone, then took a few steps toward them. After a barked order from Nick, Alex stopped and threw the bag on the ground at his feet.

Nick moved forward, pushing Gina in front of him, his gun still at the ready. He had to let her go to pick up the bag.

While Nick's head was bent, Alex raised his eyes to hers. She was startled by the intensity blazing in them, completely at odds with his shambling appearance. With his free hand, he motioned to her to move away.

Nick stepped back, the bag in his hand. He was so intent on retrieving the bag, he didn't bother to pull her with him. She took a small step back, standing clear of the two men but with a clear view of both. Nick put the gun into his pocket and moved to open the bag.

Her father had always told her, 'a gun in your pocket was a great way to shoot your balls off'. Right now, she hoped he was right.

The moment he put his hand into the bag, Alex brought up his crutch and lashed out at Nick's head. "Run, Gina!"

Falling to one knee, Nick clapped one hand to his ear while fumbling for his pocket with the other. Alex swung the crutch again, striking him on the wrist. The gun fell from his hand and skittered across the concrete as Nick lost balance and fell to the ground.

As Gina stood frozen, Alex yelled at her. She couldn't help with her hands tied behind her back. She turned and ran through the warehouse, out into the street. It was empty, apart from a little Fiat parked on the other side of the road. At first, she thought no one was inside the car—then a dark head appeared over the sill, the door opened.

Sophie climbed out of the car. "Thank God," she said, hugging her. "Where's Alex?"

"Back there, with Nick. We have to get help."

Sophie hesitated. "The police are on their way. Shouldn't we wait for them?"

"I won't leave him." Gina turned around to present her wrists. "Untie me!"

"They're cable ties. I'd need a knife or scissors. Come and sit in the car, the police'll sort it out."

"I can't leave Alex there on his own!"

The argument was solved when Alex appeared at the warehouse entrance. He held Nick's gun in one hand. He didn't look up as Gina and Sophie approached.

"Alex…" Gina paused, her delight fading as she took in in his appearance. His face was pale, his mouth set, his eyes looking into the distance. "Are you hurt? Where's Nick?"

He shook his head. "I'm fine. Nick got away."

"Who cares?" Now the danger was over, Gina felt giddy with relief and had a ridiculous urge to giggle, but his expression stopped her. She moved close, wishing her arms were free to wrap around him. "We're both safe, that's what matters. It's over."

Finally, some life came back to his eyes. He almost smiled and nodded.

The *wah-wah* of a police siren alerted them to the arrival of a squad car. It drew up and two policemen jumped out.

All Gina wanted to do was go home, but she had a feeling it was going to be a long, tedious day at the police station.

****

She didn't see Alex for the rest of the day, which turned into a round of waiting rooms, interrogation rooms, and cups of bad tea.

A balding detective called her into a bare, gray interview room for a final review of her statement. "You met Nick Rostov on holiday in Greece and moved straight in with him?"

He made her sound like a slut. "I didn't move in with him, I'd known him for about a month, and he invited me for a holiday."

"And you saw him bribing an officer of the law?"

"I wasn't sure if it was a bribe. I asked him about it and he said that was how business was done in Greece."

"So you knew he was a smuggler?"

"No!" Honestly, who was the victim here? She'd expected the detective to be more sympathetic. "I'd seen so much black-market stuff going on in Thessaloniki. Everyone fiddled their taxes, paying in cash and giving backhanders. I thought it was the same thing."

"Ms. Tarasco, you're either very naive or you're not being entirely honest." The detective paused. "On that score, I notice your passport gives your surname as Williams. Can you explain why you're using a false name?"

The man's an idiot. Gina took a deep breath. "It's not a *false* name. It's a stage name. I'm a performer."

As the questions went on, the cop eventually accepted she had no more information for him. Sighing, he put the statement down on the desk. "As Rostov is still at large, we would recommend you not to go home for a week or two. Is there somewhere you could stay? We recommend avoiding close friends, he might be able to track you there."

Gina considered. She could go back to Aunt Teresa's—but that would mean leaving the show. "No. Al—Mr. Korolev said he's going to a hotel and I could stay there."

The detective looked frosty. "We would not recommend associating with Korolev, either. It's a fair bet he's just as mixed up with the Russian *mafiya* as Rostov."

"The *mafiya?*" And here she'd been imagining Nick as a small-time gangster. "I don't think Alex—"

"Face facts, Miss Tarasco. We know Rostov was involved with them in Moscow. There is an outstanding warrant for his arrest. Since then, he has toured with Korolev in various countries. What's the likelihood he wasn't with the *mafiya* during that time? And how likely is it that Korolev wouldn't know? A lot of these high profile Russkis are up to their necks in it. "

"But if he's in league with them, why would he take such risks to rescue me?"

"There's a good chance your rescue has more to do with a rivalry between gangs, than anything to do with you. Korolev is not to be trusted, as far as we're concerned."

Struggling to think straight, Gina shook her head. The Greek police had been suspicious of Alex, too. What if they were right?

On the other hand, if Nick had police connections in Greece—why not here?

Her legs almost gave way as she walked out to the front desk. After the euphoria of the escape, the reaction had well and truly set in. She couldn't stop shaking.

Sophie was waiting for her. "You poor thing, you were in there for ages. As if you haven't been through enough already. How are you feeling?"

"Awful. The doctor gave me something." Gina stroked her forehead. "I just want to get clean."

"Alex has organized a safe house for a few days, we can go straight there."

Gina bit her lip. "The police told me not to trust him. They say Nick's mixed up with the Russian *mafiya* and so is Alex. I don't know what to do."

Sophie put an arm around her. "I don't know, maybe he is. But what matters is, he's on your side. He wouldn't have done all that if he wasn't, would he?"

"No."

Better the Devil you know, she decided as she allowed Sophie to lead her to the car.

Chapter Twenty-Three

The "safe house" was an elegant, renovated Georgian apartment near Holland Park. On the third floor, Alex stood at the window, peering impatiently around the edge of the blind. A car drew up and Sophie emerged.

He hurried across the room and opened the door of the apartment, ready to embrace Gina. But when he saw her turn into the corridor, head down and clinging to Sophie like a lifeline, he stepped back. As they entered the apartment, Gina looked up at him, eyes wide with shock and dark with shadows.

How he wished he'd been able to pull the trigger on his brother.

"Come on, let's get you in the shower," Sophie said to Gina.

In answer to Sophie's questioning look, Alex indicated the direction of the bathroom with a brief nod of his head. After a few minutes, he heard the sound of water running, and Sophie emerged from the room.

"I know Gina wanted you to perform tonight, but I think you should stay here," he said. "She needs you."

Sophie shook her head. "She doesn't want me to let the circus down, not with my understudy sick. I tried to insist but she was getting really upset. I didn't want to push it."

Alex bit his lip, then leaned forward to kiss her

cheek. "I don't like it, but if that is what she wants, I've detailed one of the security guards to stay with you."

"I don't think I'm a target, really."

"Perhaps not, but it's important to make sure you're not followed. Theirs is no point in a safe house if Nick tracks you here."

Alex shooed her through the door, double-locked it, then walked over to flop on the plush sofa by the window to wait for Gina.

The sound of a door banging woke him. Opening his eyes, he saw Gina halfway to the bedroom, a white toweling robe swamping her petite frame. "I didn't mean to wake you."

He sat up, blearily running his hands through his hair. She took a few steps towards him. "You ought to clean that up."

He frowned, then looked down at his blood-encrusted knuckles, where he'd scraped his hand on the concrete reaching for the gun. "It's only a graze."

"You can't go to bed like that," she said, heading for the kitchen cupboards.

Closing his eyes again, he slumped against the big back cushions of the sofa. He jumped when he felt a sharp, cold wetness on his hand. "Ouch! That stings!"

"It's antiseptic, it's meant to. Sit still."

She kneeled on the couch beside him, a plastic bowl filled with cloudy water in her hand. He sank back again, submitting to her ministrations. Her face was tantalizingly near as she leaned over him and dabbed at his cuts. He shut his eyes so he wouldn't see her soft hair so close to his lips. Instead of helping, it only made him more aware of the clean, warm smell of her, fresh from the shower.

He opened his eyes again. Her head was bent forward, a tumble of wet curls falling across her face. A stray strand fell on her face and she kept shaking her head to shift it. He reached over with his free hand and swept the curl gently away, his fingers brushing her forehead. She jumped. "Sorry. I'm on edge."

"I'm the one who's sorry."

She put the bowl down and backed away. "I think I'll go to bed now, if you don't mind."

"Sure."

She turned and fled to her bedroom.

Alex hauled his shirt off over his head and threw it aside. Damn the circus, he should have insisted Sophie stay. Gina needed comfort, but clearly not from him.

****

In the bedroom, Gina climbed into the furthest of the twin beds, switched off the lamp on the table between them, and dived under the quilt, still wearing the bulky cotton robe. The material crumpled around her in awkward folds, but she had nothing else to wear and she didn't want to sleep naked. She closed her eyes and told herself to get some rest.

Clink. What was that sound? For one second she froze, wide-eyed, holding her breath. Then she switched the light on, got up and checked the window. It was an old-fashioned sash window, open a crack at the bottom. She closed it and flipped the catch then climbed into bed and turned off the light.

Thud. She was alert in an instant, her entire body tense. The sound had been far away, she told herself, probably from the apartment upstairs. Nothing to worry about.

Logical or not, she had to check the window again.

Still shut, but it didn't have a key lock, only a catch. Couldn't they be opened by sliding in a screwdriver blade? She supposed it was unlikely on the third floor, but there was a ledge...

She had felt in control earlier, while she had things to occupy her—having a shower, tending to Alex—but now, in the quietness, unwanted thoughts crowded her mind. Setting her jaw, she climbed back into bed and clicked off the light. She wouldn't let Nick beat her. She started her toe-to-head relaxation exercises.

"Your toes are relaxed. Your feet are relaxed. Your ankles are relaxed. Your calves are relaxed. Your knees are relaxed. Your..."

She woke to the sound of a woman screaming. The robe and the quilt had tangled themselves around her, trapping her in the bed. She flailed around, desperate to get free and run to safety. A bright light beamed into the room—a menacing figure stood silhouetted against the light from the open door.

She needed a weapon. She lunged for the lamp and pulled hard to free it from its socket—then cried out as the plug refused to budge and the force wrenched her arm and shoulder.

"Gina, Gina, it's all right, it's me, Alex."

Cradling her arm, Gina gazed around the room, slowly recalling where she was. No Nick. No danger. She breathed deeply, trying to calm her racing heart.

He stood close now, looking down at her. He sat on the edge of her bed. "Did you hurt your shoulder?"

His voice was so tender, so caring. Something gave inside her and the tears welled, uncontrollable. She collapsed onto his chest.

His arms closed around her like a protective cage.

"Would you like me to stay with you?"

Relieved, she nodded. He got up and found a blanket in the closet, then lay on top of Sophie's bed and covered himself with the blanket. When he reached to switch off the light, she yelped, "No!" then, sheepishly, "do you mind if we leave it on?"

"Of course not. Try to get some sleep. If I fall asleep and you need me, please wake me up." He turned away from her, trying to tug the blanket over his shoulder.

The sight of his broad back made her feel more secure, regardless of the policeman's warning. Alex had been willing to risk his life for her—he had thrown himself at Nick even though he was carrying a gun, for God's sake.

She could never doubt Alex. Not after all that.

Chapter Twenty-Four

Alex arrived back at the apartment at lunchtime, in time to change shifts with Sophie, who had rehearsals to attend. He had spent a few hours to work at the National then, security guard in tow, made a quick visit home for a change of clothes. They had seen no sign of being followed. The more Alex thought about it, the more convinced he was that Nick would have left the country already. With Silverback's men on his heels, he would be foolish to delay.

Sophie answered his knock and scurried out of the door as soon as he entered. When Gina ran to meet him, his heart leaped. She put her arms around his neck—but then there was a moment when her smile slipped away, and her head turned at the last moment so they bumped cheeks in an awkward peck.

"How was your morning?" he asked, pulling clothes from the case.

She sat down on the sofa, twisting round to speak to him. "Quiet. We watched a lot of television. And I made a couple of phone calls."

He stopped, a pair of socks in his hand. "You didn't tell anyone where you were?"

"No, of course not, what do you think I am? I rang my cousin, the one who runs *Circo*." She fiddled with the piping on the sofa. "I didn't tell him where I was, but I did end up telling him all about what happened.

He was really understanding. He told me I didn't have to come back until I was ready."

She paused. He didn't like that—it gave him an ominous feeling.

"He said that maybe I shouldn't come back at all, and he would be happy to find me a job with one of the other shows outside London. In fact," —she took a deep breath, and Alex's sense of foreboding rose another notch— "he said there's a role for me on the Asia tour."

A shirt slipped through his fingers and landed on the floor.

"It makes a lot of sense, you know," she continued in a rush. "I can't go on being followed around by bodyguards forever, and I'm never going to feel safe in London. Or anywhere in England, for that matter. The further away I can go, the safer I'm going to feel."

He couldn't speak.

"*La Setosa* is a major role," she continued. "It's a huge compliment. My big break. The show's being launched in Australia, so I can go there now, straight away, no worries about visas or anything—I could start living a normal life again."

"That's great," he managed. His voice sounded strangled, even to him.

As the silence hung between them, he threw the shirt back in the carryall and faced her. "That's great," he said again. That sounded better, almost as though he meant it. "You deserve it. I should take you out to dinner to celebrate."

"No, we don't need to. There's stacks of frozen meals in the freezer, and even a bottle of champagne." She came off the sofa and into the kitchen.

He followed, watching the exquisite curve of her bottom as she took the champagne glasses from the top shelf of the cupboard. He stepped closer and touched her arm. "Please don't go." The words were out before he had time to think. He pulled her round to face him, his hands on her shoulders. "I can take you to Paris, or Madrid, or Berlin—wherever you want to go—"

She shook her head. "Alex, I'm very grateful—"

"Christ!" He threw his hands up and stepped back. "It's not gratitude I'm looking for!"

His sudden movement made Gina stagger back against the kitchen bench. She nearly dropped the glasses.

He was instantly apologetic. "I didn't mean to frighten you."

"It's fine."

"No it isn't. I'm being selfish. Of course you must go," he said, silently begging her to contradict him. "It's a great opportunity. You'd be mad to pass up a chance like that. I have to fulfill my contract, but I can join you later, we can—"

"No," she said, turning away from him to put the glasses back on the bench. "Please don't."

He moved closer, willing her to look back at him. "Gina, I love you. I've loved you ever since you came to the island. I don't want to lose you again."

He felt foolish, exposed, as the silence went on and she didn't move or speak. What had he expected? He'd built up a dream on the basis of a brief acquaintance and a kiss. All that really told him was that she found him attractive—he had read too much into it.

She put the glasses down on the bench. She was avoiding his eyes. Now she would say something comforting about being very fond of him. He didn't want to hear it. He turned on his heel and went back into the lounge room.

The world had been turned upside down. How the hell had he arrived at this? He had never begged a woman for anything, ever. Even Karen. He resisted the urge to go back into the kitchen and get down on his knees.

He was sitting on the sofa in front of the TV, flicking through channels without seeing them, when she joined him. "I'm sorry, Alex, it's not—."

Oh God, please, not this conversation. He knew exactly what she was going to say. He'd used every variation himself over the years. "It's not you, it's me." "I don't deserve you" If she wanted to get complicated, "You're amazing but I have so much going on in my life, it's not the right time."

He stared fiercely at the screen, the picture blurring. "It's fine, Gina, you don't have to say anything, I had no reason—"

"No, you don't understand." She sat beside him on the couch. "I can't imagine anything I want more than going to Paris with you. "

His head whipped around to look at her, but the hope surging in his chest died in seconds. He could see in her eyes that there was a "but."

"But how can you guarantee Nick won't follow?"

His mouth opened, ready to swear anything to convince her. He closed it again. She deserved more than empty promises, and there was no denying they would be empty.

Nick still did not have the money he wanted to start a new life, and Alex had been his piggy bank for too long. He wouldn't hesitate to use Gina as a lever again, given half a chance. Unless she traveled with a permanent bodyguard glued to her side, Alex could never assure her safety. That would be no life for her.

He had one last chance. "We don't have to go to Paris. Or Madrid. We can find a place in the country somewhere, disappear."

"And never work again? We're performers. You know what it's like to give up dancing. It's what I've worked my whole life for." Her eyes were glimmering with tears. "But you know what? I would. If only I felt sure it would be safe. But I'm not sure it would be, living somewhere isolated, miles from anywhere. If Nick did track us down, we'd be sitting ducks."

He knew she was right. To ask her to stay with him was to ask her to risk her life for him. He couldn't expect that. He wouldn't want that. "You're right." He rested his elbows on his knees, shoulders sagging. "I've put you in enough danger already. I hate to admit it, but you have to go. You can't live every day in fear. The only place you can be safe is away from me."

"I'm not even sure I'll be safe on my own. But it's all I can think of."

He stood and took her by the shoulders. "Don't worry about that. Nick told me that he has no interest in you, except as a way to get at me. You'll be in no danger."

The urge to kiss her was overwhelming, but he was barely holding it together as it was. It would be too painful to taste what was about to be snatched away from him. "When will you go?"

She shrugged. "As soon as I can get a seat on a plane, I guess."

He didn't want her to go. He wanted to throw his arms around her and hold her, and never let her out of his sight.

"Use my phone," he said. "You may as well start booking now.

Chapter Twenty-Five

Gina lifted her suitcase onto the bed, unzipped it and found a space to squeeze in her cosmetics bag. She was ready.

She couldn't wait to get on the plane. Being with Alex messed with her head and she couldn't cope with it much longer. Not because she didn't want to be near him, but because she wanted it too much. She craved the comfort and security of his arms around her, but if she allowed herself to weaken, he might persuade her to stay—and that way lay a life of endless fear, always looking over her shoulder for Nick.

It wasn't as if she could ever put Nick out of her mind. While she was with Alex, his hair and eyes were a constant reminder, and if she caught sight of him at the wrong angle, it triggered a flashback. Then she'd look again and drink in the differences. Nick's eyes had been sunken and bloodshot, unlike Alex's clear blue gaze. In spite of his weight loss, Nick's jutting chin had looked coarse and mulish compared to the sharp planes of Alex's face...

Giving herself a shake, she balanced her tote on one of the suitcases and dragged the case to the bedroom door. Nothing could be gained by mooning over Alex's jawline. While Nick was on the loose, she and Alex had no future. Period. End of story. Absolutely no question.

Alex smiled at her as she stood in the open doorway. She abandoned her suitcase and scurried back into the bedroom.

"The car's waiting," he called. "Do you need help with your other case?"

"No, no! I'll be a minute. I forgot something." She dabbed her eyes and blew her nose. She mustn't let Alex see how hard it was to leave him.

A moment later, she was stepping into the lounge room again, pulling her second case, her lips pulled back in her best stage smile. "I'm ready.""

Alex took the other suitcase and together they went downstairs to the car, where Sophie waited. While Alex and the driver put her luggage into the trunk, Gina jumped into the front seat. She had managed to avoid Alex most of yesterday, by taking forever to pack her meager belongings. Best to keep a distance now, too. She wished he hadn't insisted on coming to see her off.

Sophie tried to keep up a stream of conversation, but only the taxi driver seemed in the mood to talk. Gina didn't trust her voice, and Alex was monosyllabic. The drive to the airport took an age.

When they finally arrived at the terminal, Gina scrambled out of the car, desperate for the ordeal to be over. She grabbed a case and set off, leading the way into the terminal, intent on finding the right check-in desk, leaving Sophie and Alex to catch up.

"Hey, Gin, where's the fire?' Sophie called, behind her, as Gina approached the check-in desk.

"You okay?" Sophie whispered, touching her sleeve. Gina sniffed and frowned, giving a little shake of her head. Sophie put an arm round her. "Won't be long now."

The line was unusually short. She could have delayed going through security for half an hour or so, but she didn't want to drag out the goodbyes. "Well, I guess this is it," she said, turning to hug Sophie. "Bye, Soph, and thanks for everything. You know you're welcome in Sydney if ever you're coming to Australia. Even if I'm touring—you've got my mum's address."

With a nod, Sophie stepped back. Gina couldn't put it off any longer. Swallowing hard, she looked up into Alex's eyes. "I'll never forget what you did for me. I'm so sorry—" Gina broke off, the tears she'd promised not to shed overwhelming her.

Alex reached out for her but when she backed away, he let his arms drop. His voice was stiff. "You have my number. If ever you need me, call."

Head down, she nodded, not daring to look at his face again. "I'd better go," she said, turning on her heel to go through the gate. She had taken only a few steps when she felt a hand touch her shoulder and pull her round. She almost screamed, but then she recognized Alex and the panic subsided. He held her by both shoulders so she couldn't avoid his gaze. For a long moment, she thought he wasn't going to say anything, but then he spoke.

"I want to say…I wish I could say that I'll find Nick and make it safe, and then I'll come for you and we'll be together." He shook his head. "But I can't. The reality is, I may never find him. You must not put your life on hold for me. You deserve so much more. Forget me, Gina. Live your life. Goodbye."

He lifted a stray curl from her forehead and kissed where it had rested. And then he was gone.

****

Alex waved goodbye to Sophie and climbed into the car. He'd sent her off in a separate taxi, on the pretext that sharing a ride through the city would make her late for the theatre. In truth, he didn't want company. Seeing Gina off with a smile on his face had taken every shred of self-control he possessed.

Had he just touched her for the last time? He thought he'd hit the depths of despair when they told him he would never dance again. He was wrong. Losing Gina...he wanted to punch something. Scream at the top of his lungs. Run back into the airport and drag her off the plane. He smacked the armrest with his fist. *Fuck Nick! What did I do to deserve such a bastard for a brother?*

"You okay, mate?" the driver asked.

"Yes, yes I'm fine, thank you." That was a lie. He'd sworn he would never feel helpless again yet here he was, utterly unable to do anything to rescue a relationship which, he now realized, had become more important than anything else in his life. Why, oh why hadn't he been able to pull that fucking trigger?

He couldn't let it end here. There had to be something he could do.

Alex knew only one person who had the knowledge to help him find Nick. He pulled out his phone and thumbed the number. A woman in a cultured English voice answered. "Can I help you?"

"Alex Korolev. I need to speak to your boss."

"Hold please." The line went quiet for several minutes, then, "Where are you now?"

"On the M4 heading into the city."

She named an exclusive Mayfair restaurant. "Be there at twelve thirty. Booking for John Bank."

Alex was heartened by the quick response, but as he entered the black marble portal of the restaurant, his mood darkened.

The old man had said he wanted to look after Alex, but he hadn't scrupled about getting Nick to exploit him. There would be limits to how much Silverback would do without some kind of return for the favor, and Alex feared he knew where that might lead.

Silverback had said it himself. Once you got involved the *mafiya*, there was no going back. Their ranks teemed with the thousands who thought they could walk away after just one "favor." If Alex agreed to do something in return for finding Nick, he would be ensnared forever. And then he would have to say goodbye to Gina, even if Nick ceased to be a threat, because he couldn't involve her in that kind of life.

Besides, what exactly did Alex want the *mafiya* to do? Did he really want to ask someone to murder his own brother? The idea was unthinkable, no matter what Nick had done. And it would be naive to ask them to capture Nick and hand him, alive, to the authorities.

If Nick's death was the only thing that secured Gina's safety, then the least Alex could do was pull the trigger with his own hand. But he'd had that opportunity at the warehouse, and he could not do it.

The old man was already at the table. The waiter hovered, ready to hand Alex his menu as the *maitre d'* drew out his chair, but Silverback waved him away. "My guest will not eat."

Once the staff left, Silverback added in Russian, "You cannot eat, because you are not here. We did not meet."

"This is a conspicuous place to not meet," Alex

replied in the same language.

Silverback shook his head. "It may appear so, but it is quiet, and discreet."

Alex looked around and had to admit it was so. The few diners in the spacious, low-lit dining room were near the windows, far from their table in the innermost corner, shielded by a Grecian column and a large potted palm.

Silverback poured some white wine into Alex's glass. "What can I do for you?"

"I—," Alex picked up the glass and took a mouthful, grateful for the chance to gather his thoughts. "I'm assuming you know you were right about Nick planning revenge."

"I am aware he kidnapped your girlfriend. I understand you showed some courage in her rescue."

"Girlfriend is too strong a word." Alex's instinct was to hide the relationship from the *mafiya*, but he needed the godfather's help. "I would like to see her again, but while Nick is out there, I can't take the risk. He might try to harm her again. I wondered if you knew his current location."

"I am afraid not. We would like to find him, too. As I told you, he failed to deliver a very valuable consignment. It was *mafiya* property and we take such theft very seriously indeed. For that reason alone, I expect he has already left the country. He would know it is much too dangerous for him to stay here."

Great. That only left the rest of the world to search.

"He would be a fool to go to Russia, Greece or Albania, because he is a wanted man in those countries," Silverback said. "In fact, he would be well advised to avoid the whole of Europe, due to Europol and our own extensive network there. If he is sensible, he will choose a country where we do not operate."

Alex raised his eyebrows. "There are countries where you don't operate?"

"Oh, yes. There are many branches of the *Bratva*. In some parts of the world, we agree not to compete. Your brother could go to India, parts of Asia, Australia—"

"Australia?" How ironic if Gina had chosen one of the very places where Nick might take refuge.

"It would be a reasonable choice for him. He speaks English…of a sort. In any case, I do not think he speaks any other language, so he would be more comfortable in an English-speaking country."

"He speaks some Greek, but as you say, he can't go there." Alex frowned. Silverback had a point. He and Nick had never toured extensively in Asia, but they had visited Australia several times, and Nick had liked it. He might even have some contacts there.

There was one silver lining. When he'd come to demand the ransom, Nick had made it clear that he had no interest in Gina, except as a way to hurt Alex. If Alex could convince his brother that Gina no longer mattered to him, she would be safe, even if Nick was in Australia. The longer they were apart, the safer she would be.

Especially if Alex had a conspicuous relationship with someone else—and that, he could do.

Chapter Twenty-Six

Along the foreshore at Manly Beach, slender Norfolk pines speared into a vault of bright powder-blue sky. A perfect winter's morning in Sydney. At their favorite café on the promenade, Gina and her mother sat at an outside table, finishing their brunch—avocado on toast and poached egg for Gina, blueberry pancakes for her Mum.

As the morning warmed, more customers arrived. Gina felt surrounded by contented couples. The nearest pair sat with their elbows on the table, fingers intertwined. They leaned towards each other, touched foreheads, and exchanged a kiss. Gina's eyes prickled. She had sent Alex her contact details as soon as she was settled, but he hadn't responded. Almost ten weeks now, and not a word. It seemed he'd really meant it when he told her to forget him.

Alex certainly seemed to be managing to forget her. The women's magazines were full of photos of him, squiring the Aussie singer Summer Leigh to parties and galas. The latest darling of the Australian press, Summer was in London in a bid to become the next Kylie Minogue.

No chance, Gina thought. Leigh was all looks and no voice and would be flying home to Melbourne soon enough. But then some other glamour girl would take her place on Alex's arm. She sniffed.

Her mother touched her hand. "Are you sure you're going to be okay on your own now?"

"Yes, Mum, of course I am." Gina widened her mouth into a smile. "Anyway, you've got to go. You've got a hot date."

"It's only the bridge club dinner."

"If it's only the bridge club dinner, why's your face red?"

"Don't be silly." Her mother sat back, consulting her watch. "I told your brother to be here by eleven, so we've got time for another coffee."

Gina laughed. Matt was famous for his lateness. "But you do have a train to catch."

"If I miss the one I'm aiming for, there's another in an hour. I'll still be home in plenty of time."

"Hey, gorgeous!"

The shout made them turn to see a tall, tanned surfer approaching, his long dark hair flying in the sea breeze. Her brother Matt was on time, for once.

"I'll get this, Mum," Gina said, taking out her purse. "You go on. Have a great time tonight."

They embraced all around. Matt grabbed the handle of her mother's wheeled suitcase and Gina watched until he and her mother disappeared around the corner of the street, on their way to the car park. Then she paid the bill at the cashier desk, and set off for home, at the other end of the Corso, Manly's wide central boulevard. She window-shopped as she strolled along, knowing she had plenty of time before her ferry was due to leave.

She reached the back gate, unlocked it, and stepped through into her sunny private courtyard, inhaling the rich scent of gardenia. Seconds later, she yelped as sharp claws embedded themselves in her left leg, right through her denim jeans. "Mephisto! Get off!"

The cat refused to budge. She limped through the back door into the kitchen with him clamped to her leg. Only then did he let go to jump to the top of the retro refrigerator, tucking his front paws in so he looked like one great mass of jet-black fur. His copper eyes regarded her with disdain.

"You know, there is a perfectly good cat flap if you wanted to get in," she said. "But of course, you're much too grand to do things yourself, aren't you? You need your servant to do it for you."

Her instinct was to tickle him under the chin, but by now she had learned better, and had the scratches to show for it.

When she'd been offered the chance to house-sit the apartment while the owner was in Europe, she'd been looking forward to having a pet to keep her company. But that was before she met Mephisto. She couldn't complain, though. The elegant apartment, decorated in Art Deco was much grander than she could afford to rent, and all she had to do was water a few plants, keep the place clean and feed the demon cat.

She refreshed the feline's water bowl and got ready for work.

****

She timed her arrival at the Manly ferry wharf to arrive just as the ramps were extended from the ship to the quay. The crowd of passengers trooped aboard, some hurrying to grab the window seats in the main cabin, others climbing to the upper deck.

A Japanese couple went through the door to the open seating at the bow. An elderly woman exchanged a knowing glance with Gina. "They won't stay out there long, once we're out in the harbor."

Gina nodded in agreement. The bow would be a cold, wet place once the ferry reached open water. The open walkway, running the length of the ship from bow to stern, would be chilly too—but she lingered there anyway. She loved this part of her morning commute, with its stunning views of the harbor and the city.

As the ship left the quay, the breeze began tugging at her clothes and tousling her hair. She drew her fleece jacket closer around her but stayed on the walkway, taking a seat on the slatted wooden bench. They passed the high cliff of South Head, and the ship began to pitch and roll as the wind strengthened. The waves became longer and higher. She gripped the edge of the bench and laughed in delight at the swish of the water surging by, and the salt wind stinging her face. It could be dangerously rough, this crossing between the two headlands, where there was no protection from the open ocean beyond—but on a good day like today, it was simply exhilarating.

Too soon, the ferry turned to starboard, and they were in sheltered waters again. She retreated to the warmth of the main cabin for the remainder of the trip to the city terminal. The bus from Circular Quay traveled only a short distance through the city streets before it descended into a concrete canyon.

This was her least favorite part of the journey, the bleak gray walls of the freeway tunnel giving her too much time to think about things she'd rather forget, like Summer Leigh. She distracted herself by concentrating on the number she would be performing, going through all the moves in her head.

****

The bus disgorged passengers onto a wide suburban road. From there, it was only a short trip through leafy streets to her destination. She reached the Big Top with time to spare, greeting the stage doorman with a cheerful "Hi, Pete!"

Most theaters were rabbit warrens, filled with cavernous spaces, storage rooms piled high with junk, and unexpected cubbyholes. By comparison, the interior of the Big Top was simple and uncluttered. She reached the women's dressing room quickly, shed her track suit, and made her way to the practice room.

The rest of the day passed quickly in classes and rehearsals, with a short break for a light snack before the show. As show time approached, Gina sat down for the long session in front of the mirror to create her fantastical make-up. The glittering result looked more like a carnival mask than a real face, with huge eyes and a scarlet mouth. At least getting into her costume was simple and quick: a flesh-colored unitard sewn with red silk ribbons, twining around her limbs and torso. Its hood, decorated with ribbon ringlets, covered her hair. She was ready. At the five-minute call, Gina headed for the stage.

The Sydney tent wasn't a true Big Top, with a circus ring in the center and the audience ranged around it. Instead, it had a stage with a proscenium arch, and the audience out front, like a conventional theatre. Gina preferred it. She found performing in the round difficult, never quite knowing where to direct her energy.

Limbering in the wings, she waved at the puppeteers on the other side of the stage, readying the elephant. In her head, Gina knew Sanook was just a life-size puppet, made of nothing but sackcloth on a spindly aluminum skeleton, driven by stilt walkers. But to see him lumbering around, lowering his great head and offering his trunk, was to believe Sanook was one hundred per cent a living, breathing elephant. She adored him.

The music for *The Three Sisters* began. With Francesca and Grazia behind her, Gina cartwheeled out to the center of the stage. Three pairs of red silk ribbons hung from the gantry, long enough to reach the stage. Each woman grabbed a pair and backflipped into a sitting position. For this routine, the silks had to be lifted by a mechanism, to clear the floor for the elephant to make his entrance.

As she rose, Gina took a moment to scan the audience, a blur of faces beyond the glare of the lights, before shifting her focus to the silks. Suspended high above the stage, she twirled in a series of long, slow movements, wrapping herself in the silken fabric. The music reached a high note and she spun into a fast unroll. As she braked sharply to hit the final pose, she heard a metallic clunk. The sudden stop always jarred, but this time, she had felt a fractional drop. Or had she?

She peered above her head, but the gantry was lost in the gloom. If the silks had torn or a carabiner had come loose, she was in danger. Equally, she could be imagining things. The equipment had been checked thoroughly this morning. If she called for help, she would ruin the performance.

Better safe than sorry, she abandoned the choreography, inching down the length of the silks, making graceful movements so the audience would see nothing amiss. From the corner of her eye, she caught Francesca frowning at her, and gave a small, "don't worry" shake of her head.

She had almost decided it was a false alarm, when she felt herself drop again, this time with an audible cracking sound above her head. She opened her mouth to call for help, but there was another crack, and she was falling, the silks in a flutter around her, flapping across her eyes.

She expected to fall through space, but instead something soft and feathery whipped past her cheek, her hand touched velvet, then there was a cacophony of crackling and ripping as she was enveloped in a confusion of sharp spikes and rough material. She collided with someone, and they fell to the floor together with a thud.

Pushing herself up on one arm, Gina unwrapped the silk from her face and saw the puppeteer lying beneath her. "Oh, I'm so sorry!"

She tried to scramble off him but her feet were entangled and there was something pressing on her back. "Hey, take it easy, you'll hurt yourself," he said, putting a restraining hand on her shoulder. "Let them get this shit off us first."

All at once, the chaos of the last few seconds came into focus. The pink feather, the red velvet cap, the great hessian-and-aluminum head: poor Sanook had broken her fall, and now she was lying in his wreckage. She closed her eyes and laid her head on the puppeteer's chest, grateful to be alive.

The stagehands were always so careful. Every piece of equipment had been checked and rechecked. How on earth could this have happened?

****

Emerging from the TV studios, Alex smiled for the cameras, most of which were focused on Summer. She flipped her long blonde hair and lifted the fur collar of her jacket to frame her face. The warmth of her smile didn't reach her eyes, though. He would never understand why a twenty-one-year-old needed to freeze her face with injections, especially one with the natural beauty of Summer Leigh, "the new Australian singing sensation."

Everything felt wrong. He took Summer's elbow to shepherd her through the photographers, curbing his urge to rush. Unlike him, she relished their attention. She took her time climbing into the back of the studio's limo, making sure to show plenty of leg. He closed the door and hurried to get in the other side.

The car pulled into the light traffic. Summer unbuttoned her fur coat. "That took forever. I can't be fucked going to dinner. I might just get room service."

Alex frowned a warning, tipping his head towards the driver. "Come on, *darling*, you wanted to eat at Catalina's and you know how exclusive they are. If we're a no-show tonight, you may not get another chance."

"They'll make an exception for me." She sighed. "But I guess you're right. Can't let the papps down."

So she had tipped off the paparazzi. Alex stifled a groan.

The role as the dance judge on the TV show *Triple Threat* had seemed like a good opportunity. Make an impression on this one, Anthony said, and there were hundreds of other similar shows around the world in need of judges. It could be the start of a new career.

When the producers had wanted to spread rumors of a romance between him and singing judge Summer, he had gone along with it. A high-profile new relationship was exactly what he needed to convince Nick that Gina was no longer important to him. Luckily, Summer was no more interested in a real romance than he was, so there was no risk of complications. But he had forgotten how much he hated playing the celebrity.

In his old life, the hoopla of fame had been bearable, because all the tedious photo opportunities and celebrity gigs served their purpose. Back then, he'd enthusiastically pursued anything that would further his dance career because that had always mattered to him more than anything. He had politely tolerated all the rest, recognizing—with an occasional nag from Monika—the need to build a nest egg for his eventual retirement. Now, he had no dance career to promote, and since the sale of the island, he had no burning need for a high income, either. Life as a reality TV judge, all show and no substance, did not appeal.

The limousine turned onto the freeway approach. In the evening traffic, the trip into Central London could easily take an hour. Alex sighed and closed his eyes, pretending to doze. He was in no mood for small talk. His phone broke the silence. He pulled it from his pocket and answered.

"Hello?" A woman's voice, hesitant. "Am I speaking to Alexander Korolev?"

"Yes. Who is this?"

"You don't know me. My name is Mariella Tarasco. I'm Gina's mother."

Alex sat upright, all of his attention focused on this

lone woman. "What has happened?"

"She's fine, don't worry. She had an accident, but she's not seriously hurt. In fact, she asked me not to call you, but I disagree with her."

"Please, go on."

"Someone tampered with the fixing bolts that hold the carabiners—"

"I'm sorry, I don't understand what you are saying."

"Didn't you ever see her perform?" the woman asked. "She does aerial silks—acrobatics on long pieces of silk, suspended above the stage. Someone tampered with the bolts holding the silks. They gave way in the middle of her performance, and she fell."

"*She fell…?*" He couldn't keep the panic from his voice.

"My Gina's fine, really. She didn't fall too far and landed on the elephant. She has a sore back, a broken finger and a heap of superficial cuts from the skeleton, but nothing serious."

Silks, elephants, skeletons—Alex couldn't make sense of it, but he clung to the fact that Gina was not badly hurt.

"Anyway, Mr. Korolev, I'm ringing you because we think it must have been your brother who sabotaged the clamp."

"*What?*"

"There was an electrician working at the theatre that day, but he wasn't who he said he was. The police found the real electrician, tied up in the back of his van. The man who took his place was blond, with a strong accent," she said. "Anyway, we can't think of anyone else who'd want to harm her."

Nick didn't want to harm her either, or at least that's what he had said to Alex. Clearly, he had changed his mind. "Thank you for telling me, Mrs. Tarasco."

"It's Ms., but call me Mariella, please."

"Mariella. Tell Gina I'll be there as soon as I can get a flight."

"Oh, I'm so pleased to hear it!" She paused. "But I won't tell her if you don't mind. If I do, she'll only ring you and tell you not to come, she's so determined not to worry you. But I know she really wants you here."

Alex wanted to believe that, but if that was the case, why was she so against the idea? He would deal with that later. His priority was to get to Australia on the very next flight available.

"I'll text you her address," Mariella continued. "If you turn up on her doorstep, she can hardly turn you away. I'll make sure she's there to meet you, one way or another."

"Thank you. I'll let you know my arrival time as soon as the flight is booked."

"What's all this about flights?" Summer demanded as soon as he hung up.

"You get your wish," he said. "Dinner is off. I have to catch a plane."

Chapter Twenty-Seven

It was almost ten in the evening by the time Alex paid off the taxi outside Gina's apartment block, a 1920s era structure with round-edged balconies and an imposing portico. Half an hour ago, wearily checking in at the hotel after his twenty-four-hour flight, he had contemplated waiting till morning to see Gina—but no. He couldn't wait.

There was no security on the double front doors. He pushed through them, entering a short, beige lobby with a high ceiling, but poor lighting. Her door, number four, was at the far end of the corridor. He pressed a button that might have been a doorbell, but nothing happened. After a moment, he rapped on the door with his cane.

Gina opened it. She was hiding inside a loose sweater and brightly patterned harem pants, but he didn't have to see her body to picture it. Clothes couldn't hide her beautiful eyes, or the tangle of curls that he wanted to run his fingers through—but her expression wasn't welcoming.

"Alex? What are you doing here?"

"Your mother rang me."

Gina huffed, frowning, and moved aside. "You'd better come in, then."

He stepped across the threshold and stiffened as a man stood up from the velvet sofa in the middle of the living room. Tall and slender, showing off his dark tan and six-pack abs in nothing but a pair of tight jeans. Perhaps this was the reason Gina didn't want him here. It hadn't occurred to Alex that she'd have a boyfriend. God, he looked about eighteen.

"Alex, meet my brother, Matt. I didn't want to be on my own after what just happened, so he's been staying with me."

Alex let his breath out and grinned with relief as Matt came forward to shake hands. "Welcome to Australia," he said. "Jeez, you look just like your posters."

"Er—?"

"Gina had posters of you plastered all over her bedroom at home."

"Matt!" Her face went a delicate shade of pink, then her eyes narrowed. "Did you know about this?"

A lopsided smile spread across his face. "Yeah, Mum told me. Anyhow, Alex is here now, so I can get moving."

"What?"

"The boys are waiting for me at the pub," he said, his voice muffled as he tugged a rugby shirt over his head. He buttoned the collar and pulled a business card from his jeans. "Gina's told me why you're here. If you need some help catching this bastard—sorry, he's your brother, I mean—"

"No need to apologize, you are right, I'm afraid."

"If you need any help, ring. If me and Tommo can help, we'll be happy to."

Alex pocketed the card. "Thank you."

Gina followed Matt to the door. "So when can I expect you back?"

"Told ya, I done my bit. It's Alex's job now. I'll be off home after the pub." With a peck on her cheek, he opened the door, stepped through it, then turned back. "I'll pick up my stuff tomorrow. *Ciao*."

"Matt, wait, I—!"

He walked out the door. Gina stared after him for a moment, then turned her glare on Alex.

His jet-lagged brain was still catching up. She needed someone to stay with her, and Matt had just dumped that responsibility onto him. He was happy to take it on—but he could see Gina wasn't so pleased. He opened his arms. "I knew nothing about this."

She was silent.

"Your mother asked me to come, and I'm here. I had no knowledge of what they had planned. In fact, I've booked into a hotel. You'll notice I have no luggage."

Her expression changed. Doubt, rather than anger. Encouraged, he pressed on. "Matt is right, though. If Nick is around, you shouldn't be alone. I'll crash on your sofa just as I am. I'm so tired, I could sleep anywhere."

Gina pursed her lips, then sighed. "You don't need to do that. There's a spare bedroom. I'll get fresh sheets."

He stepped forward and put a hand on her arm. "Let me do it. I can look after myself."

She jumped back as if she'd been stung. "I don't know what good you think you'll do here. The police reckon they've got no chance of finding Nick. What makes you think you can do any better?"

For a split second, he considered giving up. He had misjudged Gina's feelings—she didn't want him here.

But he hadn't traveled over fifteen thousand kilometers to walk away.

"I can only try. But that's not why I came." He set his jaw. He was probably about to make a fool of himself, but he had no alternative. "I love you. Now, just as much as ever. After Nick kidnapped you, I gave up all hope of being with you, because I believed it was the only way to keep you safe. Now I know that Nick wants to harm you whether you are with me or not."

He looked up into her still wary face. "Do you not see?" he asked. "Nick is a danger, but he is not an obstacle any longer. We can be together. We can face him together."

She folded her arms. "What about Summer?"

"Summer?" Alex laughed. "She is a manufactured romance. It's part of the show. Reality television. I agreed to it because I thought, if Nick was watching me, he would see it as proof that I had moved on."

She relaxed her arms a little, massaging her forearms, but she still didn't speak.

"In London, you seemed—I thought—perhaps I misunderstood how you felt—" He ran a hand through his hair, unable to find any more words. At least he had booked the hotel. He would have somewhere to go when she asked him to leave.

Time to get himself back under control. He closed his eyes and took a deep breath.

"Alex."

He opened his eyes.

She stepped close in front of him, one hand on his chest. "You didn't misunderstand how I felt."

The kiss was just as he remembered it from that precious moment in the studio, except that she did not break away. Her lips opened. Her tongue met his. Desire flooded through him and he wrapped his arms around her to pull her closer.

A muffled scream and her whole body tensed. He released her at once, stepping back. "What's wrong?"

"I'm sorry." She clutched her lower back, her face twisting in pain. "I hurt my back when I fell. It's all been x-rayed, it's nothing serious. You just caught me at the wrong angle. I'll be fine in a minute."

"Let me." He placed his hand where hers had rested and massaged her back gently through the harem pants.

"Ooh, that feels good."

"A proper massage would help." Alex paused, all too aware what his proposal meant. To lay hands on her naked flesh, and do no more than massage her, would be an exquisite torture. But she was in pain. "If you would feel comfortable."

Her long silence suggested she was considering the implications, too. Eventually, she spoke. "That would be nice."

He took a step towards the sofa. "I'll need some towels—"

"No, not here. I can't risk getting oil on that velvet." She bit her lip, then reached out for his hand. "Come on."

****

Gina led Alex through her bedroom into the *ensuite* bathroom and pointed to a slat-fronted cupboard. "You'll find more towels in there."

She picked up a towel from the rail, selected a bottle of massage oil from the shelf above the sink, and left.

In the bedroom, she folded back the quilt, spread the towel over the sheet, and lay down on her stomach. She hitched her top high around her shoulders and wriggled her pants low on her hips, to expose her back. She wore nothing else, so she didn't need to undress. Not for the massage, anyway.

His footsteps entered the room. She turned her head to watch him as he placed the towels on the edge of the bed, set his cane against the dresser and took off his coat.

Things were moving so fast, Gina almost felt dizzy. If she counted up the days, she and Alex had known each other for less than two weeks. What's more, he had walked through her door only five minutes ago and hadn't even had a chance to take his coat off. Yet she had never felt more certain that she was ready to make love to a man. And she was positive, even though he had only offered a massage, that sex was in Alex's mind, too. She lowered her head to the pillow.

"I'll have to kneel on the bed, so I need to remove my brace first," he said. The edge of the bed dipped, and she heard the click of the brace fastenings. Then a rustle as he changed position, and an exclamation. "My God! All these cuts!"

"Oh, they're nothing. They're healing already. When I fell, I landed on an elephant puppet. It had a metal skeleton. They're fine, honestly."

"If you're sure…"

She squealed as the cold oil plopped on the small of her back.

"Sorry," he said. "I should have warmed that up."

His hand was warm as it spread the oil. The smell

of orange blossom and hyacinth filled her nostrils. She had never noticed its perfume was so sensual.

It was her lower back that needed attention, but Alex worked on her upper back and shoulder blades first, his hands sliding under her top to reach her neck, steadily and firmly driving out her tension.

He took his hands away. She stirred to look around, but he hushed her and she let her head fall again, breathing deeply to inhale the delicate perfume.

"I'm going to massage your lower back now," he said softly, and she felt him tug the pants even lower, then his fingers grazing the top of her buttocks as he tucked a towel into the waistband. "Is that okay?"

"Fine," she squeaked.

This time he must have warmed the oil in his palms. His moist hands slid smoothly over her skin. Strong thumbs went to work on the indentations of her lower back, his fingers curving around her hip bones. "I need to come around behind you. I can't get the right angle."

She felt totally relaxed, limbs warm and heavy, eyes sleepy. The mattress sagged as he moved behind her, then in an instant she was awake and alert again, as she felt his leg nestle against her thigh. Both his hands, slick with warmed oil, pressed flat on her lower back and began a steady journey along her spine, up and down, with a firm pressure that slowly banished every trace of tension. The rhythmic strokes continued, becoming hypnotic. She felt her body melting into the mattress.

His hands became hotter, radiating warmth into her back. He worked the pads of his thumbs into her lower back again, and she found herself wishing that his fingers would curve a little further round her hips. The thumbs traveled up to her shoulders, his hands still curving around her sides. His fingers were so close to touching the edge of her breasts. She wished he would. Just brush them, gently.

His hands left her back. She was too lazy to move, or even to open her eyes. A moment later, she was covered in something soft and he was pressing it gently over her. She opened a drowsy eye and saw the corner of the towel in her line of vision. He lifted it away.

"Get some sleep," he said, swinging around to sit on the edge of the bed and reached for his leg brace.

She rose up on one elbow. "Don't go."

He knew what she meant. She could see it in his face. "You're injured. I don't want to hurt you."

She rolled to her back. "You won't hurt me."

She saw the flare of desire in his face, then he was in her arms, his mouth finding hers with a raw hunger that would have frightened her if she hadn't been instantly swept up in the same overwhelming need. His lips frantically traversed her eyelids, her cheeks, her chin, the hollow of her neck. He lifted her top and closed his lips around her nipple. She moaned at the tremors it sent down to the pit of her stomach.

At the sound, he lifted his head to read her face. "Are you sure you want this?"

"Yes."

The look he gave her was almost one of anguish and he seemed about to say something, but instead he closed his eyes and kissed her mouth again, his hands caressing her breast, sending lightning bolts through her every time his fingers brushed her nipple. She tried to take off his shirt, but it was hard to concentrate on undoing his buttons. Her fingers froze as his hand slipped inside her pants. The shirt forgotten, she let her arms flop on the bed, her body dissolving into a puddle of ecstasy. He hooked his thumbs into her pants and slid them down, kissing his way down her body as he did so. His lips tickled as they brushed her stomach. Surely he wasn't going to—

She gasped as his tongue sent liquid fire through her veins. She reached down for him as she arched in pleasure, threading her fingers through his hair. Too much, too much! The need to have him inside her was more intense than anything she had ever known. She tightened her grip on his hair and hauled his head up from between her thighs. His eyes came level with hers and she reached for the buckle of his pants. She could taste herself on his mouth.

When he looked up at her again, the tenderness of his gaze made her heart turn over. "Stay there," he whispered, and she obeyed, lying still on her back while he shrugged off his clothes. For the first time, she saw his legs without the fixators, horribly scarred below the knee.

She reached out, and he moved to stop her. "Be careful. Your back."

He lowered himself on top of her and kissed her again, his tongue deep and demanding. Eventually, he lifted his head and looked into her eyes. "Tell me," he said, his voice thick, "I'll stop now if you have any doubts."

She lifted her head and kissed his mouth and he pressed down on her eagerly in response. She closed her eyes and tilted her pelvis towards him, willing him to thrust into her, needing him to penetrate to the hilt and relieve the intolerable pressure building inside her. Finally, finally he understood that she was ready, he didn't have to be gentle anymore. She cried out as she felt his length filling her, possessing her, and then she was lost in a swirling, convulsing orgasm that obliterated every coherent thought.

Chapter Twenty-Eight

Gina licked a trail of melting ice cream from her hand, then frowned at Alex's grinning face. "What?"

"You look like a ten-year-old with that huge cone."

Gina pouted. "We're all allowed to express our inner child sometimes."

"Of course." He put his arm around her, bringing her head to his shoulder. "But it is winter, you know."

Gina waved at the bright sun and blue sky with her cone. "You call this winter? It's ice-cream weather all year round here."

They continued their walk on the broad promenade along the beachfront, under the pines. She was exaggerating the weather, a little. Alex wore his pea coat, unbuttoned, and she had pulled on a lightweight fleece over her jeans and blouse. Only a few intrepid souls braved the cool water to swim. But a morning in bed with Alex, the ice cream matched her mood.

They had got up, briefly, to make coffee and toast, which they'd taken back to bed—but most of the breakfast had been left uneaten. Now, she felt pleasantly spent, loose-limbed, a little sore but above all else, blissfully happy.

Raspberry-Ripple-ice-cream-happy.

"We have to talk about Nick," Alex said.

"It's such a gorgeous day, let's not spoil it."

"We can't afford to delay. You are at risk. Now

I'm here, perhaps I'm at risk." He stopped and looked at her, his expression serious. "We need bodyguards."

"That's a bit extreme, isn't it?"

"I don't think so. He has already proved he can be violent. We don't have the choice here to carry a gun or a weapon to defend ourselves—" Alex side-stepped to avoid a boy on roller blades.

"I wouldn't anyway."

"I would not expect you to. But we have to protect ourselves somehow. For the short term, at least, while we decide what we will do for our future."

Our future.

She wanted to feel thrilled that he was so sure of their relationship, but his certainty troubled her too. She felt as though she was losing control of her life. Here they were, on the way to the hotel to pick up his suitcase, but she hadn't actually invited him to stay with her. Her mother and Matt had decided he should move in and Alex had gone along with it. No one had asked her what she wanted. She didn't object, exactly—but it was her home. It should have been her decision.

"When do you have to get back to London?"

"I don't. I have pulled out of *Triple Threat*, and I have no other firm bookings. I will stay as long as it takes."

I will stay. Not, "Can I stay as long as it takes?" The decision out of her hands, again.

"What's wrong, Gina?"

She didn't know how to explain it. Her expression must have given her away because Alex stopped and put a hand on her arm to stop her, too. Something brushed her leg—a poodle. Its owner, walking on the path behind them, looked down her nose and tugged on the dog's lead to skirt around them.

"Let's get out of the way," Alex said. "There's a seat here. Careful of your ice cream."

The arm of her jacket was dripping with raspberry trails. She gave the cone to Alex—"Here, you eat the rest"—and mopped at her jacket with a tissue as they sat on the wooden bench.

Alex took one lick at the ice cream and dumped it in the rubbish bin next to the bench. "Something is wrong, Gina. Tell me."

"I'm so pleased you're here, Alex, I really am. It's just…" She hugged herself. Her feelings were contradictory, and she wasn't sure she could explain them. "I love having you with me but—" She tried again. "Moving in together—it's a big step. It should be something we've thought about and discussed beforehand, not just an accident of circumstances, like this. I feel—I feel a bit railroaded. I mean, we've never even been on a proper date…"

"Is that how you see it?" He sat back, staring out to sea for a long moment, before turning to her again, his face serious. "It did not occur to me. I didn't mean to railroad you. To be honest, I am not sure what that word means. In this moment, all I'm trying to do is keep you safe, and enjoy every moment I have with you, because I can be here for such a short time."

"I thought you said you didn't need to go back?"

"No. But I have a tourist visa. In three months, I must go home, whatever happens."

She had forgotten about Australia's strict immigration system. "I don't suppose there's much chance of you getting a longer visa?"

Alex shook his head. "If one of the Australian

dance companies will hire me for a project, perhaps. But that will take months to arrange."

She laughed. "I'm not making much sense, am I? One minute I'm complaining because I think you're moving in for good, next minute I'm upset because you're going to leave."

"I understand, I think. I feel as though we've known each other so long, but it's not true."

She leaned into him. "I know what my mother would say. We love each other, but that's not enough. Now we need to get to know each other."

"Then we will take her advice. We have three months. And I promise to take you on a proper date tonight."

Chapter Twenty-Nine

Alex sat back in the spindly chair to let a waiter remove his plate. His ears rang from the loud music, but at least the steak had been tender. The waiter leaned close to take his order for a "long black," as Alex had learned to call coffee here.

He'd left Gina at the Hilton only an hour ago, and already he missed her. For the last six days, they had spent almost every minute together, many of them in bed, on the sofa, in the shower…the wonder of her body was inexhaustible. He hoped he satisfied her as completely as she satisfied him—but he knew she was unhappy in other ways. She felt embarrassed and annoyed by the constant presence of their bodyguards and frustrated at being unable to go back to work. A broken finger was such a small thing, and yet it would prevent her performing for at least five more weeks.

Tonight's party should lift her spirits. He had fretted at the idea of her out on the town, but Gina was determined to live a normal life, Nick or no Nick, and he had to respect that. The security firm had provided two female bodyguards, dressed appropriately to blend in with the guests at the event, a hen party for Gina's cousin Bettina.

Alex had decided to have his own night out, too. Not because he craved excitement, but because it would give him a chance to look for Nick. He knew his chances of success were poor, but he needed to feel he was making some contribution. The private investigators had achieved nothing.

The waiter brought the bill with his coffee, and Alex offered his credit card. Unusually for Sydney, the brew was bitter and undrinkable. He pushed back his chair and began making his way through the crowded tables. From the corner of his eye, he saw his bodyguard, Bob, rise from his table.

Out on Darlinghurst Road, the crowds were already milling, although it was only nine. Outside every strip joint, peep show and night club stood a nattily-dressed man called a *spruiker*—another word Alex had learned from Gina. The spruiker's job was to accost passers-by and entice them to come into their establishment. Alex needed no enticing. These were exactly the kind of places he might find Nick.

The first strip club was in a basement, down a flight of dimly lit, red-carpeted stairs. Inside, the walls were black and the lighting low, except on the stage where two women gyrated halfheartedly in G-strings and nothing else.

He bought a stupidly expensive drink and sat down, as if to watch the show—but his eyes were scanning the patrons. Bob had settled on the other side of the central runway. No sign of his brother.

Alex sighed. He was wasting his time and Bob's. But the alternative was to sit in the apartment and worry. If only there was more he could do. He had already sent a message to the *mafiya* number—not to ask for help, but to let the old man know Nick was in Sydney.

A reply came back, from a different number.

"Thank you. We have no representation currently in Australia but will endeavor to address this matter in due course." Alex took this to mean that although they wanted to catch Nick, they were in no hurry.

A woman in fragments of pink lace shimmied in front of him. He shook his head, she shrugged and moved on. Another woman, almost dressed in something black and shiny, took her place.

He'd had enough. Draining his drink, he stood and left the club, slowing just enough to be sure Bob was following him.

Another basement, another club. Pole dancers this time, but the drinks were just as expensive and the hostesses just as persistent. The next place had both male and female performers on stage, doing things Alex would not have expected to be legal. But knowing it might appeal to Nick, he forced himself to linger for longer.

A couple of hours later, Alex stepped out of yet another club into a downpour—huge droplets that bounced off the concrete and created rivers in the gutters. For a city famed for its blue skies and sun-kissed beaches, Sydney seemed to have more than a reasonable share of rain. The inky-black skies and growling thunder echoed Alex's mood.

He turned to see Bob behind him and beckoned. They might as well drop all pretense and travel together—getting one taxi would be difficult enough tonight, let alone two.

Finally, they managed to grab a taxi dropping someone off. The driver refused to take them at first, saying he couldn't drive as far as Manly because it was the end of his shift, but he agreed to take them as far as

Circular Quay in time for the last ferry.

Waiting under the canopy on the Quay, Alex watched lightning arc across the sky, and hoped the storm wouldn't get worse. If they canceled the ferry due to bad weather, it would be impossible to find another taxi on a night like this. At least Gina wouldn't have to battle the weather—she was staying the night at Bettina's.

The ship docked, a few passengers trooped off, and Alex and Bob boarded. An older woman, slender, with scarlet lipstick and the dress sense of a teenager, simpered at Alex as he entered the cabin. He found a seat on the far side, by the window. Bob went to check out the rest of the boat.

A few more passengers trickled on board, most heading for the cabin on the upper deck. Finally, the engines rumbled and the ferry plowed through the sea, already white-capped even in the shelter of the Harbor. It would be rough at the Heads, but at least the rain had eased off.

Bob returned. They sat together in silence, Alex preoccupied with thoughts of Gina. There was a strange "whuff" of sound outside and all the windows rattled as the ferry lurched.

"Sounds like the wind's getting up," Bob said.

Inside the cabin, the air was stuffy. The ship began to pitch and roll in earnest. Bob, looking pale, excused himself to go to the bathroom. Feeling a little queasy himself, Alex got up and slid open the door to get some fresh air. The chilly blast felt welcome after the fug of the cabin.

"Sasha."

Nick stood on the narrow walkway along the side

of the ship, towards the bow. Alex stepped out. Instinct prompted him to reach for the rail to steady his balance, but that would mean swapping his cane to his left hand. He looked at the dark shape in front of him, grasped a hook on the wall instead, and shifted his hold on the walking stick to an overhand grip.

"You cannot have bodyguards forever," Nick said in Russian. "You cannot keep your precious tart safe."

The boat slammed into a wave and sea spray showered over them.

After gaining his balance, Alex demanded, "What's your proposal?"

"If you want me to leave her alone, I need money to start a new life somewhere else. You have sold the island now, I think. A million will do. Do not try to trick me this time."

The figure stung Alex into anger. "Do you really expect me to just hand over that kind of money? What will you do, blow it all on drugs? Then if you don't kill yourself, you'll be back for more."

He cursed himself at once for losing his temper. Advancing on him, Nick launched into a torrent of Russian insults, finger jabbing the air. The heaving motion of the boat made him sway from side to side. "You think I can't handle money. You treat me like a child, you always did. Tell you what, forget it. I've had enough of you and your lectures. You and that little whore. I'll finish both of you."

Nick thrust his hand in his pocket and brought out a knife, flicking the blade open with his thumb. Alex lashed out at the knife with his stick, but Nick jumped back, holding it high out of reach. At that moment, a huge wave crashed onto the walkway, knocking the knife from his hand and slamming him against the wall of the cabin.

Alex kicked at the knife. It spun across the walkway and under the rail, into the water—but if he'd hoped Nick would give up now he was disarmed, he was wrong. Nick lunged, hands reaching for Alex's throat. Alex dodged aside as a wave surged high above their heads and dumped onto the walkway, soaking them both.

"Hey!"

Bob stood in the doorway. He broke into a run, ignoring Alex. Nick was scrambling up the steps to the bow deck, Bob close behind. Alex followed. The ship was bucking, a violent see-saw motion. The stairs were at a crazy angle, the bow high out of the water. Alex had to use the railings to haul himself up.

He stepped onto the steeply angled deck and felt the world tilt. The bow was beginning its downward plunge into the next trough. Ahead of him, Bob felt it too, and he moved back to grab a rail. Nick was standing at the very front of the ship, facing them.

"Hang on, Nick!" Alex yelled, but his words were whipped away by the wind.

The hull hit the water. The impact would have sent Alex flying if he hadn't hooked his arm around the rail. The bow disappeared. Waves towered over the prow and crashed onto the deck, drenching him. He couldn't see Nick and prayed he'd had the sense to hold on.

Alex felt the change in angle under his feet. The water drained from the deck. Nick was not where he had been standing.

"Man overboard!"

Bob's yell made Alex jump. At Bob's urging, he

made his way back to the cabin, his feet slipping on the wet deck. As they entered the cabin, the woman came forward to offer help, but Bob waved her away. Crew members appeared and there was a flurry of activity.

Bob had disappeared. Alex couldn't sit quietly. He stepped out on the deck again. The rain had returned, pelting into his face and stinging his eyes as he peered out over the roiling sea. He frowned. Why was the ferry still moving?

Alex caught the arm of a passing crew member. "Why have we not stopped? To search for the missing man?"

"The weather's deteriorating fast. The Captain has to consider the passengers. We have to get them safely into port before conditions get too dangerous. The police launches are on their way and they're much better equipped than we are."

Before Alex could protest, a wave smashed over the guardrail, soaking them both. The crewman gave him a "see what I mean?" shrug. "I have to ask you to step inside, sir. No passengers allowed on deck in this weather."

Reluctantly, Alex returned to the cabin, slicking his wet hair off his face. His shoes squelched and water dripped from the hem of his coat, but he scarcely noticed. Nick was gone, no longer a threat. The joy of relief—Gina is safe!—clashed with a sharp sense of loss.

He snorted. What loss? He had lost his baby brother twenty years ago, the day of his parents' funeral, when he'd watched Nick being led away. The brother who'd been "returned" to him as a teenager, although recognizable on the outside, had changed beyond all recognition. Traumatized by his years on the street and corrupted by the mafiya, Alex had simply refused to see it.

If only their parents had lived. It would have made little difference to Alex—his future had been sealed the moment his mother enrolled him in ballet school. He would have had a treasure trove of memories of holidays with family, but very likely he would still be where he was today. He might have been more likely to stay in Russia...but no. The lure of overseas fame would have been too great, and he would have put career before family, just as he had with every other relationship in his life.

Until Gina. Thank God for her.

The ship jolted and the engine note changed. They must be close to docking. Alex stood up, feeling suddenly exhausted, and made his way to the exit.

Bob stood waiting for him on the quay. They were about to pass through the turnstiles when there was a shout from the ferry. "Call an ambulance!"

Alex and Bob exchanged glances, then Bob launched into a sprint back to the ship, Alex following. A few passengers hovered on the quayside, drawn by the commotion. Alex shouldered past them, until a crewman barred his way onto the bow section.

"What's happened?" Alex asked, trying to see around the man's bulk.

"They found the guy. He didn't go overboard. Hey, you can't—!"

Alex had shoved him in the chest and barreled past him. Another crew member stepped forward, but Alex held up his palm shouting, "Please, I'm his brother."

He reached the row of molded plastic seats that ran

across the bow, bolted to the deck. Something lay in the deep shadow under the seats.

As he moved closer, a uniformed man with a peaked cap intervened. "I'm sorry sir, he's gone. There's nothing you can do for him. It might be better if you stay back."

Alex couldn't speak, but his expression must have said enough to make the man step back. He knelt on the deck, dipping his head below the level of the seats.

He might have believed Nick had simply hidden here and gone to sleep: his eyes were closed, and his arms and legs were curled into a fetal position to keep warm on such a cold night. But the mass of crusted blood in his matted hair, and the black pool under his head, told a different story. He must have been knocked over by the wave, then smashed his head against one of the wrought-iron seat legs. He had bled to death while Alex sat inside the cabin, only a few meters away.

Alex reached out a hand.

"Best not to touch the body, please, sir," said a voice behind him. "Police and ambulance are on their way."

Alex let his hand drop. "Oh, Kolya," he whispered, in Russian. "I thought I'd done my best to look after you. I got it so wrong. I am sorry."

"Sir."

The official hovered at his shoulder. Alex sniffed, took a deep breath and wiped a hand over his face as he got to his feet.

Bob waited for him by the railing. "We'll have to wait for the police. They'll want to talk to us."

Alex nodded, only half-listening, his eyes still drawn to the dark shape under the seats.

"I've called the girls and told them they can stand down," Bob continued. "Miss Tarasco's asleep. Would you like one of them to wake her and tell her the news before they go?"

At Gina's name, Alex's head snapped round, giving Bob his full attention. "Uh...no. No. I'll tell her myself when she gets home."

He pictured himself in a few hours' time, telling Gina what had happened. That irresistible smile on her face when she realized what the news meant for her future. No more shadows hanging over her.

He would always mourn the loss of his brother, but for Gina's sake, he would be glad.

Epilogue

Six months later

If she hadn't spent most of the day gawking at the palaces of St Petersburg, Gina might have been impressed by the foyer of the Maryinsky Theater. As it was, she took in the wedding-cake interior at a glance and began searching the crowd. If this were Covent Garden, she'd be sure to spy some well-known dancers. Not that she knew many famous Russians by sight, but it didn't hurt to look.

She didn't expect to see a familiar face.

"Alex!" She almost knocked over an usher in her headlong dash to grab him. "What are you doing here? I didn't expect you till tomorrow! "

He enfolded her in a bear hug, lifting her off her feet. "Filming finished early, so I was able to catch an earlier flight."

She surrendered to his kiss, relishing the feeling of his arms crushing her against him. When they surfaced, he looked over her shoulder, one eyebrow raised. Following his gaze, she remembered her three companions.

"Sorry," she said. "I'm here with a tour group from the cruise ship. This is Deborah, Nancy and Marylou. Ladies, this is my fiancé, Alex."

Marylou's plump face dimpled in a smile. "We

kinda worked that out."

Marylou seemed about to say more, but Nancy plucked at the sleeve of her faux fur jacket. At least, Gina hoped it was fake.

"Now, Marylou, I'm sure these two want some time together," Nancy said. "We should find the cloakroom right now in case there's a line. The tour guide said they won't let us take our coats in."

"It's that way," Alex said, pointing. He waited until they had moved off. "Did we shock them, do you think?"

"No. They may be little old ladies, but they have a racy sense of humor. You should have seen them checking out the nude statues at the Hermitage." She looked into his eyes and forgot her companions. "Gosh, I've missed you. How did you know I'd be here?"

"Because you told me about it in every phone call for the last three weeks." He stroked her cheek. "Has it only been three weeks? How are we going to survive a whole year like this?"

A hot wave of guilt washed over her. "I should have taken the London gig. I—"

"Ssshhh." He placed a finger on her lips. "I was joking. Don't even think it. Your career is precious. You must make the most of it while it lasts. They offered you a promotion, you took it. It was the right thing to do."

Gina managed a smile, but she wasn't convinced. Yes, she loved her job. But if it meant not seeing Alex for weeks on end, was it worth the price? Of course she'd considered it when she accepted the contract, but the reality was so much harder than she had imagined.

He had one hand on the lapel of her puffer jacket.

"Here, let me take your coat."

She took a step back. "I can do that. Or—" She looked him up and down, finally noticing that he wasn't wearing an overcoat. "Don't tell me you got a ticket! How did you manage it?"

"I still have friends here. Our seats are this way." He took her arm and began to steer her towards a doorway.

"Wait, I have to tell the others. And I have to leave my coat—"

"All taken care of. Give me your ticket."

Gina found her ticket and shrugged off her coat as they walked and gave them to Alex. He handed them over to an usher at the bottom of the stairs. Gina had no idea what they said, but the usher seemed to know Alex, and greeted him warmly.

After the flamboyance of the foyer, the staircase and tiled corridors above were surprisingly plain, more like a Victorian hospital than a theatre. Their starkness left her unprepared for the vision that unfolded before her as she stepped into the auditorium.

She had expected a vast, grand space, but she had assumed it would be covered in rich, glowing, garnet red, like the Royal Opera House or the New York State. The Maryinsky sparkled with whites and creams and golds. And what a view of it she had. Their seats were in a box in the middle of one of the circles, directly opposite the stage, with the whole theatre laid out beneath them.

"You have influential friends," she said as they sat down. "These must be the best seats in the house."

"They are, but they're not so hard to get. This is the Tsar's box. They always hold these tickets until a few days before the performance in case a politician or a diplomat decides to visit at short notice. On Monday, I saw the filming was ahead of schedule, so I called a friend and asked him to watch the box office for me."

Gina snuggled into his arm as she watched the auditorium fill with people. A family filed into the box and settled themselves into the seats behind them. The sounds of the theatre coming to life became steadily louder—the creaks and groans of the wooden chairs, the shuffle of feet, the riffle of pages as people consulted their programs, the buzz of conversation, the occasional chord from a violin or toot from a clarinet as the orchestra warmed up.

"I meant what I said, earlier," he said, his lips close to her ear. "I've told Anthony I won't be accepting any more offers. No more TV, no more ballet."

"Gosh, he must be devastated." She could guess what he was thinking. "You're still thinking about the winery idea, aren't you?"

"Do you think it's foolish?"

"No. I'm worried you're choosing it for the wrong reasons." She lifted her hand to count the reasons on her fingers. "You're worried about how we'll see each other if we're both constantly traveling the world for work. And you know, I'd like us to make our home in Australia at some point. So you're choosing a new career that will let you stay in one place, and something you can do in Australia. I'd much rather you choose something you love doing, even if it would mean seeing you less often. For your sake. Really."

"I won't deny those advantages, but I am interested in the winery business too. After this tour, perhaps we can visit Oscar and Jeanne. You'll see what I mean. I found it satisfying." He leaned forward and kissed her forehead. "For now, my priority is to be with you. Even if it means spending the next three months sailing in circles around the Baltic."

Gina raised her head. "Darling, I can't ask you to do that."

"It will give me time to think. Besides, it will hardly be a hardship. You haven't seen our suite."

"*Suite?* You should see where I am now. I thought the principal artists would get a decent cabin—but no. We're all down in the bowels of the ship, four to a cabin." She clapped a hand to her mouth. "Oh God, they'll think I'm a stuck-up bitch if I move to a suite."

"Not if we throw them a party. Or two." Alex glanced at his watch. "The conductor is running late."

An usher entered the box and murmured something into Alex's ear.

"Excuse me, darling," he said. "Someone is here to see me."

He was gone for only a moment, returning with a frown on his face and a book-sized package in his hand, wrapped in white tissue paper.

"Who was it?" Gina asked as he sat down.

"I don't know. A messenger. He said this is an engagement present from my *krestny otets*. In English, that's…" Alex huffed as the English translation came to him. "My godfather."

"Who?"

"He's—a family friend. I met him only a couple of times in my life."

"What is it?"

"I'm afraid to look."

Nevertheless, he tore off the wrapping—and

gasped at the photograph in his hand. It showed a woman, posed beside a classical statue in a formal garden, with two small boys standing in front of her. The boys were so swaddled in woolen hats, scarves and thick jackets, Gina could barely see their faces, but she could guess who they were. They stood close, the taller boy holding tight to the toddler's hand. The collar of the woman's fur coat came high around her ears, but she was bare headed, her long blonde hair being whipped by the wind. She was laughing.

"Your mum?" Gina whispered. "She looks like you. Her eyes."

"I've never had a photograph of her." Alex's voice was thick.

Gina reached up and put her arms around his neck. He leaned into her. They held each other close as the hubbub of voices increased around them and the lights dimmed. A scattering of applause built into a roar as the conductor finally took the podium.

Eventually, Alex sat back. "This was taken at the Peterhof Gardens. I recognize the statue. I was holding onto Nick because he kept wanting to run into the fountains." He took a deep breath and sighed, staring unfocused into the distance. "That's how I try to remember him. My mischievous baby brother. Before it all changed. I sometimes wonder if it could have been different..."

The first haunting notes of the *Swan Lake* overture floated up from the orchestra pit. Alex pulled her closer. "But what is the point? He's gone. You're my family now. And we're safe. That is all that matters."

As their lips met, Gina could hardly believe her luck. To be in the theatre of her dreams, with the man of her dreams, with the music of *Swan Lake* swelling around them—it was all too wonderful to be true. But the warmth of Alex's mouth was real. The strength of his arms around her was real.

And the woman in the seat behind them, tapping her sharply on the shoulder, was also real. Gina sat back in her own seat and put her hands in her lap. Trying to suppress a giggle, she stole a glance at Alex, who was also sitting bolt upright. His eyes, equally amused, met hers. Still keeping ramrod straight, they reached out and joined hands.

The curtain rose.

A word about the author...

Scottish by birth, Australian by choice, Marisa's love of dance was sparked at the age of three by a performance of La Fille Mal Gardée by the Royal Ballet.

When childhood illness thwarted her dreams of a ballet career, she turned her creativity to writing, finishing her first novel by the age of 17. As her health improved, dance again took center stage in her life. In recent years, she has returned to her typewriter (or rather, her laptop) to revive her love of writing romance.

Lightning Source UK Ltd.
Milton Keynes UK
UKHW020156240223
417572UK00014B/777